looking for lady

by
dennis apperly

authorHOUSE

AuthorHouse™ UK Ltd.
500 Avebury Boulevard
Central Milton Keynes, MK9 2BE
www.authorhouse.co.uk
Phone: 08001974150

© 2009 Dennis Apperly. All rights reserved.

No part of this book may be reproduced, stored in a retrieval system, or transmitted by any means without the written permission of the author.

First published by AuthorHouse 2/6/2009

ISBN: 978-1-4389-2047-4 (sc)
ISBN: 978-1-4389-2048-1 (hc)

Printed in the United States of America
Bloomington, Indiana

This book is printed on acid-free paper.

Author photograph by Clint Randall.
Cover photograph by Sarah Randall.

In memory of Janice Holbrook,
who was murdered in Gloucester
on October 16, 1999, age 36.

1

MIDNIGHT Sam sat in the alcove of The Mitre with half a pint of Olde English cider. He took a small sip, pushed the glass to one side and rolled a cigarette. He fumbled for some matches, patted the pockets of his navy blue donkey jacket, got to his feet wearily, pushed the flimsy table forward with his hips and walked over to the bar. Bobby, the landlord, flicked a cigarette lighter without being asked and Midnight leaned towards the flame.

It was Thursday, benefits day, 4pm in the afternoon and Midnight was alone in the alcove he used to share with The Professor, Lady Jane, Scots Robby and occasionally with strange and sullen Fen. But now they were gone – only Nobby and Splodge were left. There were new faces, new names, new mysteries, new tragedies – new but paradoxically the same – yet something was missing. The spark – albeit a sad, often hopeless hint of a spark – was no longer there. Midnight had difficulty remembering the new names, recognising the new faces. But worse than that, he had difficulty caring about them and that was not like him.

"You going to have another?" Bobby looked up from the beer mug he was polishing and draped the tea-towel over his shoulder.

"Just a half," said Midnight, draining the remains of his drink and wiping his mouth with the back of his hand. An inexplicably graceful gesture, vulgar in the case of most people but not so with Midnight Sam, who possessed a natural and gentle grace. Even when he broke wind, a frequent occurrence, he would apologise with a winning, ingratiating smile. And when he got drunk, again a frequent occurrence, he simply went to sleep and snored peacefully, wherever he happened to be at the time. On a bench in the park or in the bus station or in an alleyway or propped up in a doorway. When the police came across him – comatose but harmless in the middle of the city's 'alcohol free' zone – they tended to leave him where he was, maybe relieving him of the ubiquitous bottle of White Lightning or Strongbow or whatever.

"That's all right," mumbled the landlord gruffly, waving aside Midnight's money. Midnight's deep brown eyes twinkled and he ambled back to the alcove, where he sat on the seat underneath the frosted glass window and sighed loudly. Bobby looked up for a second and shook his head with empathetic melancholy: he too missed the old days. He even missed surly Fen and the loud-mouthed Scotsman he had barred more times than he cared to remember. Who else could he bar for life on a weekly basis, now that Scots Robby was gone? No, things were not the same.

Midnight glanced at the little brass plaque screwed onto the faded back of the wooden window seat. It gleamed, but then it should. Both Bobby and Midnight Sam had spent many hours casually but lovingly polishing the two-inch square of metal – the landlord with Brasso and Midnight with the frayed sleeve of his donkey jacket. 'Prof's Place,' read the inscription. And nobody was allowed to sit there. Regulars understood this, but whenever some unwitting stranger sidled into the alcove and sank innocently onto the sacred seat, the offender's bottom had barely touched the cushion before Bobby materialised in front of the luckless individual with surprising speed for one so chubby and inclined his head in the direction of the plaque. It was The Professor's place and, for as long as Bobby was landlord of The Mitre, which would probably be forever, it would remain that way.

Hardly a day passed (and certainly never a Thursday) without Midnight Sam thinking about The Professor, at first painfully but as time went by with sweetness and nostalgia. Midnight began to forget the agony The Prof had endured so bravely as the cancer ate into his frail body; he began to forget the dreadful coughing fits; he began to forget the impotence he himself felt as he watched the older man fade away in front of him; and he began to forget the guilt which gnawed at his mind – an irrational and undeserved guilt – for not being able to help The Professor in his hour of need. But he would never forget the funeral – and by God, it had been one hell of a funeral – and Bobby was unlikely to forget the wake. After all, it had cost him enough.

As soon as he found his friend dead amidst an assortment of abandoned fridges, cookers, sofas and general rubbish on the wasteground, one-and-a-half miles from the city centre, Midnight Sam headed for the Bishop's Palace, which adjoined The Cathedral. It was a cold and spiteful November morning and the rain, whipped by a north-east wind, stung his face as he strode, tears streaming down his cheeks, into the city. People stared at him. Those who knew and therefore liked him asked what was wrong, two concerned police officers tried to engage him in conversation, but all to no avail. He was a man with a mission and he was going to speak to nobody apart from Bishop John.

A guilty conscience is a powerful thing but a collective guilty conscience is superhuman: 250 people took their pews for the funeral service in The Cathedral. Every able user of the night shelter and the day centre plus the staff; Commander Eric Pankhurst, headmaster of King's College; several teachers who remembered The Professor from happier days and scores of pupils who did not, but who had heard the legendary and tragic tale; three detectives, the governor of Leyhill Open Prison and two cell mates; Bobby, his wife and the locals from The Mitre; the editor and a photographer from the Evening News; and numerous curious citizens who had read about The Professor's death in the local newspaper.

In the front row, directly beneath the aloof and imposing pulpit, sat The Professor's ex-wife Janet, his 24-year-old daughter Louise and a three-year-old boy who was clearly overawed by the occasion. The Professor's grandson looked over his shoulder and up, up into the magnificent but loveless, vaulted ceiling. The child was excited: something exciting was about to happen, something to do with somebody called 'granddad.' The same sort of thing as grandma, he had been told, only he had never met this particular person. He had only ever seen a photograph of this 'granddad' dressed in a long, black gown and wearing a funny flat hat with a tassel on the top. But he had heard a lot about the man.

"Keep still, Davey," Louise bent down and whispered in the boy's ear, "and don't keep turning round … it's rude." But she stroked her son's unruly hair from his eyes and kissed him lightly on the cheek. He automatically rubbed the kiss away, but he grinned up at his mother.

"Why are you crying, mummy?"

Louise dabbed her eyes with a handkerchief, forced a smile and put a forefinger to her lips. Davey fell silent but he could not resist half-turning from time to time to inspect the congregation. One very strange man, in particular, caught his attention: he *was* a man because he had a black moustache but he was wearing a red-and-black check skirt with a white, furry thing hanging down the front. And although everybody else was seated, this funny man, who occupied a row at the back of the church on his own, was standing up. Ramrod straight with a fiercely challenging glare on his face. Scots Robby certainly knew how to stand up straight: he had "been in the army, you know."

The church organist struck up the Funeral March and the rest of the mourners joined Scots Robby, bustling to their feet. Chairs squeaked, hymn sheets rustled, people coughed and cleared their throats and The Professor's coffin was borne down the aisle of The Cathedral, which adjoined King's College where he had flourished as Head of English all those years ago. Borne by Midnight Sam, Splodge, Nobby and Brian Davies, the proprietor of the night shelter and day centre. As the solemn cortege passed Scots Robby on its way to the altar, tears trickled down the Glasweigan's cheeks and into his moustache. He twitched his nose and saluted.

Bishop John, who had always believed the disgraced teacher to be innocent, spoke poignantly and controversially of injustice, of how Jesus Christ himself had been the victim of injustice and of how David Browning (The Professor) too had suffered such a fate.

Brian Davies, who had done everything in his power to look after The Professor, read the parable of The Good Samaritan and spoke passionately about the plight of the homeless: "Mary and Joseph, on that night in Bethleham more than two thousand years ago, were homeless and there was no room at the inn for them," said the Welshman. "And I know many fine, good people who are homeless through no fault of their own, people like David Browning, The Professor as we all knew him. Despite man's so-called progress since the days of Christ there is still no room at the inn for far too many people."

Bobby, conscious of where the wake was going to be held, heard the words with a sense of panic: The Mitre was not a large pub and where the hell was he going to put all these people? What if there was no room at his particular inn?

Bishop John – tall and spidery and kindly – loomed in the porch of the West entrance to the Cathedral, magnificent and yet humble in his ecclesiastical finery, holding his crozier like an avuncular shepherd, determined to shake hands with every mourner, which included little Davey Browning, who skipped out into the dark and dismal late-November afternoon.

"I knew your granddad," the bishop stooped down to an undignified squat to be on level terms with the boy. "He was a good man. I want you to be proud of him, I want you to know how lucky you are to have had such a granddad." Davey took a backward step (after all, he had never met his grandfather) and he looked up at his mother, apprehensive and confused by the attention. Louise extended a hand and Bishop John straightened with some difficulty (stiffness was accompanying his 75 years). He took her hand fondly, folding his other enormous hand over hers.

"He is at peace now," he said, softly and inadequately. "Just make sure that you never forget him and that goes for this little lad too. And you must never feel guilty." He turned to The Professor's ex-wife: "Nobody here need feel any guilt, none whatsoever. Nobody. There is only one person – and we all know who that is – who should hang her head in shame."

Janet nodded but her shoulders shook with raw emotion and she wept silent tears of regret. Her daughter reached out and hugged her but she too was crying. For all the what-could-have-beens, for all the what-should-have-beens. And in the midst of it all, poor little Davey started to cry, although he wasn't exactly sure why.

One member of the congregation managed to avoid the bishop's outstretched hand: a morose and lone mourner who, throughout the proceedings, had lurked behind one of the massive pillars near the West entrance, where various leaflets and tourist information were displayed, well away from the main event.

Mark Fenemore hung around outside the cathedral until the hearse pulled up and the coffin was carried in. And then he sidled into the church and hid behind a pillar at the back. Fen did not shed a tear – he had long forgotten how to – but he was there. He remained for the service, but as soon as the coffin was carried back up the aisle he scuttled out of the West entrance, untethered Charlie from a bench and loped out of the cathedral gardens into town, yanking his dog after him with unnecessary violence.

****

The Mitre had never experienced such a feast. Paper plates groaned beneath sandwiches, sausage rolls, Scotch Eggs, pork pies, cheese and pineapple chunks on cocktail sticks, chicken drum sticks, sausages, crisps, pizza slices, garlic bread, quiches, cheese and biscuits. Hardly an even surface of the pub was spared. Bobby's wife had spent the past three days preparing the spread with an occasional word of advice from her husband, wisely ignored. She had also had the sense to decline the flood of offers of help from residents of the night shelter, on the intuitively correct assumption that a great deal of the food would have disappeared.

Conscious that many of those at the wake would be skint and unable to afford a drink – it was a Wednesday, the worst day of the week for the Thursday benefits brigade – Brian Davies, Bishop John, a detective inspector who would not give his name, Commander Pankhurst and the editor of the Evening News (who knew a good story when he saw one) clubbed together and put enough money behind the bar to deal with most contingencies. And if funds ran out, then the landlord was not going to quibble. Any shortfall would be on the house.

Bobby remembered only too well that bleak lunchtime the previous week when The Professor had turned up unexpectedly at his pub, earlier than usual and alone, for what was to be his last visit to The Mitre. He remembered serving the dying man three pints of Olde English cider; he remembered loaning him a wine glass; he remembered phoning for a taxi. He remembered The Professor handing over three five-pound notes and he recalled exactly the words the older man said as he did so: "Get them a couple of drinks apiece when they come in. Tell them 'cheers' from me."

And that was that. The Professor went quickly and without fuss away to die. Without a bang, without even a whimper. Just another name on a death certificate, just another no fixed abode, just another wasted body on the wasteground.

Puffing and blowing and red in the face, Bobby managed to be first back to his pub. He was a model of fluster, frantically itching a non-existent beard, scratching furiously at the back of his balding head or rubbing his impressive beer belly for inspiration.

"Get behind the bar – I'll look after the food," Bobby's wife said in a tone which only Bobby fully understood. He relaxed immediately, slumped his shoulders with relief and did as he was told.

Midnight Sam, sombrely but proudly, led the first group of mourners into the pub. Several respectful but thirsty street-drinkers, Brian Davies and Bishop John. Assessing the gathering expertly, Bobby hefted six two-litre bottles of Olde English on to the bar and began to pour. Midway through the exercise he suddenly remembered that there was a Man of God in their presence, all-but curtsied and addressed the bishop: "I'm so sorry, your holiness, what would you like to drink?"

Bishop John leaned towards the landlord and said, with a kindly grin: "I'll have a pint of bitter … in a mug, that's if you've got one."

Midnight Sam, who regarded the bishop to be his personal responsibility, considered the order worthy of repetition: "He'll have a pint of bitter … in a mug … if you've got one." Bobby was already halfway through pouring the beer but he treated Midnight to a polite nod.

"Only the second time I've been here, Sam," said the bishop, leaning against the bar and surveying the scene. He took a healthy swig of his beer and smacked his lips. "The last time was after that sponsored walk of yours. Now when was that?" He chewed his lower lip.

"June or July, I can't remember exactly when," Midnight replied cautiously, not sure what was coming next.

"And if I recall correctly we were all served with orange juice – jugs of orange juice – and I must say it was delicious, *different* but delicious."

Midnight looked away so he did not spot the twinkle in the bishop's eyes, but he mumbled his confession: "There might have been a dash of vodka, your honour, only a dash though. I thought we needed a bit of a lift after all the effort. I hope you didn't …"

Bishop John rested one of his enormous, knobbly hands on Midnight Sam's arm and interrupted, with a chuckle: "No, no Sam, I think it was an excellent idea. Resulted, later on, in quite an interesting, if unorthodox Evensong." He shuddered at the memory.

The Mitre soon filled up – Bobby had never seen so many people in his pub – and before the serious mourning got underway Midnight Sam blew a shrill blast on a whistle he had picked up (literally) from Woolworths the previous day. He nodded towards the landlord.

"Your honour, ladies and gents. The Prof had a favourite drink, which he used to enjoy in the old days … before he … well, when he was … when things were …," Midnight floundered.

"In happier times," Bishop John came to the rescue and Midnight nodded gratefully. Bobby had already begun ducking behind the bar to reappear with bottles of Chateauneuf-de-Pape – 24 in all. It must have cost somebody, doubtless nobody present, a fortune.

Midnight continued his rehearsed speech with growing pride: "This was The Prof's favourite wine. He used to drink it before we all knew him. I thought it would be a good idea to drink a glass or two in his memory now."

Janet Browning narrowed her eyes for a second, smiled, nodded along with the others and kept her own counsel. For she, more than anybody else, knew her late ex-husband's favourite wine, because it was her's as well. Chablis. Different colour, different taste, different grape, different body. But at least the first three letters were the same.

"You must be Midnight Sam," she said, sipping the deep and fulsome red wine with feigned pleasure. "Bishop John told me about you. You were a good friend to David. The bishop told me you looked after him. He said you saved his life when he was attacked …," she paused and looked down at the ground. "The bishop told me it was you who found him … at the end." Midnight shuffled from foot to foot, noticed the three-year-old boy for the first time and pulled a funny face.

The Professor's grandson giggled and hid his face behind both hands. Midnight squatted on to his haunches, inches away, so that when the boy peeped out between his fingers it would be straight into the street-drinker's twinkling eyes. Midnight pulled another funny face and, despite the crowded bar, rolled over on to his back and waved his arms and legs in the air. Davey burst out laughing and hopped from one foot to the other with delight. Janet shook her head and beamed down at Midnight. Everybody, especially children, loved Midnight Sam. He made people laugh.

Mark Fenemore slipped into the pub unnoticed. He made his way to the bar, declined a glass of wine with a sneer and asked for a half pint of lager – any lager. He turned around and leaned against the bar, his left foot hooked over the brass foot-rail. He scowled at the jolly scene with dark, lifeless, haunted eyes.

"Were you one of Daddy's friends?" A soft voice interrupted his secret thoughts and he half-turned his head. People rarely spoke to Fen; they knew better of it. He found himself looking into the gentle face of The Professor's daughter and, in spite of himself, he softened and the permanent scowl faded. He nodded and tried to look away from the kind and candid eyes, he tried to shuffle off the uninvited intrusion, he tried to be rude, he tried to be Fen. But he could see The Professor in her face and there was nothing he could do about that. Compassion and kindness – emotions long-suppressed in his own troubled being – fought their way briefly to the surface.

"Your dad was a good bloke, a fuckin' good bloke … I'm sorry, I didn't mean to swear … but he was a good bloke, your dad. D'you want a drink?"

Louise nodded: "Yes please. Can I have a small glass of cider?"

Fen looked slightly taken aback and then the corners of his eyes crinkled. For perhaps the first time in years, he smiled and the transformation on his face was incredible.

"That was your dad's drink," he said. "Never heard him ask for a small glass, though. Always a pint. He was a good bloke, your dad. Drunk too much though."

"What's your name?" Louise asked.

"Mark," answered Fen instinctively before he could stop himself. And then quickly, nervously: "But don't tell anyone. I don't want people to know. Everybody calls me Fen. Don't tell anyone." Louise picked up on the panic in his voice and she nodded gravely.

"Of course not, don't worry, I understand," she said, taking the glass of cider from him. "I'd better go and find mum, make sure Davey's not being too much of a nuisance. Thanks for the drink … Fen."

"That your boy?" Fen asked gruffly. "Must be The Prof's grandson."

Louise raised her eyebrows and nodded: "He's quite a handful." Fen frowned: "Make sure you looks after him. Don't let anything bad ever happen to him." Louise, slightly unsettled now, patted Fen's arm and vanished back into the crowd. And Mark Fenemore vanished back into Fen. He scowled at Bobby and banged his empty glass on the bar.

The party was in full swing when a furious commotion could be heard outside The Mitre. Barking, growling, snarling and an angry tirade of cursing from Scots Robby. The Scotsman had not meant to be so late for The Professor's wake but circumstances, way beyond his control, had intervened. Five days before the funeral, Scots had borrowed a set of bagpipes and endeavoured to learn to play The Last Post. The limited time factor, coupled with the Scotsman's lack of musical acumen, produced an interesting result.

Scots Robby stood erect and dignified at the graveside in a drab and soulless cemetery on the outskirts of the city and delivered a loud and muddled combination of notes, while the mourners crept quietly but quickly away. Eventually, some 15 minutes into the curious cacophony, Scots stood alone. Exhausted with pride, he gave a final salute and marched stiffly from the graveside. He reasoned that before he could face the adulation of the others in The Mitre he needed to steady himself and The Fox and Hounds – a convenient two hundred yards from the cemetery – was the perfect place to do that. Scots 'steadied himself' with two-and-a-half pints of cider and five double whiskies in the space of three-quarters of an hour. And by the time he reached The Mitre, he was in no mood for Fen's mongrel. Charlie and Scots had developed a dislike for one another from the outset and the Scotsman had the scars of two very sharp teeth on his right hand to show for it.

Fen heard the commotion and barged through the swing doors. What confronted the young Brummie was a strange spectacle. Charlie, straining at the rope leash that tethered him to a nearby lamppost, was baring his teeth and barring Scots Robby's access to the pub. Scots, red-faced and sweating profusely and also on all fours, was growling back at the dog.

Fen kicked Charlie on the backside – a casual but hard kick – and then cuffed Scots across the side of the head with a curled, open hand. The dog yelped and cowered down on to the pavement and the Scotsman reeled from the blow, arms revolving like a brace of windmills and toppled backwards into the side of a parked car. Fen untied the leash and loped off towards The Cross, yanking Charlie behind him.

2

THREE months after The Professor's funeral, Mark Fenemore performed one of his disappearing acts. Not a word, not a hint. One day sour-faced and sullen around town and the next day nowhere to be seen. Midnight Sam, Scots Robby and the usual suspects hardly gave it a thought and put it down to Fen being Fen. Only Splodge was slightly perplexed: he had a vague notion he had seen the young man running down Park Street, dragging his dog behind him, at around one o'clock in the morning, a couple of days before he vanished from the scene. Splodge half-remembered calling out and half-remembered getting no response. But that was Fen and, to be fair, Splodge had just woken up from a drunken coma on a park bench and was not entirely sure which planet he was on, let alone who or what he might have seen.

Nevertheless some niggle had penetrated Splodge's alcoholic force field and he saw fit to mention it to Brian Davies, who closed his eyes for a second, ushered the street-drinker out of his office and picked up a copy of the Evening News for the umpteenth time.

'POPULAR CITY SKITTLER BEATEN TO DEATH,' ran the front page headline; a second deck heading announced 'MURDER HUNT LAUNCHED.' But what had made the centre manager's heart skip a beat was one of the photographs accompanying the story. Besides an out-of-focus family snapshot of the victim – an unremarkable, middle-aged man by the name of John Wilson – and a shot of scenes of crime detectives on their hands and knees, combing the immediate area for clues, was a photograph of Fen. It looked like a police photo which had clearly been taken some years ago. The caption read: *Mark Fenemore, 24, who police are anxious to interview in relation to their inquiries.*

Two days later the Evening News carried another front page story, headlined 'MURDER HUNT: MAN HELD.' Due to legal restrictions the story was simple, now stripped of 'colour' and non-committal. This time there was no photograph or mention of Fen by name, but a repeat publication of the photograph of the victim. From a newspaper point of view, apart from the publication of the alleged killer's name, when he was charged and when he appeared at the city magistrates court for a preliminary hearing, there was little more mileage in the story until the trial.

****

Half an hour before he battered 54-year-old John Wilson over the head with one of the Irishman's own skittles trophies and attempted to set fire to the body, Fen was skulking alone across the park. It was a blustery February night with traces of sleet in the air and Fen was in an even fouler mood than ever.

He had spent the past three days in Birmingham on one of his regular but abortive quests to find his sister Penny, who had been taken into care several years ago and who was the only living person in the world he had come close to loving. All he had to go on was a faded photograph taken when his sister was 12 – she was 18 now – and a vague notion that she might be living in the dreary suburb of Langley. It was a hopeless quest, one he had undertaken a dozen times since his release from prison. And every time he slunk 'home' the bitterness and the frustration and the anger grew.

They had all suffered his quick and vicious rages: Scots Robby, Midnight Sam, Splodge and Nobby and, before he overdosed in a public toilet in the city centre, Paddy Maguire. Fen had lashed out at them all - apart from The Professor - afterwards funding his victims' drinking for several days by way of unspoken and ungracious contrition. Nobody ever reported the assaults to the police. A black eye or a bloodied nose were, after all, reasonable prices to pay for a buckshee spell on the booze.

But it was different this time. Of course he had drawn a blank in his search for Penny. Deep down in his black and damaged heart he had known that he would. But the death of The Professor – the father he wished he had had – and the sweetness of The Professor's daughter – the girl he knew he could never have – had festered in his already poisoned mind.

"You got a light?" a voice slurred from the shadows and Fen stopped and turned. He could just make out the shape of a man slumped against a tree, barely able to stand.

"No," he snapped and carried on walking.

"I'm pissed as a fart, mate, but I gotta get home. Can you give us a hand. Please, mate, I'm pissed."

"Fuck off," Fen said.

"I'll pay you, mate," said Wilson. "I've got money. I've just won the skittles at The Cross Hands. Two hundred quid. You get me home and I'll give you some."

Fen turned around, cocked his head to one side and replied disdainfully: "How much?"

"I'll give you a tenner mate, just get me home."

Fen's face twisted into a cunning, unpleasant grin: "That ain't enough, mate. Try again, you fucking piss-head."

The Irishman staggered forwards, away from the tree, and stood, swaying, legs apart and arms waving about as if he were trying to conduct an orchestra: "Okay, mate, I'll give you twenty. Twenty quid. Just get me home."

"Fifty quid and I'll tuck you up in bed," Fen said. Wilson lurched up to Fen and clumsily draped his arms around the younger man's neck.

"Okay, mate, fifty quid it is then ... just get me home."

"Where d'you live?"

"Number 53, Park End Road, big block of bedsits, flat nine, here's the key." He slurred the words and they all rolled into one.

Fen took the keys and frog-marched the drunk out of the park, dragging Charlie behind him. The dog, for some reason, became uneasy with the situation. He sensed something sinister and he yelped and pulled at his leash. The dog tried to stand his ground but Fen was having none of it: he yanked the leash roughly.

When they reached the address, Fen tied Charlie to a nearby lamppost, bundled Wilson up a flight of steps, wriggled a key in the Yale lock and pushed open the front door. The Irishman lurched into the darkened hallway and Fen followed, closing the door behind him. He found the light switch and the dismal hall was bathed in the pallid light of a 40 watt bulb. An oily smell of fast food – Indian or Chinese, it was hard to tell – mingled with a faint odour of urine. The air was also heavy with the smell of cigarettes. Fen followed Wilson up the stairs, two flights, to the second floor, elbowed the drunk aside and unlocked the door to Flat 9.

"I'll put the kettle on – d'you want a cup of tea, young fella?" Wilson asked, more coherent now that he was in home territory. He automatically, if a little clumsily, flicked on a number of light switches, turned on the gas fire in the living room and threw his coat onto a sofa.

"Where's my fifty quid?" Fen asked flatly, standing with his back to the living room door, arms folded across his chest. Wilson, who was halfway to the kitchen, stopped in his tracks, turned and treated Fen to a drunken, lopsided and lascivious smirk.

"You've got to earn your fifty quid, my lovely," he said, unbuckling his belt and letting his trousers slither to the floor. Staring at Fen from hooded eyes, he then slid his Y-fronts down to his knees and began to masturbate his semi-erect penis.

"You said you were going to tuck me up in bed, my babe," the Irishman spoke huskily and took a couple of steps closer to Fen. "But let's have a bit of fun first … that's got to be worth fifty quid of anybody's money."

Mark Fenemore's eyes widened and what colour there had been drained from his face. His hands clenched into tight fists and the knuckles showed white. His breathing quickened and then slowed to a flat calm. This calm – a deadly calm – washed over his body, mind and spirit. It had happened only once before and with similar consequences. A thin, cold smile spread across his face and he walked easily, unhurriedly towards Wilson. The Irishman suddenly sensed his miscalculation and frantically tried to pull up his underpants. But it was too late.

Fen shoved Wilson in the chest with both hands and the older man went down with barely a whimper. He rolled over on to all fours and looked up at Fen with a weak, apologetic, bewildered expression. "Sorry, mate, I didn't mean anything. A bit pissed. Let me give you some money. Thanks for getting me home. How much is it I …"

But he never finished the sentence, his last sentence. Fen cut him short with a savage kick underneath the chin. Wilson's head snapped back and he collapsed in a heap, groaning. Fen stood over him for several seconds, legs apart, and watched the stricken man squirm, half-conscious on the floor. He stepped carefully over Wilson and walked over to the mantelpiece. Fen selected one of the man's skittling trophies, the biggest he could find – 'League Three, 2004' read the engraving – tested the weight, raised it above his head and brought it down on to the Irishman's head. He repeated the exercise, quite methodically, half a dozen times, until the man's head was a pulp of blood and yellow brain fluid. He threw the trophy across the room, scooped up a newspaper from a coffee table, scrunched up the pages, turned Wilson's body over with his right foot and stuffed the balls of paper down the front of the dead man's trousers. He set fire to the paper and left the flat.

It was only when Fen was outside the block of flats and looked down at his blood-drenched shirt, that he realised the enormity of what he had done. He untied Charlie, who had been barking incessantly the whole time, and ran down Park Street. Three wandering down-and-outs, including Splodge, saw him, as did Wilson's landlady – a blousy, disgruntled old hag of a woman who missed nothing and who apparently never slept. Rumour had it that her curtains had learned to twitch on their own accord.

****

Two days after he killed John Wilson, Fen was arrested aboard a Virgin Inter-City train bound for Blackpool. He was taken to the main city police station in handcuffs, while Charlie was deposited in the animal shelter. He wasn't a very agreeable creature and six weeks later he was put down. By this time Fen had been formally charged with murder.

It was a big story for the Evening News. Wilson was a well-known and well-liked local chap, a keen skittler and an even keener drinker. But the murder coincided with one of the Chief Constable's tiresome career-building crusades – "to rid the streets of the blight of aggressive begging" – and so maximum publicity was guaranteed.

The 'aggressive beggars' such as Midnight Sam, Splodge and Nobby, were shell-shocked. They knew that Fen had a short fuse and a decidedly unpleasant disposition. But murder? The Chief Constable's 'aggressive beggars' were, in the main, very gentle and non-violent people. Hopeless drunks, yes; pathetic and sad, yes; a nuisance and an eyesore, yes. But aggressive? No. However, the exception is said to prove the rule, and Fen was undeniably that exception.

"Why d'you think he did it, Brian?" Midnight asked, close to tears. The centre manager shook his head and gazed bleakly out of the window, pearled with rain. He had asked himself the same question a dozen times and a dozen times he had drawn a blank. And, as usual, whenever one of his 'clients' got into serious trouble, he felt a niggle of guilt, of personal failure.

"Sam, I have no idea, no idea at all. We all know what Fen can be like, we all know he can fly off the handle at the slightest thing … but to do what he did to poor John …" Brian left the sentence unfinished and slumped his shoulders.

"What's going to happen now?" Midnight asked.

Brian shrugged: "There'll be a trial, ofcourse. He's pleaded not guilty to murder, so there'll be a trial. His lawyers will probably say it was manslaughter."

"Lawyers? How can Fen afford lawyers?" Midnight Sam was incredulous. He leaned forward, his head to one side.

"It's everyone's right – to legal aid. If they cannot afford to pay themselves."

"So who pays? Must cost a bloody fortune."

Brian frowned, a shade irritated at the direction the conversation was going: "The State pays, Sam. That means the taxpayers. You and me – well me, anyway."

Midnight down-turned his lips and stroked his chin pensively: "How much do you think it will cost?"

"Oh, for God's sake, Midnight, I don't know. What the hell does it matter anyway?"

****

During the preliminary hearings at the magistrates court, while preparations were made to commit the case to the crown court, Midnight Sam, Brian Davies and Bishop John took their places in the public gallery, a rather grand term for the two rows of wooden bench seats at the back of courtroom one. Fen, flanked by two security guards and in handcuffs (he had proved to be an unpredictable prisoner), was brought up a flight of steps from the police cells to the dock.

Mark Fenemore (his cronies heard his full name for the first time) stared straight ahead and did not acknowledge the three people who had dutifully come to lend him their moral support. He did not really acknowledge anything – but then he never had – and that included the court. And himself.

looking for lady

Six months elapsed before the trial and life carried on, moreorless the same, for the motley crew who scratched a subsistence around the backwaters of the city. The high spot (or low spot, depending how you looked at it) was when Scots Robby got into another fight and lost. He took a swing at a patient WPC who tried to break up the muddled fracas. Unfortunately for the WPC and unusually for the Scotsman, he made contact, splitting the young lady's upper lip and fracturing her nose.

Scots being Scots, he was fast-tracked through the legal system and sent down for 12 months, by far his longest stretch to date. He was told he would only serve half the sentence but that if, upon his release, he transgressed in any way whatsoever – "if you so much as breathe out of tune" the judge had put it eloquently – he would find himself back inside before he could draw his next breath.

Midnight Sam was in limbo; he had turned in on himself and had lost his sparkle. Of course he was still seen about town, half-heartedly peddling his pile of Big Issues, but something had happened to him. He did not seem to care whether or not he sold the magazines. He still played with children, who always persuaded their mums to make a detour so that they could bump into him, but that semi-permanent, infectious smile was no longer so convincing. Midnight Sam was not the old Midnight Sam anymore. He could not himself understand the change, so he put it down to the imminent trial of Mark Fenemore. But he was not entirely convinced.

****

Bishop John, Brian Davies and Midnight Sam sat side by side in the front row of the public gallery in courtroom three at Bristol Crown Court. They formed an unlikely trio – a bishop, the manager of a night shelter for down-and-outs and one of the occasional residents – but they drew little attention. Nobody, apart from human-interest-story hungry journalists ever took much notice of people in the public gallery. There was far too much drama in the mainstream court itself. Bishop John wore a sedate, working dog's collar, Brian an ordinary suit and Midnight sat huddled but defiant in his ageing, dark blue donkey jacket. Brian offered to buy him a shirt and tie and a new jacket and trousers, but Midnight had declined.

"Court rise," the practised, stentorian voice of a frail, grey-haired court usher drew back the curtains for what surely is one of the most electric examples of true theatre imaginable. Never mind Big Brother and the tiresome plethora of 'real-life telly' which blight television screens night after night after night. For pure, unadulterated Drama, with a capital D, a murder trial, in the flesh, takes one heck of a beating.

The judge, a busy little fellow with chestnut brown hair peeping out from his wig, bustled to his place on the dais. He bowed briefly, business-like, to the packed courtroom and sat down. The door to the enclosed dock clicked open after a momentary pause and Fen shambled in, a security guard on either side. He looked neither left nor right but stood, hands on hips, head held to one side and stared across the courtroom at the judge. The clerk to the court, sitting below and in front of the judge and also facing the dock, stood and began the proceedings. Act One.

"Are you Mark Fenemore?"

"Yep," replied Fen.

"Mark Fenemore, you are charged with murder, the particulars being that between January 12th and January 16th you murdered John Wilson, a male. To this charge, are you guilty or not guilty?"

"Not guilty to murder, but guilty to manslaughter by way of diminished responsibility." The words were rehearsed and without emotion. Fen knew the score: he had been there before.

"Sit down," the clerk spoke with practised but tired authority. The prosecuting barrister flowed effortlessly to his feet and scratched the back of his head.

His Honour Judge Tom Crichton nodded: "Are you ready to proceed, Mr Grumbolt?" The barrister shuffled the sheaf of papers on his lectern, adjusted his wig, hoisted his black gown back over one shoulder and half-turned to face the jury. Act two.

Midnight Sam was both terrified and mesmerised at the same time. It was his first time in a court of law (miraculous given his views on the ownership of property) and he found the experience intimidating. His mouth sagged open at the stern entrance of HHJ Crichton and virtually remained that way for the next ten days. He tried to catch Fen's eye on a number of occasions but the defendant was not interested. He either stared straight ahead or up at the ceiling. He was evidently bored with being there and did not appear concerned who knew it. He had written himself off, but then he had done that a long, long time ago – from the moment paedophile Charlie Stanton had corrupted him at the age of eleven.

The prosecution case was academic, fleshing out what everybody knew had happened, and Fen's three moral supporters were saddened at what they heard. But it was the case for the defence which staggered the trio, along with many others in court. Mark Fenemore's barrister – Carol Hogen QC – had decided upon the bold and risky gamble of revealing her client's past. She was after the sympathy vote and brutal honesty, she reasoned, was the best policy.

The astute barrister gave a lurid and detailed account of Fen's dark and dreadful life. She told his grim story exactly the way it was, even dwelling on the unpalatable – drawing out the agony, revelling in the sheer repugnance. A jury of nine women and three men heard how the defendant and his little sister Penny had been systematically sexually abused by their step-father and then by their step-father's friends. They heard how one of those friends, one Charlie Stanton, had 'eloped' with Fenemore when the lad was barely 17 and lived with him in squalid secrecy in Blackpool.

But what truly shocked Midnight Sam, Bishop John and Brian Davies was the barrister's account of how her client had then battered and stabbed Stanton to death, butchered the body, stuffed various body parts in black, plastic bin liners, packed them into the boot of his car and driven the grisly cargo back to Birmingham, where his sad life had begun.

They had had a murderer in their midst without knowing it. A man who had stabbed and bludgeoned another human being to death and then calmly cut off his head, arms and legs. Midnight Sam had rolled cigarettes for Fen, shared a drink with him, slept next to him on the same patch of wasteground. And Fen had carted him home, albeit roughly, and put him to bed. And, all the time, he was a killer.

The jury took 45 minutes to reach a unanimous verdict. Hogen's brave and eloquent gamble had failed and her client was given the obligatory life sentence. Fen showed no emotion, not a flicker of reaction, and when the judge finished pronouncing sentence he turned around as if to leave the dock without a word, without a sign. But then, just before he was ushered through the door at the back of the dock, he stopped, turned his head and looked directly into the eyes of Midnight Sam, the man he had casually and repeatedly racially abused from the moment the two had met.

Fen's face softened for a second and a small smile tested the corners of his mouth. Mark Fenemore said goodbye to Midnight Sam.

3

LADY JANE went away without a word to anyone, a matter of weeks before The Professor took his last trip to the wasteground. She had drifted, like a wisp of warm, good air, into their lives, and stayed for a short while, gracing the group with kindness and even with a breath of feminine gaiety (and by God they could all have done with that.) But then she was gone, gone as swiftly and as inexplicably as she had come. Gone with Gordon Blacklock, her dark and violent partner, the man who regularly beat her but the man she was drawn to, drawn by a masochistic and guilt-ridden force. Blacklock, like all the other violent men she had been with, represented her punishment, punishment for, in her mistaken view, being responsible for the suicide of her younger brother.

As Midnight Sam sipped his fourth half-pint of Olde English in the alcove of The Mitre one Thursday afternoon, more than a year since The Professor's funeral, he realised that he missed Lady Jane. He had always regarded her as The Professor's woman – not sexually, although Blacklock had never been able to understand that, but in a sweet and spiritual way, which was far more intimate – and he had been more than happy to play second fiddle. He saw his role as a friend, a guardian to them even. And he had grown to love them both equally.

Bobby waddled over to the alcove with a pint of cider. "On the house," he muttered, plonking the glass on to the table and returning to the bar, not waiting for a response. The paradox of a pub landlord trying to increase a customer's drink rate by supplying him with free drinks failed to register or maybe his business acumen ran to long-term investment. However Midnight's by-now legendary pledge to cut down his drinking was never going to descend to the cardinal sin of turning down a freebie. And they both knew that.

"Cheers, Bobby, but I'm trying to cut down," said Midnight, swiftly tilting the glass to his lips.

Nobby and Splodge were the only ones left of the old gang. Nobby and Splodge were inseparable, either flopped out on some park bench, propped up in some doorway, snoring drunkenly in the bus station or staggering, arm in arm, down the street, harmless but completely smashed. They were, however, the unlikeliest of couples.

Nobby was six-foot three inches tall, a bent beanpole of a man with an elongated, sad, bulldog face and a straggle of shoulder-length, brown hair. His hands and feet were too big, his jeans ended two inches above his ankles and he never wore socks. The Green Flash tennis shoes which he constantly wore (even to bed) were at least 20 years old – and they looked it. The big toe of his right foot poked out proudly, both soles flapped noisily with every step, rather like the call of a seal, and neither shoe had experienced laces for a considerable time. Nobby was 37 years old and severely asthmatic. Unbeknown to him, he was dying of emphysema.

Splodge was shorter than his mate by a good eight inches. He had a barrel chest, short and chunky legs, beefy arms carried by necessity at twenty degree angles from his body and no neck. His shaven, bullet head appeared to have been stuck on straight between his massive shoulders. He always wore shorts, even in the depths of winter, and heavy, faded black industrial boots (also without laces) even in the height of summer. Splodge was also 37 and he suffered from haemorrhoids, varicose veins and kidney stones. And unbeknown to him, he had a potentially fatal heart condition.

Neither man had married but they had both dipped into a number of doomed relationships; neither had ever held down a proper job but they had stacked supermarket shelves, dug holes in roads, worked half-heartedly on a variety of building sites, picked up litter for the council, cleaned windows and, of course, sold the Big Issue. And neither had known a real home, not even when they were kids. Because that was how they met: two abandoned 11-year-olds in a grim residential children's home on the outskirts of Lincoln, frightened and defensively aggressive and indescribably lonely. No mothers, no fathers, no brothers, no sisters, no love. Just each other.

Midnight Sam knew none of this of course; he only knew them as Nobby and Splodge, two homeless street-drinkers who got drunk with him from time to time.

Down-and-outs came together with a clean slate, their backgrounds hidden safely away, their former lives tacitly respected no-go areas. Nobody asked questions, everybody told lies. All that mattered was their company on a lonely night, a shared dog-end, a swig from a bottle of strong cider and those all-important, boredom-relieving, aimless arguments about nothing of consequence. All that mattered was now. The past was dead, the future unthinkable.

As with all vagrants, when Nobby and Splodge drifted into town they gravitated to where the haphazard homeless fraternity dwelled, instinctively seeking out like people, drawn by an invisible magnetic force to The Park, the bus station, the underpass, the Cathedral gardens, the Railway Triangle and inevitably to the wasteground.

When the distinctly odd couple met The Prof, as with Midnight, Scots Robby and even Fen, they immediately wanted to protect him, to look out him, to care for him. But these two drifters from East Anglia went a step further: they appointed themselves The Professor's unofficial and not always welcome minders. And whenever trouble brewed, as it often did on the street, they would materialise magically by the frail man's side, Splodge puffing out his vast chest and Nobby straightening himself to his full six foot three.

Their one regret – and it would haunt them for the rest of their lives – was that on the two occasions when The Professor needed them most, they were not around. The first occasion was the night The Professor got badly beaten up and robbed down at the Railway Triangle. At the time, Nobby and Splodge were busy stealing 36 boxes of Walkers crisps (cheese and onion) which had been inadvertently left unattended outside a delivery bay at the back of Sainsbury's. The second occasion was when The Professor had slipped quietly away to die on that cold, rain-swept November night. His self-styled minders were sleeping off a monumental bender in one of the cells at the main city police station.

Midnight Sam was on the point of leaving The Mitre – emotionally exhausted by his reflections – with a view to wandering down to the day centre, when Nobby and Splodge stumbled through the swing doors. Bobby looked up sharply, correctly deduced they were merry but not drunk, relaxed his shoulders and resumed polishing a pint mug. Since the others had gone, the landlord had allowed the two street-drinkers looking for lady

into his pub on the same conditions that applied to Midnight and company: Thursday afternoons only, between three o'clock and five o'clock (after the lunchtime trade and before the office-leavers popped in for a quick couple on their way home); no bottles of booze secreted about their persons; and NOT roaring drunk.

Splodge was very excited; he was clutching a well-worn copy of the Daily Mirror, which he waved in Midnight's face before he sat down in the alcove. Nobby, head bent and shoulders hunched (for some reason resembling a walrus) meandered to the bar, studying the contents of his benefits envelope and frowning with the effort. He was the more phlegmatic of the two.

"Only a pound," Splodge gasped, "only a sodding pound. Can't bloody well believe it. A sodding pound!"

Midnight scratched the side of his head as Splodge flopped on to a stool and pushed the newspaper across the table, stabbing a chubby forefinger at a full-page advertisement. It was a cross-Channel day trip promotion – Dover to Calais and back – aimed at filling the ferries during the slow and unprofitable winter months. A booze cruise. And the only reason Splodge had got hold of a copy of the newspaper was to camouflage the bottle of cider he had bought from the One-Stop Shop earlier that day. He had forgotten to ask for a carrier bag and had experienced a few recent run-ins with the police about his street-drinking. The city centre had been declared an alcohol-free zone and a certain community police support officer – a young, over-zealous specimen who strode about town peering disapprovingly from beneath the peak of his hat like an SS commandant – had taken an instant dislike to Nobby and Splodge.

Splodge had been on the point of scrunching up the newspaper and tossing it away as soon as he reached the underpass when the front page 'teaser' for the promotion caught his attention: 'STOCK UP ON

YOUR CHRISTMAS BOOZE – FRANCE AND BACK FOR JUST £1.' For the first time in many years, Splodge engaged with the Fourth Estate.

"How are you going to get to Dover – it's miles away?" Midnight asked. Nobby shuffled lugubriously to the alcove, concentrating on not spilling the two pint glasses of Olde English he was clutching, and placed them reverently on the table. He had overheard Midnight's question and answered with a pensive nod: "We're going to hitch-hike. Shouldn't take us too long. I know where Dover is. I've seen it on a map." Splodge nodded encouragingly but Midnight looked puzzled. Nobby understood and explained: "There are maps in that Tourist Information place at The Cross. Never been there before. I popped in on the way here after Splodge showed me the paper."

When Nobby entered the Tourist Information Centre, the manager immediately stepped out from behind the counter, perplexed and shocked, to usher him back out (he'd obviously wandered in by mistake). But Nobby picked up a leaflet with a map of the United Kingdom on the front cover and raised a friendly hand to the bespectacled and bemused manager before leaving.

"So how far d'you reckon it is from here to Dover?" asked Midnight.

"Hundred and fifty miles, something like that," Splodge replied knowledgeably, downing a third of his pint in one go.

"How long do you think it's going to take you?"

Nobby and Splodge exchanged glances and paused for several seconds. Nobby stroked his long, narrow chin and his lips moved in silent calculation.

"Probably a couple of days," he replied and Splodge nodded sagely. "Give or take an hour or two."

Fortunately the Daily Mirror promotion was available for four weeks. Nevertheless they only just made it to Dover in time. The 136-mile trip took them 26 days, but to be fair seven of those were spent in a prison cell on a joint (and spectacular) drunk and disorderly charge. Nobby had been interrupted in mid-stride pushing Splodge through the pedestrianised centre of Swindon, at speed, in a supermarket trolley. The police officers who interrupted them would probably have let them go had it not been for Splodge defiantly, accurately and profusely urinating over one of the constable's shoes.

It had taken them 18 lifts and more than two weeks to cover the 40 miles to Swindon. At that rate Christmas would have come and gone by the time they reached Dover, as would the promotion. But luck, in the shape of a 74-year-old diminutive but scary nun driving an old and battered chocolate brown Citroen Diane, intervened. The fierce Catholic took severe and matronly pity on the bedraggled pair, bundled them into the back seat of her car and took them all the way to Dover. Sister Mary was only going as far as Maidstone, but she felt unable to be partially responsible for Nobby missing his grandmother's funeral. However there was a moment's panic when the Citroen rattled into the port town and Sister Frances demanded where the church was located. With a flash of inspiration, Nobby came out with: "Just drop us near the town centre, sister. I need to find a flower shop so I can buy my dear departed gran a wreath. We'll get a taxi to the church, no problem. Thanks to you, sister, we've got plenty of time now."

Which was true: the ferry (which Brian had booked for them) was not due to sail for two days. They spent that time infiltrating the town's homeless community, drinking cider, sleeping on the beach and acquiring their mode of transport for the cheap booze they intended to buy in Calais: a Tesco supermarket trolley. This achievement merits relatively detailed description …

Nobby and Splodge were extremely drunk when they decided to embark upon their mission and for some obscure reason it had become absolutely vital that the supermarket trolley they selected still had a pound coin in the slot. A pound was a pound, after all.

When Mrs Anthea Browning pushed her loaded trolley out of the supermarket onto the pavement outside, having ordered a taxi on the customer freephone, she was in a fluster. The bill still haunted her. She had estimated four pounds less and suspected she had been swindled; she had forgotten the milk and eggs (the reason she had gone shopping in the first place); her trolley had an irritating list to the left; she was unsure whether or not she had the correct fare for the taxi; and it had started to rain. All in all, Mrs Browning was not at her best or at her most alert.

Nobby kindly offered to help the pensioner empty the trolley and stack the various plastic bags of groceries into a neat pile on the pavement near the kerb, while Splodge awaited his moment. As soon as the last bag was offloaded, he darted from the doorway in which he had been skulking and hastened the trolley away from the supermarket and into a side road at breakneck speed. Mrs Browning was puzzled but not overly concerned – after all, a pound was *only* a pound – but Nobby went through the motions of valiant indignation and charged off like a knight in shining armour to apprehend the villain. Mrs Browning, however, shrugged her shoulders – it had been one of those days – and waited for her taxi, which arrived 15 minutes after the promised ten.

A great deal of effort went into separating the pound coin from the trolley. A borrowed screwdriver, a hammer, a pair of pliers and plenty of sweat and colourful language. Nevertheless Nobby and Splodge went to sleep in the sand that night, cold but content, with an extra £1 to spend on cheap booze in France.

As far as anybody knows, they boarded the ferry to Calais the following morning, armed with £250 in saved-up benefit money, a Tesco supermarket trolley that listed to the left and a bent pound coin. Nobby and Splodge were never seen again.

4

ARMED with a dozen cans of Strongbow, Midnight Sam headed for the wasteground, a mile-and-a-half south of town, hugging his ubiquitous dark blue donkey jacket around him. The date was November 17th, a very special day, the first anniversary of The Professor's death and also the birthday of The Prof's daughter. Midnight Sam was honouring a promise he had made himself: on that day, every year, he would revisit his beloved friend's 'happy hunting ground' and he would raise a glass (or in this case a can) to the man's memory. It would have been a two-litre bottle of cider but Midnight Sam was endeavouring to cut down his drinking.

The afternoon sky was a pale, washed blue and there was not a flutter of wind, although the air was cold. A late-autumn moon hinted that night was on its way. Midnight picked his way through the detritus of the vast and unofficial rubbish tip which bordered the canal until he reached the exact spot where he had found The Professor. Little had changed. The ageing, doorless cooker against which The Prof had rested his spent and diseased body and in which he had stowed his final bottle of alcohol (Chablis, in memory of his former wife and of his former life) was still there, just a year older.

Midnight Sam pulled a neatly packaged bundle of kindling wood from the front of his jacket (unwittingly donated by Tesco's for the occasion two hours beforehand) and he made a small fire. Midnight knew how to make a fire. The flames licked through and around the pyramid of kindling and Midnight added twigs and then little branches and finally a couple of chunks of wood. The blaze soon caught and held and brought a bristle of satisfaction from the man.

Darkness crept in across the wasteground and Midnight watched the circle of firelight brighten and widen, casting an intimate orange glow, but his heart was heavy. He was remembering how it had been before. Fen sulking or bitching or insulting him; Nobby and Splodge happily and harmlessly drunk; The Professor smiling enigmatically and slipping Midnight a cigarette from time to time; and Scots Robby pontificating inaccurately but loudly about something or other, waggling a forefinger for emphasis, colourfully cursing the uselessness of "you fuckin' Sassenachs" and marching off with furious disgust in the wrong direction. Scots Robby, Midnight whispered the name affectionately. Poor Scots Robby. But despite his mood of triste, Midnight was unable to suppress a sad smile at the turn of events that memorable night in September, the Scotsman's last.

"*It's my fuckin' birthday, tomorrow,*" *Scots bellowed accusingly, eyes flashing with defiance. He shot up from a park bench by The Tree, took a couple of military paces away from the others, turned sharply and stood facing them, hands on hips, chin and chest puffed out belligerently. Midnight, Splodge and Nobby and a newcomer – Tattoo Terry – looked at the Scotsman without enthusiasm.*

"Happy birthday for tomorrow," Splodge slurred and tilted a bottle of cider to his lips. Scots glared at him and continued.

"I'm going to have a fuckin' party, down at The Docks, behind that old warehouse, you know the one, the one they haven't reverated yet…"

"Renovated," corrected Midnight Sam.

The Scotsman took a deep and angry breath: "That's what I fuckin' said. Anyway, it'll be nice and private."

"Good idea, Scots," said Midnight kindly. "How old will you be?"

"Thirty-three," Scots Robby chanced a guess, but carried it off with authority.

"What time, Robby?" Tattoo Terry shielded his eyes from the slanting rays of the sun, the letters of the words 'Love' and 'Hate' clearly visible on his eight fingers. His left and right thumbs sported a dove and a skull-and-crossbones respectively. A wreath of barbed wire encircled his forehead and the back of his neck was a sanctuary for wildlife: sea-horses, butterflies, a snake and the proud and regal head of a Bengal Tiger. His torso and limbs boasted an amazing riot of images, too numerous and often too obscure to list. From a distance Tatts appeared to be dark blue in colour. Actually his name was Graham but 'Terry' ran off the tongue with more alliterative ease.

Scots rubbed his chin: "Better wait until dark. Say around ten?"

"What about booze?" Nobby asked. He was lying on his back with his hands behind his head and his eyes closed. Scots braced himself with a flush of pride: he had been hoping (and expecting) that somebody would bring up the all-important subject.

"I've got hold of some Scotch whisky – fuckin' good stuff it is too, none of your blended rubbish. Half a dozen bottles. That should see us all right. But bring your own as well. More the fuckin' merrier. Better safe than sorry."

Midnight carefully added more twigs to his little fire, inched closer to the flames and opened a fourth can of Strongbow. In his determination to cut down on the booze he reasoned that if he bought half-litre cans instead of two-litre bottles of cider, then he was bound to drink less. In reality he was consuming approximately a third more and it was costing him twice as much. Midnight's brown face glowed orange and his eyes twinkled in the flickering firelight as he remembered Scots Robby's party. The crackle of the embers and the sharp smell of burning wood made him squirm with pleasure.

Besides Scots, Midnight, Nobby and Splodge and Tattoo Terry, there were three others – Barry Morgan, a bad-tempered Welshman; a violent young Kosovan asylum-seeker known as Johnny because nobody could pronounce his real name; and Mickey, a small and fierce Irish tinker who was passing through the city en route for London and had decided to hang around for a day or two or maybe more. They all had two important things in common: alcohol and nowhere to live.

Scots Robby had picked a good spot for his party: out of sight and not too far from the One-Stop Shop, should they run out of supplies. They sat in a ragged row on the quayside, legs dangling over the side, passing a succession of whisky bottles down the line. Glasses had been deemed superfluous as the palms of eight pairs of hands ensured that the tops of the bottles were clean. One by one the six whisky bottles found their way into the shiny black water, bobbing up and down like tiny periscopes. The lights from three surrounding warehouses – converted into fashionable dockside apartments – twinkled over the basin and the rigging of several ocean-going yachts and three magnificent Tall Ships chinked against their masts. It was a clear night, with a lovely, honey-coloured moon and an intimate but infinitely distant tableau of stars pulsed from the black and domed sky.

Mickey pulled out a small mouth-organ, shook the battered instrument and began to play. A repertoire of Irish folk music, which included several fervently patriotic Republican songs, climaxing with When Irish Eyes Are Smiling. *It was an indescribably sweet sound, all the more so considering the circumstances: a group of alcoholic, rootless, shunned and despised vagrants with nothing much to look forward to save for the next drink, draped over the quayside, getting pissed in the moonlight. A mood of melancholy, nurtured by the whisky, descended like a warm and invisible cloak and Midnight Sam brushed away a tear.*

Suddenly fearful that the party was in danger of running out of steam, the Irishman announced: "Dis being a birthday party and all dat, I tink we should all wish Scots Robby here – d'birthday boy – a happy fuckin' birthday in d' time-honoured tradition." He staggered to his feet and cleared his throat. The others followed suit and formed a vague circle around Scots. Mickey began to sing Happy Birthday *and, in a variety of keys, Midnight, Nobby and Splodge, Barry Morgan, Tattoo Terry and even 'Johnny' joined in. The troubled young Kosovan's English was limited but he managed to get his tongue around the principal words of the song and bellowed out " 'appy birthday" in a deep and heavily-accented, mid-European monotone whenever required.*

The song kicked the party back into life and Midnight Sam clapped Scots affectionately on the shoulder: "Come on Scots, give us a party piece. Do one of those Eskimo Rolls you did at Christmas."

"Commando rolls, you fuckin' idiot," Scots growled, wriggling free of Midnight's arm but straightening imperceptibly with pride. "I was in the army you know. They taught us this in the fuckin' army – gets a soldier out of trouble. Clear a space, for fuck's sake." And those were the last words he uttered.

The circle of friends spread out to make room for the demonstration and Scots Robby crouched, arms outstretched, chest heaving and eyes wide with concentration. He set off along the quayside at a furious pace, arms pumping, and hurled himself onto the ground with a strangled grunt. To be fair, it was an impressive example of a commando roll, but it went on for too long. And nobody, least of all Scots Robby, recognised the danger until it was too late. The Scotsman's head clipped one of the cast-iron bollards on the edge of the quay with a loud crack. The dishonourably discharged soldier executed a perfect cartwheel in the air before plunging feet first into the water. It was not a very loud splash, more like a deep gurgle, and he disappeared from sight immediately. Scots had fractured his skull and was out cold before he hit the water. He drowned without discomfort.

The other partygoers stood completely still, in stunned silence, for several seconds until their booze-befuddled brains caught up with what had happened. And then, as if responding to a command, they galvanised into action at the same time in a quasi-military fashion. Midnight Sam kicked off his boots, tore off his donkey jacket and dived in. It was a near-noiseless dive. He remained underwater for half a minute before he burst to the surface, gasping for breath and shaking his head. (Midnight had been brought up in The Gambia and had learned to swim before he could walk.)

"Can't see a thing," he spluttered, took a deep breath and went under again. Three times he disappeared beneath the black, cold waters of the docks and three times he surfaced, his face a picture of despair.

Splodge sat on the quayside, head in hands, and groaned, while Mickey hopped from one foot to the other, howling directions to Midnight Sam or rocking his head back with anguish and intoning "Mary, Holy Mother of Jesus." Barry Morgan and the Kosovan scarpered: they predicted a load of imminent trouble and they both had very good reasons for avoiding the police. Tattoo Terry ran up and down the quayside, perilously close to the edge, calling out the Scotsman's name, while Nobby (who had recently acquired a mobile phone) frantically tried to call 999. He finally mastered the procedure and summoned all three emergency services.

Midnight dragged himself out of the water, assisted by Tatts and Splodge, and sat down on a bench, without a word. He dropped his head and wept. An ambulance was first on the scene, followed shortly by the police. Fire and Rescue divers, along with an inflatable dingy, turned up twenty minutes later. There was no hurry.

****

Midnight Sam stared sadly into the flames of his busy and private little fire. He had tried to save Scots Robby – he had really tried. But what haunted him most was the unarguable fact that had he not egged Scots on to perform a commando roll, his mate would still be alive. In the weeks following the accident, Midnight's guilt troubled him to such an extent that he went to see Bishop John. And the kindly old cleric had come up trumps, as usual. There would always be the occasional twinge of conscience, but the bishop managed to gentle away that crawling pain of guilt which was poisoning his mind.

Midnight poked a wayward ember back into the fire with his foot. Tonight would surely be the time for twinges: November 17th, the anniversary of The Professor's death. An appropriate time to grieve The Prof, Scots and even Fen. But something else was troubling Midnight and he could not identify what it was. A sudden sense of unfulfillment, incompletion, restlessness. A feeling that something important was missing from his life. But what was that *something*?

The fire was beginning to look tired and Midnight had run out of cider. He got to his feet and waded through the litter of empty cans, rattling them one by one and occasionally polishing off the dregs. It was time for another chat with Bishop John.

5

LADY JANE hugged her knees and gazed unblinking across the bustling but bleak waiting room. She was one of forty-five people awaiting attention in the Accident and Emergency department of Bradford Royal Infirmary in the early hours of a dismal Sunday morning in November. Her big, once-brown and beautiful eyes stared out like a deer caught in the headlamps of an approaching motorcar. The hair at the top and back of her head was matted, flattened and caked with dried blood and fresh, crimson blood had begun to trickle down the centre of her forehead, along the side of her nose and into the corner of her mouth. She rocked rhythmically to and fro.

When Lady limped into the hospital she whispered that she had fallen over and banged her head on the floor. She did not tell the reception nurse (who should have asked) she was suffering from double-vision and was drifting in and out of consciousness. She was concussed. Lady also failed to mention that she was bleeding, quite heavily, from her vagina and that her left kidney and rib-cage ached abominably.

She told nobody about Gordon Blacklock, the man responsible for her injuries, and she was only advanced to the front of the queue after she gasped and fell forwards on to the floor. Somebody screamed and suddenly there were white coats everywhere …

Detective Sergeant Chris Sellwood was a patient man. He had waited in a small, bare ante-room for three hours before a miserable, sour-faced porter poked his head around the door and said: "Doctor says you can see her now. No more than five minutes, though." Sellwood got up without speaking and followed the porter along a labyrinth of dingy corridors until they reached a small ward adjacent to the intensive care unit. There were three beds: a teenage boy with tubes growing from every orifice lay unconscious on the top of one bed; the second bed was empty but still ruffled from a previous occupant and Lady Jane lay flat on her back on the third. Her eyes were wide open and she was staring fixedly at the ceiling. Her head was swathed in bandages and a cage kept the bedclothes from her lower body.

A surge of anger welled up inside the policeman as soon as he saw her. It was the third time in six months he had witnessed such a scenario but it had never been as bad as this. The legal terms 'grievous bodily harm' and 'malicious wounding with intent' and even 'attempted murder' crossed his 'official' mind. He looked down at the frightened and injured scarecrow of a woman, not yet 30 years old, battered and bruised and alone, and his heart ached.

"How is it, Jane?" he asked, perching carefully on the edge of her bed. He squeezed her outstretched hand and closed his eyes for a second. Lady Jane flopped her head to one side so that she could see the detective, forced a wan smile of recognition and raised her eyebrows with an even mix of despair and defeat. And also an element of guilt, because she knew she was about to lie. Detective Sergeant Sellwood knew that too.

"I'm okay Chris," she replied drowsily, the general anaesthetic working its way through her veins. "I'm okay." She smiled too quickly and added too quickly: "I don't know why you're here Chris. Thanks anyway, but I don't know why you're here. It's just silly me again. Accident prone, that's me. Drink too much, but you know that. Fell down the steps to the flat, cracked my head and whatever. Silly me ...," she trailed, fully aware that Chris Sellwood believed not a word. She closed her eyes, tears burning behind them, and waited for the inevitable lecture.

"For God's sake, Jane, this cannot go on, it really can't," the detective began. "You know and I know that Gordon Blacklock is responsible for your injuries. Jane, you didn't fall down any steps. You were hit on the head with a blunt instrument and then you were kicked repeatedly. For God's sake woman we know you were kicked – there was the imprint of a size ten boot or shoe on the small of your back. The bastard stamped on you Jane ... he stamped on you." Sellwood's eyes were bright with anger. "You have got to get your head around this. Blacklock very nearly killed you this time. Do you understand what I'm saying. He very nearly *killed* you. And it is only a matter of time before he succeeds."

"I fell down the steps," she repeated obstinately. "I was very drunk. In fact it was Gordon who picked me up and telephoned the ambulance." A vague touch of inspiration, but Sellwood drooped his shoulders and shook his head.

"No it wasn't, Jane. The person who dialled 999 would not give *her* name. It was a woman, not a man, not your Gordon bloody Blacklock, Jane, not the bloke who very nearly killed you."

Lady Jane would not meet Sellwood's gaze: "I fell down the steps, Chris."

"Why?" he asked incredulously.

"Why what?"

"Why the hell do you protect him? For God's sake why?"

Jane did not answer; she stared ahead. Her mind was full of far more pain than her body. The detective made a decision: "Okay, Jane, I know you're going to stick to your story and there's nothing I can do about that, but this is the last straw. The bastard has landed you in hospital three times now. And it's been worse every time. When you leave here in a day or so you are going into a women's refuge, no argument, and I am going to see to it."

Jane stirred herself for an argument but Sellwood continued, brutally: "And if you don't, then I am going to run Blacklock in and put him through the mill. And believe you me that won't do you any favours, because I've got nothing to hold him on and I'll have to let him go. And then what …?"

"Please don't do that, Chris," Lady Jane looked at the policeman imploringly. "You know what he'll do. He'll take it out on me, like he always does."

Hating himself but determined to drive the message home, Detective Sergeant Sellwood got up from the edge of the bed, fastened his jacket buttons, smoothed out the creases in his trousers and waggled a forefinger close to Lady's face: "I'm sorry Jane but enough is enough. Gordon Blacklock, as I'm sure you know or at least you must have guessed, has a record as long as your arm. Mainly for violence with the odd burglary and robbery thrown in for good measure. He has done time for wounding with intent and for GBH. He has numerous convictions for ABH, common assault and for threats to kill. Jane …," the detective softened his tone and rested a hand on her forearm, "… it's only a matter of time before he kills somebody. And that somebody could so easily be you."

Lady Jane shrugged as if to say 'so what, what am I worth anyway?' She really did not care; she possessed such abysmally low self-esteem that death at the hands of a brute like Blacklock was, in her view, probably what she deserved. Sellwood understood, so he changed the subject.

"How long do you think you'll be in here?" he asked, quite abruptly, angry with her for not caring about herself but even angrier with Blacklock.

"They said about ten days. My kidneys are badly bruised and I've got three broken ribs. Fortunately there are no complications with my skull fracture. There was some damage to my girlie bits … but I'm sure it'll be okay." Lady forced an embarrassed giggle, but the detective was not amused and his eyes widened again with anger; it welled up inside him from deep down and seemed to invade his whole being, filling him with a fire of primeval violence. "He kicked you *there*," he said, his tone dangerously soft. Lady did not answer and Sellwood did not pursue the matter. He got up from the edge of her bed and stood rock still, hands on hips, and looked down at her sternly: "I shall be speaking to the doctors and when they discharge you I will be here and I will pick you up and I will take you to the refuge. No ifs, no buts, Jane, no arguments … absolutely no arguments."

"Okay Chris, okay, if that's what you want," she whispered, too weak and in too much pain to object. "But there is one thing, Chris …" The policeman waited, the sternness gone. "Why don't you call me Lady Jane or just Lady?" A tinge of mischief in her voice. Sellwood looked puzzled. "It's what my friends used to call me, my friends down south, before Gordon brought me up here. I was Lady Jane to them – that's what they called me, that's what The Professor and Midnight Sam used to call me." Chris Sellwood nodded and left the ward.

dennis apperly

****

Lady was dreaming. She was in a deep, morphine-induced sleep and she was back in The Mitre, sitting between The Professor and Midnight Sam in the alcove. Fen was surly and aggressively methodical at the gaming machine and Scots Robby was arguing with some bemused stranger at the bar. And Bobby was busy polishing a long-suffering (but very clean) beer mug with a tatty teatowel. She was listening to the wise words of The Prof and savouring the gentle strength of Midnight. She rested her head on The Professor's shoulder and pinched Midnight Sam affectionately on the arm in response to some silly but seriously-delivered remark he had just made. Scots marched over to the alcove with a glass of whisky which he slammed down on the table in front of her, roaring something about it being "the only fuckin' drink for a bonnie, wee Scottish lassie" (which she was not). Bobby shook his head, choosing to ignore the profanity, while Midnight Sam caught Lady's eye. He pulled a funny face – he was the world champion at pulling funny faces – and he looked sweetly into Lady Jane's soul with those warm and wonderful eyes of his. She shivered with delight and awoke abruptly, a smile on her face, a smile which evaporated the instant the here-and-now replaced her dream.

Lady was in intensive care for three days before she was transferred to a general ward, where she remained for a fortnight. She had made a good recovery but was still weak and clearly unable to fend for herself. But Chris Sellwood had seen to that side of things. Fully aware he was exceeding his duty as an officer of the law, the detective, with Jane's reluctant permission, went round to the dreary bedsit in downtown Bradford where she lived and collected her belongings. She had told him what to take and it did not amount to much. And fortunately

Blacklock was not there – although Sellwood did not expect him to be.

Lady Jane was sitting on the edge of her hospital bed, fully clothed, both hands clasped on her lap, when Sellwood walked into the ward. He carried a holdall in each hand – his holdalls – which contained all of Lady's worldly goods.

"Are you ready, Lady Jane?" he asked, using her nickname for the first time. She looked up and treated him to a quick but radiant smile. She levered herself to her feet, winced, straightened carefully and smoothed herself down.

"You really are a bossy bugger," she said. "Talk about laying down the law …," she trailed, tut-tutting and shaking her head. "So where are we off to?"

Chris Sellwood took her arm: "You know damn well where we're off to and you haven't got a say in the matter, young lady. I'm a policeman and I'll have no hesitation in arresting you for obstructing a constable in the execution of his duty if you start playing up. Now come on."

Lady allowed herself to be ushered from the ward, taking cautious steps. Her ribs throbbed, a dull pain at the back of her head pulsed with every step and the stitches in her groin pulled. And yet she felt okay in herself, even experiencing an alien wave of excitement.

It was a rare and beautiful thing to have a kind, strong and good man in control. For Lady Jane it was a novelty, apart from her father a lifetime ago. But since then, since the heroin and the suicide of her younger brother, she had been drawn masochistically to a succession of violent men, men who abused her, men who confirmed her own low opinion of herself.

Detective Sergeant Sellwood thought about his own life as he accompanied Lady Jane to the women's refuge. He had a wife about the same age as Lady, two children – Tom aged seven and five-year-old

Ruth – a three-bedroomed, detached house on a pleasant estate on the outskirts of the city, security, happiness and a future. And, above all, he had love. And then there was Jane. Obviously a once-pretty girl but now a street-ravaged victim who looked twice her age. He felt overcome with despair. How and why had it happened?

****

The women's refuge in Bradford was a red-brick, Victorian mansion two miles from the city centre; it housed approximately fifteen women, half of them with young children. The sign on the gate read 'Residential Care Home' but neighbours suspected what the place really was. And mostly, to their credit, they maintained the pretence.

Men were not allowed into the building, but that did not include Chris Sellwood, who was a familiar face there, either bringing in somebody like Lady Jane or taking out and arresting somebody like Gordon Blacklock. He was trusted and he was welcome. But he was a sensitive and tactful man and he knew when to leave, which he did as soon as he had seen Lady to her room. He lowered the two holdalls on to the floor, turned and made for the door.

"Just a minute, Chris," Lady spoke softly. She walked up to him, placed both hands on his shoulders (a shade nervously) and kissed him on the cheek. "Thanks … thanks for this. You really are one of the good guys, Chris. There aren't many of you out there."

Sellwood pushed her gently away, to arms length, his hands resting on her shoulders, and frowned solemnly: "No, Lady Jane, that's where you are wrong. There are plenty of good guys out there. You just appear to gravitate to the wrong sort."

Lady tested the springs on her single bed and tried to make light of the conversation, laughing gaily but falsely. The laughter made her wince with pain: the fractured ribs would make their presence felt for a good three months or so.

"Oh yes, Chris, and a knight in shining armour – Richard Gere in Pretty Woman – will call around in the morning and whisk me off my feet," she said, the smile hardening on her pale and sad face. The eyes were bloodshot with alcohol, the nose not healed straight from a previous assault and her once heavy and lovely hair straggled limply this way and that. Where Blacklock had fractured her skull her head had been shaved – a circle some three inches in diameter – and six stitches rose harsh and black.

"You've still got time ... Lady Jane," the policeman looked into her elfin eyes and experienced a wave of despair. "Lady Jane ...," he repeated with sudden curiosity, "who gave you that name?"

"Midnight Sam," she spoke the name with extraordinary tenderness. "It was Midnight Sam ..." She paused and nodded slowly, remembering the old days, when for a trice of time she had been happy.

"Midnight Sam?"

"Yes, Midnight Sam. He was a friend of mine, a good friend – him and The Professor, bless his soul – that was before Gordon took me away and brought me up here."

"Why the name Midnight Sam?"

"Not altogether sure, really," Lady pursed her lips. "Maybe because he was of mixed race or maybe because he was known to be something of a night owl, always trudging the streets when everybody else had gone to bed. I don't know. He was just Midnight Sam ... and he was lovely."

Lady Jane looked up at the detective but her eyes were turned in on herself. She was staring back into her past and Chris Sellwood understood.

6

TATTOO Terry and Mickey the Mouth were sitting side by side in the alcove of The Mitre. They were waiting for Midnight, who was uncharacteristically late. It was Thursday afternoon – benefits day – but the time was nudging five o'clock and they should all have been in place no later than 4.15pm.

Bobby was getting twitchy. In about half an hour his after work regulars from the nearby Bank of England headquarters – twenty-something posers with conversation topics confined to motor cars, mortgages and money – would swagger into his modest and cheerfully scruffy pub for a "slice of ethnic reality." Bobby heard one of them use those actual words on one occasion, but he was a businessman and he was fully aware that the twenty-something posers spent a lot of money in a thankfully short period of time.

The swing doors creaked open and Midnight Sam appeared. Bobby breathed a sigh of relief. He knew that, if need be, he could rely on Midnight to usher the other two out in time.

"Thought you'd got lost," the landlord mumbled, reaching for a pint glass. "Your mates are waiting for you in the alcove. They're about four pints ahead of you."

"Just pour me a half. I don't want a pint. I'm trying to cut down."

Bobby nodded, replaced the pint glass underneath the bar and reached for a half-pint glass on an upper shelf. He had been there before, many times, since Midnight Sam had sombrely pronounced to the world that he was cutting down his drinking. And Bobby was not in the slightest perturbed. His profits were safe, in fact they were enhanced, because Midnight Sam was now consuming around three half pint glasses of Olde English for every pint glass he had drunk before his decision to cut down. Midnight's 'cutting down' was a miracle of self-delusion, but there was no delusion about Bobby's bank balance.

"How you doing, Sammy?" Mickey the Mouth asked. Midnight nodded, shrugged his shoulders and squatted on a stool opposite the alcove window. "We were both getting worried, wondered where you'd got to. Eh, Terry?"

Tatts nodded vaguely and inspected the red and green seahorse on his right forearm, a recent addition.

Mickey was a self-contained, little but lithe man. Five feet and five inches tall, thin but fit and as hard as granite. His craggy face bore more than its fair share of the lines of life, his auburn hair hung dankly to his shoulders and his narrow, fiercely blue eyes ever twinkled with energy. When the Irishman arrived on the scene he had made it abundantly clear to anyone who was interested that he was only passing through. He was on his way to London (where he had "connections") and he would be gone in a matter of days. But Michael O'Connor remained in the city for the next 12 years, which was the rest of his life. Midnight Sam liked him. In one respect they were kindred spirits, in another a million miles apart. They shared the same sense of optimism and the glass, for both men, would always be half full. But Mickey was a violent and devious man and Midnight was not.

The Mouth indeed had a murky past, murkier than most. He had, for several years, been an active member of the IRA and on occasion had used firearms in the furtherance of the cause. To his certain knowledge he had killed two men – a bank cashier (the IRA always needed funds) and a corporal in the British Army, stationed in Londonderry. He was neither proud nor ashamed of these two incidents. For him, as for many others, it was simply the cost of war. However it was more Mickey's criminal tendencies than his political ones that prompted him to quit the Emerald Isle.

"So Midnight, where the fuck have you been – you're nearly an hour late?" he asked with a good-natured frown. Tattoo Terry nodded in agreement with the Irishman and Midnight downed his half-pint of Olde English in one go.

"I've been to put some flowers on The Professor's grave – well not his grave, actually, just a plaque where they buried his ashes."

"Tell us about him, Midnight, tell us about dis Professor bloke of yours," Mickey said kindly. He had heard the stories before, naturally, but good stories had an unlimited lifespan. He reached for his pint of Guinness, blew across the creamy head and took a cautious but ecstatic sip. "Not as good as back home," he said, patriotically but inaccurately.

Bobby ears pricked up and he craned his head to hear better: Midnight Sam's ability to exaggerate was legendary and the landlord did not want to miss a word. He too had heard it all before, but no matter …

"You want to hear about The Professor, the finest man who ever set foot on this planet of ours? It was a privilege to have known him, a privilege to have been his friend. A bloody privilege." Midnight leaned back, gazed through the frosted glass windows of the pub and continued: "Most intelligent man I ever met and the nicest, apart from my father of course. An inspiration to us all …," Midnight slipped effortlessly into a different gear. "Top headmaster, he was, in charge of the best public school in the country, he was (neither accolade was true). Wouldn't have been at all surprised if he hadn't have been awarded a knighthood. Sir Professor, he should have been. As a matter of fact I'm pretty certain they made him an MEB …"

"Don't you mean an MBE – Member of d'British Empire?" Mickey interrupted. "Dat's what I tink you mean."

Midnight nodded solemnly and stroked his chin: "I think that's it, I think you're right, but I'm not sure. Had a feeling it might have been something else though … D.S something … D.S.O. – Distinguished Services Order." An air of triumph. "That's it, I think they gave him a D.S.O."

"That's a military award, Midnight," the Irishman, uneasy in the company of British army honours, said flatly.

"Well, whatever it was, The Professor deserved it," Midnight Sam closed the subject.

"So what happened, what went wrong?" Mickey the Mouth asked.

"He was stitched up by one of his pupils – a young tart who fancied him – and it all turned nasty. The young girl – 15 I think she was – accused him of interfering with her and he got sent to prison. The Professor, of all people! Bloody disgrace it was, a bloody disgrace."

"Well, maybe he did it," Mickey said thoughtfully. "It does happen, you know. We're all human. Randy little schoolgirl with a skirt the size of a belt pouting her lips and fluttering her eyelids. Come on, Midnight, you can't really blame …"

The expression on Midnight Sam's face stopped the Irishman in mid-sentence (as would the expression on the landlord's face, had he been looking). Bobby, in fact, had his hand on the bar flap in expectation of trouble. Midnight Sam was not a violent man; a very powerful man, but not a violent one. But there were certain no-go areas and any criticism of The Professor was one of them. Midnight treated Mickey to a lazy but murderous look, which scared the Irishman half to death.

"Okay, I'm sorry. Of course he didn't do it. Look, I'm sorry, Sammy. Okay?"

"Finest man you'll ever meet," Midnight gazed into the middle distance, his eyes moist but steady, as if he hadn't heard Mickey's apology, which he had. The landlord's shoulders slumped with relief.

"He must have had a bad time in prison," said Tattoo Terry. "How long did he get?"

"Seven years, I think it was, but he was out in four," Midnight replied. "Funny thing is, I didn't know any of this until after he died. It all came out in the Evening News after the inquest. Death by Misadventure was the verdict. Suicide, more like, or murder by that bloody girl …," Midnight choked and glared the tears back from his eyes. "The Prof went away to die, just like the elephants do in Africa. My father told me about it. The elephants decide that enough is enough and they go away to die. And that's what The Professor did … he went away to die. November 17th it was. That's when he went away to die."

The swing doors opened and four men, clutching brief cases, umbrellas and mobile phones, walked into The Mitre. One of the quartet was being ostentatiously loud and intense on his phone, gesticulating wildly and saying "cool," "awesome" or "wicked" a number of times. His hair stuck out carefully in all directions. The newcomers immediately commandeered the bar, laughing loudly for no particular reason, slapping their mobile phones on the counter and feigning deep conversation. Bobby waited patiently for two minutes until they deigned to acknowledge his existence.

"How's the Hookey today ... Bob?" a tall, lanky lad wearing a dark blue pinstripe suit, lilac shirt and a wide, pale blue tie with big lilac spots, treated the landlord to a wink. Bobby's Hook Norton beer was always the same – only just okay – but the landlord effortlessly entered into the gameplay. After all, they were paying.

"Good," he nodded seriously, with convincing authority, "got a good barrel on this morning and it settled well." Bobby was a lager man or a keg bitter man and he knew as much about Real Ale as he did about the tiresome young men who had just walked into his pub. But as usual it did the trick and he shifted a gallon and a half of the beer that his other regulars would not touch.

A short but very upright member of the group, swipe card dangling from a chain around his neck and a brushed leather 'man's' handbag draped over one shoulder, indicated the three down-and-outs in the alcove with a thinly-veiled snigger. The young businessmen swivelled their eyes towards the alcove without turning their heads. Midnight Sam, Tattoo Terry and Mickey the Mouth were oblivious of the ridicule but Bobby was not and he felt defensive towards the street-drinkers. The words "ethnic" and "this is what I like about this place" and "this is what I call a real pub" drifted across from the group.

Tatts got up from his stool, gathered the three empty glasses and tried to make it to the bar unobtrusively, without the four youngsters noticing. He was unsuccessful and the group opened theatrically to let him through. One of them smiled and helped Tatts on his way with a gentle hand on the shoulder, while the others went through the pretence of a deep and meaningful conversation about CD Roms or iPods. As they stepped back they raised their heads slightly and appraised the heavily tattooed street-drinker with youthful arrogance.

"Three of the same please, Bobby," said Tatts in his soft and husky voice. His eyes swiftly checked out the tattoo on his upper left arm: an anchor with the inscription 'Susie' across the top. It would always be his favourite.

The year was 1997, the port Rio de Janiero and the name of the dodgy, unlicensed merchant ship he had come to regard as home was Susie. It was not the name of some 'port girl' he had transiently fallen in love with, although there were plenty of those, some of whom were immortalised on various areas of his skin. But Susie was his dearest memory. He had sailed the High Seas aboard the old rust bucket which occasionally flew the Greek flag, visiting (often at the dead of night and unannounced) small harbours up and down the coasts of West and East Africa and of South America, mainly Colombia. And also a number of unnamed bays, where faceless people were waiting to offload some illicit cargo. Guns, ammunition, grenades, explosives, mortar shells, cocaine.

The progeny of a wayward Liverpudlian family, Tatts had left 'home' at the age of 16 and had hung around various dockside bars, getting labouring jobs wherever he could. It wasn't very long before he drifted aboard a series of merchant ships as a deckhand, earning fairly good money. And so he became a seafarer, never bothering with a land-based home. Whenever he returned to Liverpool he would doss down in sailors' hostels, friends' sofas, even the occasional guest house and on rare occasions the warm bed of some big-hearted woman of easy virtue. He always found somewhere to rest his head ... when the boat came in. And his life, while ashore, consisted of consuming vast amounts of alcohol, shagging numerous prostitutes and playing snooker – and he was pretty good at all three.

Tattoo Terry's maritime adventures came to an abrupt end in the early hours of the morning one hot and humid July night when Susie crept into the small port of Marka, a short distance south of Mogadishu in war-torn Somalia. This time the wrong guys were waiting for them, bristling with Kalashnicovs and serious attitude. The crew never saw their captain again and Terry spent the next terrifying two-and-a-half months languishing in a Somali jail, where to describe conditions as Dickensian would have been a huge compliment. When he was released from prison, suddenly and inexplicably, the British Embassy reluctantly paid for his flight back to the UK, where he spent an uncomfortable week being interrogated by HM Customs and Excise officers, who didn't take long to realise that he was very much a bit player in the Somali troubles.

Upon his release, Tatts hitchhiked due west from London, spending a couple of nights in Swindon, where he added a python to the various animals inhabiting the calf of his left leg, before he meandered down to Bristol. And there he stayed for two years, working intermittently on a number of building sites, drinking and whoring and kipping in a succession of horrible hostels, before an ugly incident with a Rastafarian pimp in the St Paul's red light district prompted him to leave town in a hurry. He headed north and the first person he spoke to when he turned up in the day centre was Midnight Sam.

Tatts negotiated the three drinks back to the alcove, apologising profusely but insincerely to the Bank of England quartet for spilling a little cider on to their polished shoes (not altogether accidentally), and sat down heavily on a stool facing Midnight and Mickey the Mouth. They all blew imaginary froth from the tops of their drinks and sipped in reverent silence. Mickey pulled his harmonica from the inside pocket of his well-worn, shiny, brown suede jacket, caught the landlord's eye and cocked his head to one side. The boyish inquiry on

looking for lady

his heavily-lined face and the twinkle in his narrow but humorous eyes were irresistible. Bobby nodded.

Mickey never played loudly or flamboyantly; the only movement was the feathery flutter of his fingers across the stops and the pulse of concentration on the twin-temples around his closed eyes. And the sound that emanated from his scratched and dented mouth organ was one of such exquisite beauty that even the four young men at the bar stopped to listen for a second or two before resuming their conversation. Something caught in the back of Midnight's throat and Tatts sought out 'I Love You Helen' inscribed within the outline of a heart on the palm of his left hand. He had had a deep and meaningful relationship with said lady in a lesser-known hotel back room in down-town San Francisco for approximately three-quarters of an hour.

Mickey stopped playing after five minutes – much to the disappointment of everybody in the bar – because he was thirsty. He slipped the harmonica back into his jacket pocket, licked his lips and tackled his pint. He looked up at Midnight Sam and asked, for no obvious reason: "You ever been in love, Sammy?" Tattoo Terry felt mildly excluded – after all, he had been in love a thousand times – but he said nothing.

"I loved my father," Midnight ventured, after some thought, "and of course I loved The Professor."

The Mouth pulled a frustrated face, scratched the back of his head and closed his eyes: "I don't mean dat sort of love, for the love of God. I mean … have you ever been in love with … a woman? With some sweet colleen?"

Midnight pursed his lips, acknowledging the question with a thoughtful nod: "No, I don't think so. There was a girl up in Edinburgh – when I was in university – but that was a long, long time ago."

"University!" Mickey exploded. "You were never at fuckin' university."

Midnight ignored him: "I liked her a lot, but that was all. I don't know what being in love is. What does it mean? I don't know."

"I loved a girl in Singapore – she was bloody lovely," reminisced Tatts. "She had a dragon tattooed from the middle of her back all the way down to the crease of her arse. Bloody lovely she was."

"You must have met ladies dat you liked, Sammy," Mickey persisted, "ladies dat was special."

"I did like Lady Jane a lot," Midnight conceded, pursing his lips. "I suppose you could call her special. Yes, she was pretty special. She was a lovely lady, she made me feel okay, okay about everything."

"So whatever happened to dis Lady Jane of yours?"

"She was not mine," said Midnight Sam. "She was more The Professor's friend. I just liked her a lot … and I think she liked me. But she went away."

Mickey the Mouth's lively little eyes sparkled.

7

AMY BROWN was in a bad way. The 19-year-old single mother was battered and bruised by her pimp boyfriend and internally damaged by a sadistic client.

After the prolonged ordeal which earned her £50 and her pimp £150, she squatted on the toilet in her dingy Bradford bedsit for half an hour, watching, with growing horror, the steady trickle of blood. Unable to move from the WC, she phoned her older friend Charlotte and explained what had happened. Charlotte, who was having a night off to look after Amy's three-year-old daughter Emily, told her friend to lock her front door and to stay where she was. She then contacted the women's refuge (she knew the number off by heart), phoned for a taxi and woke Emily. She carried the child down six flights of stairs (the lift hadn't worked for two weeks) and waited. It was a bitterly cold February night and she hugged Amy's daughter underneath her own coat for warmth until the taxi arrived. She collected Amy and took her to A&E, explained the situation as best she could to the reception nurse, got back in the taxi and directed the driver to the refuge, two-and-a-half miles away.

The night staff knew and liked Charlotte and had already sorted out a room for Amy and her daughter. Emily – exhausted from the trauma of the night – fell asleep almost the second her head touched the pillow. Charlotte sat on a chair next to the bed and stared, unblinking at the wall opposite, valiantly resisting the temptation to smoke. Her friend did not return that night and Charlotte fell asleep in the chair.

An ambulance car brought Amy to the refuge the following afternoon; she looked confused and drained and the stitches pulled painfully. Charlotte had sorted out the formalities, for what they were worth, and helped kit out the modest room with another single bed and a selection of cuddly toys – rather tatty cuddly toys, but cuddly toys nonetheless. One of the refuge support workers had given Charlotte a lift back to Amy's bedsit, where the 36-year-old prostitute had hurriedly packed her friend's worldly goods into a small holdall and returned to the refuge. Fortunately the pimp was nowhere to be seen. En route, Charlotte detoured to a pharmacy and bought pain-killers, antiseptic cream and sanitary towels. She also called in at a supermarket and bought a selection of sweets for Emily. She was a good friend.

Charlotte visited Amy every day for the next three weeks, bringing in little treats – a packet of cigarettes, a magazine, a lip-stick – and taking Emily out for walks to the play area nearby. But then one day she didn't turn up. No phone call, no text message, nothing. And that was the last Amy and her daughter ever heard or saw of her. Something had obviously happened, something invariably bad, and she had taken off. But not before she had satisfied herself that her friend and her friend's daughter were relatively safe and sound. Three days after she disappeared, Amy received an envelope in the post which contained

£110 in £10 notes and a scrap of notepaper upon which was written, in a scrawl, 'Love you both, take care, Charlie xxx.'

Armed with the money, Amy headed for Gap, where she spent £70 on the latest designer gear for kids: two tops, a skirt and a jacket. It was her way of making up to her daughter – in reality a sad and pointless gesture and quite wasted on Emily. And then, with Emily still in tow, Amy made her way to a telephone kiosk at the end of a grim row of terraced houses, dialled a number, exchanged a few brief words and waited. Ten minutes later an ageing red BMW with the windows blacked out, screeched up to the telephone box and the passenger window was wound down. Amy handed over £30 and three cling film wraps containing a brown substance were handed back. The window was wound up swiftly and silently and the BMW accelerated away. The remaining £10 paid for their taxi fare home.

* * * * * * * * * *

Lady was cautiously happy. She crept around her private sanctuary – a dull room measuring twelve foot by nine foot – and she hugged herself with delight. She was free, she was blissfully alone, away from him, in a place that appeared to be safe, surrounded by people who were kind to her, people who did not threaten or shout or abuse or hurt her. She was away from Gordon Blacklock and from the likes of him. She felt free, but the concept frightened her and she wasn't sure whether or not she trusted it.

Lady Jane first met Amy Brown in the communal lounge two days after Chris Sellwood had virtually frog-marched her into the refuge. The teenager was huddled in a corner of the room with her daughter standing close, clutching the hem of her mother's skirt and staring down at the floor. The first thing that struck Lady was the eyes – they reminded her of her own some years ago – and they rekindled a dark memory. They were the unmistakeable eyes of a drug addict, desperate for the next fix. A heroin addict, a junkie, like she had once been.

"I'm Jane," she said with a half-smile. "I got here a couple of days ago. It's quite a relief, I can tell you. Usual story, I'm afraid. How about you?"

Amy's face registered nothing; it was as if she hadn't heard a word. She stroked her daughter's head with nervous little jerks and shuddered. She had had no money for several days and her body and mind were locked in the agonising vice-grip of 'cold turkey.'

"We've been here for two months, I think, maybe longer," she murmured and pulled Emily closer to her. "I don't feel very well ….," she added inconsequentially, but Lady knew what she meant.

"How long has it been?" Lady asked in a matter-of-fact voice, but there was kindness in the tone. Amy recognised the empathy, closed her eyes with a sudden wave of relief and replied (as one junkie to another): "A week. And it feels like a fucking year – sorry, Emily," she shook her head and winced guiltily, "I didn't mean to swear." But Emily had heard the obscenity before, many times, and it no longer meant a thing to her. Her main concern was that her mum was 'not very well' again.

"Have you thought about getting help?" Lady Jane asked.

Amy shook her head and smiled broadly but falsely at her daughter: "There my little poppet. Mummy's girl, aren't you, babes." She breathed in deeply and looked up at Jane, starting to shake: "What d'you mean *help*? The only thing I need is another fucking fix … sorry Em … mummy's not very well."

But Amy need not have worried: Emily was used to the language, the mood swings, the uncertainty, the danger and the fear. She was used to having a heroin addict for a mother and she was three years old. That the little girl had not been rescued from such an appalling situation was a combination of indifference and inefficiency by social services and the elusiveness of Amy Brown. Emily was on the 'at risk' register but efforts to monitor her safety were perfunctory to say the least. Boxes were ticked, notes filed, statutory obligations satisfied (at least on paper) but a three-year-old girl still remained in the sole care of a 19-year-old, who was homeless, a prostitute and a heroin addict. Amy had slipped through the net and she wasn't the only one to have done so.

****

Lady Jane took Amy and Emily under her wing, a broken wing at that. One lost soul looking after two other lost souls. She played with the little girl, tidied up their appallingly untidy room, accompanied Amy to the shops and encouraged her to buy 'sensible' things. And her repayment was cruel: it brought it all back, it brought crashing back into her fragile existence the black memory of her own tragedy; of when her once-happy life had careered off the rails and spiralled rapidly down into chaos.

Lady Jane grew up in a 'nice' home in Padstow, north Cornwall. It was a loving and happy family. Her father, a kind and solid man, was a bank manager and her mother, an artistic woman who specialised in oil paintings of the north Cornish coast, taught at the local junior school. Jane had a younger brother – Julian – a delicate boy whom she adored. She was a bright and bubbly girl, popular with the boys but with her own sex too. She had the rare quality of being both sensible and fun-loving.

The downward spiral began at an older friend's 18th birthday party. Somebody, somewhere, somehow talked her into 'trying this' – the this being a £10 bag of heroin. Jane, a bit tipsy and feeling mischievous, gave it a go …

So when Lady looked at Amy – wide-eyed, shaking and single-mindedly crazy for another fix – she saw herself ten years ago. Only she hadn't had a three-year-old child to look after. She only had herself to destroy. Nevertheless she recognised the dreadful, drug-induced mindset which shut out all else – reason, logic, commonsense, survival, safety, even the well-being of a child. She recognised it only too well. Because she had been there. And because of that – and because she was an intelligent person – Lady did not lecture or even advise her young friend. She simply helped her and her daughter on a day-to-day, practical basis and showed them both understanding and kindness. Lady realised that any advice would have to be asked for and more often than not that would not happen. Heroin addicts do not listen to anybody else, they do not listen to advice; they only listen to themselves and to the relentless craving that drives their every thought.

"How are you feeling today, Amy?" Lady asked. They were sitting on a wooden bench in a little park they had discovered, less than half a mile from the refuge. In one corner was a small and run-down play area with swings, a slide, roundabout and various climbing frames. And Emily had found a friend, a boy several months younger than she, which made her feel very important. She was explaining, in a school-ma'amish voice, what he could and could not do and what they were both going to do. Although confused, he followed her obediently.

"Shite," Amy replied, closing her eyes and breathing deeply. "Fucking shite. My whole body aches, every part of me, and I can't stop feeling scared shitless, all the time, for no fucking reason. I can't go on like this, Jane. I'm going off my fucking head."

"You've not scored …?"

Amy swivelled and glared at Lady Jane, her face twisted with anger: "Of course I haven't fucking scored. That's why I feel so shite, for fuck's sake." She slumped her shoulders and put a hand to her forehead: "I'm sorry, Jane, I'm sorry. I didn't mean ..."

"Don't worry, honey, I understand. Don't worry. Remember that I know what it feels like?"

Lady watched Emily lead the little boy up the steps to the top of the slide, but she watched only with her eyes. Her mind, her thoughts were in the past, ten years in the past.

It was December and Christmas was only a week away. Jane's home in Padstow was extravagantly decorated and boasted two Christmas trees – one in the living room, which, at eight-foot, brushed the ceiling, and the other one in the front garden. Jane's dad had made a crib and her mum had bought models of Baby Jesus, Joseph, Mary, the Three Wise Men, assorted shepherds, sheep and cattle. The illuminated masterpiece took pride of place in the conservatory at the back of the house. It was magnificent.

But the efforts that Christmas were tainted with sadness and despair. It was an over-the-top effort to pretend that everything was okay, that their 17-year-old daughter was not a heroin addict, that the once-happy family was not being torn apart, that Christmas would not be a heartbreaking sham.

The pretence collapsed on the day before Christmas Eve, when Jane stole her brother's presents from beneath the Christmas Tree, took them into Cash Converters in Wadebridge, sold them for a total of £35 and bought three 'ten bags' from some bloke in a dark alley. She spent that Christmas in a depressing bedsit with three other addicts and lost her virginity. His name was Sid as far as she could remember, but she had no recollection of what he looked like.

Lady Jane was still haunted by that Christmas and by what happened over the next couple of years: the sheer hell she put her parents through and the affect her addiction had on Julian. The worst nightmare of all was the suicide of her younger brother. In her eyes, despite what The Professor had told her, it would always be her fault.

"It's starting to rain," Lady screwed up her eyes and looked up into the grey, troubled clouds which scudded low across the sky. "We'd better get Emily home." Amy did not move. She did not acknowledge her friend's remarks. She did nothing but stare with saucer eyes at the grey grass beneath her feet.

"I need it, Jane," she muttered with breathless desperation. "For Chrissake, I need it. For fuck's sake, Jane, I've got to have some. I'm going fucking mad." She started to rock to and fro, hugging her knees and groaning. A horrible inhuman sound.

Lady Jane rummaged about in her handbag, pulled out her purse and handed the 19-year-old mother a £10 note. That left her £6.50p until Thursday, when she would be able to draw her benefit, but Thursday was two days away. Amy took the money, nodded and scuttled out of the playground. She was halfway down the street, almost out of sight, before she stopped in her tracks and turned: "Could you look after Emily … take her home … give her something to eat … put her to bed? Please? I'm sorry, Jane." Lady waved Amy away with an understanding gesture and turned to the three-year-old, who was making a monumental hash of the climbing frame.

"Where's mummy gone?" she asked but instinctively knew the answer. "Has she gone to get well again?"

Lady Jane hugged the little girl and kissed her on top of the head: "Yes, my darling, she's gone to get well again."

8

TATTOO Terry and Mickey the Mouth walked across the park together. Midnight Sam and a nervous young man with a stutter and a faraway look were already sitting on the bench overlooking The Tree, side by side. The young man was a newcomer who had latched onto Midnight (as many did). The Tree was one of the regular meeting places for the city's down-and-outs. Nobody bothered them there, nobody walked by with an aloof air and a disapproving stare. Nobody told them to "go and get a job."

Tatts and Mickey, from first appearances, looked as if they had been fighting. Tattoo Terry sported an assortment of plasters covering the nose area and the Irishman boasted two glorious, text-book, black eyes. Mickey's nose seemed a shade out of line and dried blood was caked in one of the nostrils and at the corner of his mouth. But first appearances were deceptive as the two men's injuries resulted from entirely separate incidents.

In the case of Tattoo Terry he had fallen victim to a well-meaning but decidedly amateur tattooist. For some weeks he had been contemplating a new tattoo and the location he had favoured was his large, misshapen nose, one of the few remaining vacant areas on his body. Tatts respected tattoos: they were, to him, personal works of art, a visible (and permanent) record of one's life, a constant reminder of something or someone. They were not to be taken lightly. The form his latest tattoo was going to take came to him in the early hours of the morning. His eyes blinked open and he sat upright in bed, overwhelmed with a surge of inspiration. Tatts loved his nickname – it gave him identity and a curious sort of street kudos; it set him apart from the common herd. He was Tattoo Terry and that's all there was to it. He could hold his head high and the rambling nose in the middle of that held-high head would soon bear proud testament to the man's uniqueness. For T.T. – his new-found initials – would be tattooed one on each side of his nose. T.T. – Tattoo Terry. Nobody would be in any doubt ever again as to his identity. What a spark of genius! Much of which was owed to Midnight Sam, who had of course dreamed up the nickname in the first place. And, from time to time, the occasional passer-by would doubtless ask him what the letters stood for. And naturally he would tell them.

Bert Finch lived in a crumbling narrowboat moored in the canal south of the docks. He had lived there, seeing off a wife and a series of women, for around twenty-five years. The love of Bert's life was Napoleon, an irascible parrot he had acquired twenty-two years ago. Napoleon adored Bert but he hated everybody else, in particular members of the opposite sex. The bad-tempered bird was, without question, solely responsible for the lack of female permanence in his master's life. Which was a pity, because Bert was a man who wanted and needed a woman. But there were limits. "Either that horrible bird goes or I do," had been said on many occasions and it was always the lady of the day who finally abandoned ship.

To supplement his Incapacity Benefit (the 50-year-old supposedly suffered from chronic arthritis) Bert pierced ears and noses and other more intimate parts of the body and he also did tattooes.

Two days after the 'operation', infection had set in and Tattoo Terry's nose swelled to twice its size. It also turned a bright and poisonous pink and began to weep in the most disgusting manner. He was forced to make an appointment with the new doctor at the day centre – an efficient but cold young man from New Delhi – and was given anti-biotics and an antiseptic cream. The criss-cross of Elastoplast was Terry's own idea.

When Tatts was through with his explanation, Mickey the Mouth pointed eagerly to his two spectacular shiners, shook his head theatrically and gazed at the floor, willing somebody, anybody, to ask how it happened.

"What happened then, Mickey?" Midnight Sam asked wearily, trying and failing to sound interested. There was a time when he would have been jumping up and down with raw curiosity and enthusiasm. But he was not the same these days and he knew it.

Tattoo Terry, who had been with the Irishman at the time, muscled in with uncharacteristic venom (he was normally a laconic and peaceful man): "I'll tell you what fuckin' happened. This Irish prat here decided to get out his fuckin' mouth organ in the middle of The Ship Inn and start playing a whole load of Irish Republican stuff.

"It wouldn't have mattered so much if he hadn't insisted on telling everyone that he was playing IRA battle songs and that the 'fucking English' should get out of his country. They wouldn't have had a clue otherwise …

"The landlord was on his way around the bar to chuck us out when Mickey, the fucking heroic freedom-fighter, stood to attention and belted out 'A Nation Once Again' while sticking two fingers up at everybody in the pub.

"Well, that was fucking it. This bloody huge skinhead, built like a brick shithouse, wearing an England shirt and with almost as many tattoos as me, squared up to Mickey …"

"He didn't give me a fuckin' chance," interrupted Mickey with a frown. "He didn't fight fair. He rushed over and head-butted me smack on d'nose. I didn't have a fuckin' chance to defend myself. He didn't fight by your fuckin' Queensbury Rules, d'bastard."

"Queensbury Rules?" Tattoo Terry looked puzzled.

"Never mind," Mickey shook his head briefly. "Anyway I was down on d'floor and dat's when dis English thug put d'boot in."

Tatts scratched the back of his head: "No he didn't, Mick. He turned around and walked back to the bar with his mates."

"Well somebody gave me a fucking good kicking," Mickey the Mouth persisted. "My ribs are as sore as fuck and I'm covered in fucking bruises, from head t'fucking toe."

"You fell down the steps when we left the pub. You went arse over tit, you did. You fell down the steps, Mickey … nobody kicked you." Terry was patient but insistent.

"So what happened, Mickey, how did you get your black eyes?" Midnight Sam asked, opening his sixth can of Blackthorn cider and staring across the park. Tattoo Terry and Mickey the Mouth exchanged incredulous looks and even the youngster, sitting next to Midnight, seemed taken aback.

"What the fuck d'you tink we've been talking about?" Mickey asked and tapped the side of his head. "Are you going soft in d'fuckin' head or what?"

But Midnight Sam was not listening. He shrugged, took a dainty sip at his cider and returned to his daydream …

They had gone on a day-trip to Weston-super-Mare – The Professor, Lady Jane and Midnight. It was the first time they had left the sanctuary of the city for a very long time and the three of them were nervous and apprehensive but also cautiously excited. Brian Davies had arranged the trip for them and, not surprisingly, had chipped in with some spending money. It was typical of the night shelter and day centre manager. He was a good and compassionate man, always exceeding his duty, always giving that little bit more, bending the rules (often his own rules) and ever championing the cause of his clients – the so-called rejects of society, the street-drinkers, the vagrants, the down-and-outs, the also-rans. Brian Davies was – and is – a good and compassionate man.

Midnight remembered how he had gone 'clothes shopping' for the big occasion, trawling a number of charity shops in the middle of the night, when boxes of donated clothing clogged their doorways. Speed being of the essence, he hadn't had time to be particularly picky and had to guess sizes and colour-coordination in seconds.

The result was fascinating and Midnight's speedy selections were destined to catch the eye. The other rather bemused day-trippers who caught the coach would have confirmed that, had they been asked. The Prof wore cream cricket flannels, an over-sized blue, green and white striped blazer, an incongruous pair of colourful Adidas trainers and, as his crowning glory, a Panama hat, far too big, which rested just below his eyebrows on the bridge of his nose. Midnight Sam cut a more complex dash: similar cream cricket flannels, proud of his ankles by an inch-and-a-half, a pink evening dress shirt, an emerald green waistcoat with a couple of silver buttons missing and a pair of Green Flash tennis shoes which had seen better days.

And of course, Lady Jane. She had politely demurred when Midnight had offered to select her outfit and the result was lovely. She had been to the hair-dressers for the first time in years, purchased a cheap but cheerful yellow summer dress, flared and calf-length, and a white cotton cardigan. She wore a small, silver-plate crucifix around her neck and a pair of white flip-flop sandals on her feet. Lady had also taken the trouble to paint her toenails pale pink.

But what Midnight Sam remembered most about Lady that day was the gay sparkle in her grey-blue eyes and the cool, fresh smell of her. The customary rancid odour of cider and sweat were gone; she smelt sweet and clean and like a young woman. Midnight also remembered the way she linked arms with both men as they strolled along the Promenade. And the way she giggled for no particular reason and gripped Midnight's arm just a little bit tighter and looked up at him. He particularly remembered the way she looked up at him.

The Professor bought them toffee apples on the beach and he packed them off across the sand while he found a deck-chair. The dying man fished out a quarter bottle of Dimple Haig whisky, snuggled down deliciously into the canvas and watched Midnight and Lady Jane kick their way through the busy wavelets in the distance.

Sam walked several paces behind Lady and he grinned when she hoisted up her dress and waded out into the sea until the water reached her thighs. He remembered, with surprising clarity, how she turned and beckoned him to follow. He remembered the tinkle of her laughter. It was the first time he had heard her really laugh and the music had warmed his soul.

Midnight sat on the park bench, steadily working his way through the six-pack of cider, occasionally passing a can to the nervous young lad who sat beside him. Tattoo Terry and Mickey the Mouth were embroiled in an animated but harmless argument about Bird Flu. Tatts was adamant that he had not heard any of the seagulls or pigeons which plagued the city sneeze or show a single sign of the ailment – not a cough, not a solitary runny beak. Nothing whatsoever. Mickey, who possessed considerably more brain cells than the forcibly retired seaman, was trying to explain the difference between human influenza and the feathered variety. Nevertheless it was a fairly even contest, seeing that neither man had the faintest idea what he was talking about.

"We had our photos taken," Midnight said to no-one in particular, during a brief lull in the argument. A faint but cold drizzle had set in and he turned up the collar of his donkey jacket. For some reason, only known to himself, the nervous youngster sitting beside Midnight jerked to his feet and scuttled off across the park towards the city centre, without a word to anybody.

"What photos? What d'fuck are you on about?" the Irishman asked.

"We went to one of those booths – you know the sort of thing. You poke your head through a hole and you might be the face of a donkey or a gorilla or a great big fat lady or whatever." Midnight brushed the rain from his forehead and treated his two mates to an irresistible smile.

"Who's the 'we'?" Mickey softened his voice, powerless when assailed by Midnight Sam's warmth.

"Me, The Prof and of course …," Midnight paused and heaved a gentle sigh, "… and, of course, Lady Jane." He squirmed on the park bench, wriggled his shoulders and his eyes sparkled at the memory. "I was King Kong, The Professor was Chief Sitting Bull and Lady Jane was Mary Queen of Scots. Scots Robby would have been proud of her." Mickey and Tatts nodded solemnly, reverently at mention of the Scotsman.

The Mouth pulled out his harmonica respectfully and began to play Danny Boy. Terry, who knew neither the words nor the key, joined in solidly with the vocals and Midnight Sam gazed across the park and remembered Lady Jane. The drizzle became a steady downpour but nobody moved.

9

SOMETHING astonishing happened to Lady Jane. She gave up alcohol or rather it was more the other way round: alcohol gave up Lady Jane. For it was not a conscious effort on her part. No Herculean act of willpower, no brave decision, no well-thought out commitment. Nothing so grand. She simply awoke one morning and didn't want a drink and she couldn't understand it at all. So much so that she was determined to carry on as normal. She marched into the nearest supermarket, bought bottles of cider, wine and vodka, and marched back to her room at the refuge. But to no avail. She winced at the taste, made herself a cup of tea and sat down, totally bemused. What the hell had happened? She didn't realise it at the time, but Amy and Emily had happened.

For the next four days Lady persevered, in desperation experimenting with a variety of alcoholic drinks. But the result was always the same: down the sink, down the lavatory pan and, on one particularly frustrating occasion, out of her first-floor window and onto an undeserving cordelyne shrub. But, to her astonishment, never down her throat.

"How long have you been without a drink?" Chris Sellwood asked her during one of his twice-weekly visits to the refuge. They were both sipping tea from steaming mugs and Emily was cautiously and clumsily flirting with the detective. She kept showing him cryptic drawings – squiggles really – which she had done earlier in anticipation of his visit. And Chris would inspect them with solemn but feigned interest (he had two young children of his own). He made the right noises and the little girl felt an important part of the occasion. She warmed to the policeman with the instinctive judgement of a child and stood a little closer to his chair. She tentatively leaned against his legs.

"Three weeks now, moreorless," Lady pulled a baffled face. "I haven't touched a drop – can't stand the stuff. Become quite a bore. Tea, coffee, Coke, mineral water … that's about it, Chris."

The detective shook his head in amazement and blew mischievously into Emily's ear. The child giggled, faked a frown and then wormed her way between his knees. She felt safe and warm.

"You look a whole lot better," Chris said, hugging Emily affectionately. "Your eyes, your face, the way you speak … everything about you. What on earth has happened? You're a changed woman."

Lady stared intently at the floor and nodded slowly, more to herself than to the man who was watching her. It was a full minute before she spoke and when she did the words were measured and strong.

"It's her," she indicated the little girl opposite. "It's Emily. I've grown very fond, very fond indeed."

"What about the mum? Amy, isn't it? What about her? She's only a kid herself, isn't she?"

A fierce fear lit up Lady's eyes and her body tensed: "You won't report her … or anything like that, will you, Chris?"

"Of course I won't Jane. I only want to help. You must know that by now." Lady's shoulders relaxed.

"What about social services?" he asked. "I'm surprised they're not involved. Emily must be on the 'at risk' register at the very least, surely?" He cleared his throat, not entirely sure that he wanted to get involved in such a conversation, and Lady came to the rescue.

"I don't think we should talk about this now, Chris," she inclined her head pointedly at Emily. The policeman nodded, raised his eyebrows and then shook his head slightly.

"I'd better go now," he said gently and Emily swivelled her head, looking straight into his eyes.

"Can you make that funny noise again?" she asked, her eyes wide and inquisitive. Chris Sellwood peered conspiratorially from left to right, before pulling Emily towards him and snuffling into her ear. She giggled and Lady smiled: "You're good with kids, Chris."

"So are you … Lady Jane," the policeman said softly, lingering over her nickname.

****

Two weeks later Lady Jane's mobile phone rang at three o'clock in the morning. Amy had gone out on some pretext and had not returned and Emily was in Jane's bed. Lady rummaged frantically for the phone on her bedside table and answered it as quickly as she could, so as not to disturb Emily, who was lying the wrong way round on the double bed, her feet inches from Jane's face. The voice the other end – Amy's voice – was garbled and hysterical. To make matters worse the signal kept fading. Lady swung her legs out of the bed, shaking the sleep out of her head: "Amy, slow down. Please slow down. Take your time, babe."

Lady paused, giving her friend time, and all she could hear was a series of muffled sobs and frantic breathing as Amy fought for control.

"I'm in the police station," Amy said. "I've been arrested. I'm sorry, Jane, I'm sorry …" Her voice broke off into sobs again and Lady waited patiently. "I don't know what's happening, I don't understand. They keep on about a caution or something and I don't know what they're talking about. They keep asking me if I'll accept a caution. I don't understand, I don't know what they mean, I don't know what to do …" Hysteria infected every word.

"Have you been using?"

"Yes," Amy replied, her tone suddenly subdued and sullen.

"Is that why they arrested you?"

A long pause and then, in an even quieter tone: "No, they arrested me in Lumb Lane."

"Oh Amy …," Lady trailed.

"I needed the fucking money," Amy screamed down the phone and then panted: "I'm sorry, Jane, I'm sorry. But I was going out of my fucking skull. I had to get some, Jane. You know what it's like. I had to have some. It's been three days …"

"Have they charged you with anything?"

Another pause and then a garbled answer and then silence and finally: "No, I don't think so. But they keep on about soliciting – on the game I suppose – and this fucking caution, whatever that is. Oh Jane, for fuck's sake come and get me. I don't know what to do … I'm going fucking mad."

Lady Jane rang for a taxi, asked the support worker on duty that night to sit in with Emily, borrowed £20 for the return fare and retrieved her friend from the police station, after persuading Amy to accept the caution. They were back in the refuge just after five o'clock in the morning. Jane put Amy to bed and took Emily, half-asleep and drowsy and fortunately unaware of the drama, back to her own room.

"Do you want them to take Emily away from you?" Jane asked harshly later that morning. Amy was sitting up in bed – sunken eyes, ashen face, bright red lipstick smeared around her mouth – nursing a mug of black coffee and smoking a cigarette. Her lips were quivering and her hands were shaking. Ash fell onto the duvet she had pulled protectively up to her chin and she tried to brush it away with a nervous and fruitless gesture. She merely succeeded in rubbing it into the material. She shook her head but said nothing.

"Look Amy, you are this far from losing your daughter," Jane raised her hand, leaving a millimetre gap between her thumb and forefinger. "Christ knows how you've managed to hang on to the little poppet for this long. For God's sake you have got to get help. And not just for your own sake, my sweet, but for the sake of your daughter. She wants to stay with you … she does not want to be taken into care."

"I don't know what to do," Amy said brokenly, tears rolling down her cheeks. "I need the stuff and the only way I can get the money is to go thieving or to pick up blokes … and picking up blokes is easier."

"Are you injecting?"

Amy hung her head, stared at the edge of the duvet cover she was gripping and nodded.

"How long?"

"Two weeks – I get my needles from a bloke down at Spargi's."

"Spargi's?"

"It's a sort-of nightclub a bit out of town, on the road to Batley. It's a bit of a dive."

Jane closed her eyes for a second.

"I'm taking you to our GP tomorrow morning," she said with gentle authority. "No ifs, no buts. We're going to get you on a methadone script. It's either that, my darling, or Emily will be taken into care. And we don't want that to happen, do we? You don't and neither do I."

"Okay," Amy whispered, forcing a bright but false smile. "Whatever you say, Jane. I want to go to sleep now. I'm tired. I just want to go to sleep." The teenage mum closed her eyes and was asleep almost immediately, her chin falling down onto her chest.

Lady Jane gazed at her young friend for a long time and her heart ached. She thought of her younger brother Julian, whose suicide would haunt her for the rest of her life, but the destructive guilt was beginning to find, after all the years, a positive focus. She was determined to do everything in her power to guide Amy and Emily away from tragedy, to protect them from the pain she and her family had suffered and to try to give them a second chance. Everybody deserved a second chance.

Lady Jane made an appointment for Amy to see Doctor Badat at the surgery the women of the refuge used. They sat in the waiting room – Amy, silent and reluctant, Lady kind but firm and in control, and Emily, playing quite seriously with a pile of plastic, multi-coloured building bricks. And when Amy's name was flashed upon the screen all three made their way to Doctor Badat's consulting room. There was no alternative, there was nobody else to look after Emily.

The doctor was understanding – he had dealt with many similar situations involving patients from the refuge – and he had a 'kiddie corner' permanently set up in his room. The first thing he did was to engage with the child, put her at ease and introduce her to a selection of toys, which included a rather grand Dolls' House. Emily was instantly engrossed and took no notice of the consultation.

"So how long have you been using?" the doctor asked, non-judgementally.

"Since I was about 15 – around four years, I think."

"And how long have you been injecting?" Doctor Badat had noticed Amy's arms the moment she walked in.

"A couple of weeks."

"Do you really want to stop, do you really want to get clean? How much do you want to do this, Amy?" The doctor's eyes were wide, his tone far from conciliatory. He wanted, quite rightly, to know the truth. What point would there be in placing this young mother on a methadone script if she was going to sell the substitute drug on the street in order to buy heroin? He had to be as sure as he could be that she genuinely meant to kick the habit.

"Yes … yes, I do," Amy replied, ringing her hands in her lap and averting the doctor's eyes. "Yes, of course I do. If I don't they're going to take Emily off me, aren't they? Jane told me … and Jane knows about these things. I've got to get off this stuff, I've just got to … for Emily's sake."

The doctor snapped: "But it has got to be for your sake too, Amy. It's no good saying that you're going to try to get clean for your daughter's sake, although that is hugely important. But the really important thing for you to realise, young lady, is that heroin, first and foremost, is destroying you. Oh yes, it's messing up everything else in your life, especially Emily, but that is a consequence of what it is doing to you."

Lady Jane frowned inwardly. She wasn't entirely sure that she agreed one hundred percent with the doctor. She knew what he was driving at and to a large extent what he said made sense. But her own recent experience with alcohol resulted from, as far as she was aware, a desire to look after Amy and Emily.

"I want to get clean, doctor … I've got to get clean," Amy said, but it was more to please Lady Jane than anything else. "I want to be a proper mother, I want to have a proper life, I want to be happy and I want my daughter to be happy." It was a short and inspired speech and there was an element of honesty, albeit wishful thinking honesty, in it. Doctor Badat, who had never met Amy Brown before, was impressed, Lady Jane less so. Nevertheless the outcome of the consultation was a methadone script, renewable weekly. Amy was also booked into twice-weekly substance abuse group sessions at a drugs and alcohol de-tox clinic attached to Bradford Royal Infirmary. It was a start …

On the way back to the refuge Amy was very quiet. She appeared to be having a silent and internal struggle: she jerked backwards and forwards, scratching her forehead and clearing her throat. Emily chose to sit on Jane's lap as opposed to her mother's as the taxi jostled with the city centre rush-hour traffic.

"Can I ask you something, Jane?" Amy said finally, staring out of the taxi window. The expression on the young mother's face was bleak and very old. Emily slipped from Lady's lap and ferreted around on the floor of the cab in search of a miniature mummy and daddy from the Dolls' House in the surgery, which Doctor Badat had given her.

"Will you look after Emily?" Amy whispered, still staring out of the taxi window. "I mean if anything happens to me." She swivelled around and her eyes were full of tears, defiant and brave tears, and there was a sudden strength and unfathomable maturity in that pale and tortured face.

Lady Jane nodded, not trusting herself to speak, and she stroked the back of her friend's head.

10

BISHOP JOHN fumbled with his pipe, tamped down the tobacco and worked his way through four matches until he got the evil thing going to his satisfaction. A heavy halo of smoke hung around his head and he sprawled back in his favourite armchair, shifting his bottom to avoid one of the springs which had patiently wormed its way through the well-worn fabric. He had stoically resisted his wife's efforts for the past twenty-three years to consign the ailing piece of furniture to the scrap heap.

The bishop was a tall and gangling man, thin but big-boned, with huge hands and feet. There was a boyishness about him: the unruly, snow-white hair which ever flopped across his long and grey face, the china blue eyes bright with enthusiasm, the quick and open smile. Despite 76 years of wear and despite the inevitable wrinkles, he was a youthful-looking man with the physical mannerisms of a teenager and yet the mental and emotional acumen of a very wise old man.

Midnight Sam was in perpetual awe of Bishop John but paradoxically always at ease in his company.

"You haven't been to see me for quite some time, Sam," the cleric said, pipe clenched between his teeth. "I was beginning to get a trifle concerned. Hope all is well …" (He had privately telephoned Brian Davies at the night shelter a couple of weeks previously to ask after Midnight. Brian and the bishop had a long chat.)

"I'm sorry, your lordship, but I haven't been myself lately," Midnight said apologetically. He reached for the schooner of sherry on the coffee table between them and took a small and delicate sip.

"Would you like a cigarette?" the bishop said, noting Midnight's agitation at the tantalising smell of his pipe. "You know where they are, old chap." Midnight Sam sprang to his feet, stepped across the room as if he were walking on red-hot coals and opened the heavy silver cigarette box on the mantlepiece. From habit he extracted two cigarettes, tucking one behind his ear for later and popping the other one into his mouth. He returned to his seat, leaned forwards and picked up the packet of matches on the coffee table.

"So what exactly is the matter?"

"Oh, I don't know, your honour. Things just don't seem to be the same anymore. I guess I never really got over The Prof's death. I used to look after him. I loved him, you know …"

"I know you did, Sam." The bishop's pipe went out and he rested it in the large, cut-crystal ashtray on the coffee table. He leaned back in his armchair, brushed a strand of hair from his eyes, folded his long arms and waited. He was fond of the street-drinker and he knew that there was more – much more – to the man than met the eye.

"I shouldn't have let him die, I …"

Bishop John jerked forwards with a frown: "For heaven's sake Sam, you have got to stop that nonsense. You of all people were a wonderful friend to The Professor, a true Christian, and we all thank you for that. *You* didn't let him die, Sam. He just decided his time had come."

"But if it wasn't my fault, then whose fault was it?" Midnight shook his head and closed his eyes for a second.

"It was nobody's fault … well," the bishop paused and gave a small and harsh laugh. "Well maybe we were all to blame, all of us. Maybe we all let The Professor die … and people like him." He was talking about society on the whole, about everybody, but seeing the expression of alarm on Midnight's face he added quickly: "But that doesn' t include you, Sam. It doesn't include you. It really is time, young man, for you to move on."

Midnight was taken aback: "But I don't want to leave here, your worship. I wouldn't know where to go."

Bishop John gazed at the ceiling patiently: "No Sam, I don't mean move on as in go away. I mean move on in your head. Stop dwelling on the past, start looking to the future."

"The future? I don't know what that means, my lord. What do you mean by the future?"

"How old are you, Sam?" Bishop John rubbed the side of his face. He picked up his pipe, knocked out the plug of dead tobacco and fiddled with a fresh packet of Old Holburn. Midnight took another sip of Harvey's Bristol Cream and noticed, with mild alarm, that he had finished the glass. The bishop nodded towards the decanter and Midnight smiled with relief and gratitude. He dutifully topped up the bishop's schooner and then made a point of only half-filling his own glass. He was, after all, cutting down.

"I'm 36," Midnight replied without hesitation. "I was born in Bristol on October 4th, 1974. Apparently I was what they call a bonny baby."

Bishop John cocked his head back, to one side: he hadn't been prepared for such a concise response. He had known Midnight for several years and had always respected the unspoken but rigid rule that one never delved into the past of such people, however tempting it was to do so. The Professor's he knew (it was a matter of record) and Fen's sad and ugly background had emerged during his high-profile trial. But the history of the others – of Scots Robby, of Splodge and Nobby, of Lady Jane and of Midnight Sam – no, they were all locked away between the covers of an unwritten book . The bishop shifted everso slightly in his armchair, as aware of the need to avoid frightening Midnight Sam back into his shell as he was of the need to avoid sitting on the sharp end of the rogue spring which protruded from his seat.

"You've got a good memory," he said casually.

"Everyone remembers when and where they were born," Midnight replied, a small smile on his face. The bishop kept silent. He blew a long and impressive funnel of smoke to the ceiling and gazed abjectly out of the stained glass window which overlooked his beloved cathedral. Midnight stared deep and long and unseeing into the depths of his drink, twirling the glass between the thumbs and forefingers of both hands. He smiled into the past and made a decision.

"My name is Samuel Midaka. I am half English and half Mandinka – that's an African tribe in The Gambia," Midnight began, still peering into his glass. "My father could speak five different languages, fluently, and he brought me to England when I was eleven years old. He taught in an English language school for foreign students in London. He was killed in a car crash …," Midnight whispered the last sentence and carefully replaced his glass of sherry on the coffee table, without taking a drink. The bishop said nothing.

Midnight was silent for a long time: he was back to that black day some 17 years ago when the principal of Edinburgh University had tip-toed into the lecturing hall and whispered into the lecturer's ear. Midnight could still remember the sudden change in the atmosphere: a darkness, a chill, an invisible but all-pervading mist of tragedy. And that was before the lecturer had called out his name. He remembered the day, as if it were yesterday, when his whole world collapsed. When Samuel Midaka became Midnight Sam. He looked into the understanding eyes of Bishop John and continued his story …

Samuel Midaka only survived the death of his father (whom he respected, worshipped and adored above all others) by subconsciously returning to the halcyon days when he was a young boy growing up in Banjul. He had slammed the door on the future, on the positive and no-doubt 'successful' direction his life was beginning to take in England (because, in his mind, without his father there could be no success, no future). He had about-turned and gone back to the unalterable safety of his childhood.

He was exploring Paradise Island, a few miles north of Banjul, where an unmarked border separated The Gambia from Senegal; he was watching the otters, the bushbuck, the many species of monkey, the hyena and the duiker. On rare and special occasions he would see a leopard – devil-eyed, lethal and belly-low to the ground – creep from Fathala Forest, or a primeval crocodile slip menacingly across the narrow creek which divided the island from the mainland. Or he was striking out in a languid but powerful crawl across the powder-blue Atlantic, often a mile from the shore. Or he was lazing on a creaky old hammock strung between two gnarled coconut palms at Madiyanna Lodge on the edge of an endless beach. Or he was with his father, talking to him, listening to him, being with him …

"You'd never believe it, your honour, you'd never believe it but I was at university," Midnight Sam shook his head slowly, not quite believing it himself. "Can you imagine … me, Midnight Sam, at university?"

But Bishop John did not appear to be surprised; he merely shrugged his angular shoulders and sipped his sherry, peering over the rim of his schooner at the man opposite, his eyes narrowing imperceptibly.

"What about your mother?"

"She left us when I was a very small boy. I can hardly remember her. Long hair, blue eyes I think. She always seemed to be busy. And she didn't smile very much. In fact I don't remember her smiling at all. I still dream about her … sometimes … but not very often." Midnight's voice was tinged with regret. "We were never close, not at all, not like me and my dad."

Bishop John struggled inelegantly to his feet, knocked the coffee table as he sidestepped his way towards the sideboard and brought the sherry decanter back with him. This was most definitely the time to overindulge the Harvey's Bristol Cream. He topped up both glasses, splashing a little on the threadbare, once royal blue, Wilton carpet and flopped back into his armchair, prising both hands together into a prism and choosing his words with care.

"At the beginning of our chat you said that you hadn't been yourself of late. So what do you think is the reason for that? What's changed?"

Midnight replied, too quickly: "Like I said, Bishop John, I miss the old days. I guess I still miss The Professor. He was the best thing since my dad …," he trailed, but a small, self-questioning frown had creased his forehead, as if something new had occurred to him. Which it had. The bishop, an eternally patient and deeply perceptive man, feigned a return to the pipe palaver.

After a lengthy pause, which entailed a number of matches and one or two sips of sherry, Midnight continued: "I wonder whatever happened to Lady Jane?" He shot the bishop a challenging look, as if to say 'and don't you dare read anything into that.' But the bishop was an expert in adopting a neutral and sombre stance.

"She was such a lovely lady, you know, a lovely lady. Lady Jane was a good nickname ... I was the first one to call her that. She was very fond of The Prof and he was very fond of her. I think she must have reminded him of his own daughter ... I expect that's what it was." Midnight nodded in agreement with himself and wriggled in his chair, a quick smile of nostalgia on his face.

"We were a real team – the three of us – a real team. We used to go everywhere together, do everything together. And *did* we have some laughs ... It was always The Prof, Lady Jane and me. Sometimes Scots Robby and even, on the odd occasion, Fen. But it was really just the three of us." Midnight grinned at some memory and the sparkle, which had deserted his big brown eyes for so long, was back.

"Lady used to link arms with The Prof and me and march us up and down the street. People used to stare but we didn't care; it made us laugh. She had such a wonderful smile. The corners of her eyes would crinkle up and she would put her hand to her mouth, just like a little girl. She bossed us about something wicked ..." Midnight was still grinning. He picked up his schooner of sherry and downed it in one. "We went on this day-trip to Weston-super-Mare – Lady Jane, The Prof and me – and, bloody hell, was it a day to remember! We caught a coach and spent the whole day on the beach or in the amusement arcades. Lady and me – well, we walked right across the beach and we paddled in the sea and we splashed each other. We had to hurry back because the tide was coming in. We had a race and Lady won. Well actually, your grace, I let her win. Oh, it was such a good day, a day to remember."

Midnight Sam's smile faded and his expression was sad: "On the way back, she told her story to The Prof – you know, how she ended up homeless and an alcoholic and all that, how she ended up the way she was – and I pretended to be asleep. But I wasn't. I heard every word.

She had a hard time, you know. And she blamed herself for everything, for all the horrible things that happened."

"But you're no different, Sam," Bishop John cut in gently. "You're just the same, forever blaming yourself for everything. And it's no more your fault than it was Lady Jane's. It's life, Midnight. Sometimes it's the way the cards are dealt."

"I know ... I do know. But Lady ... well Lady was different. She was a lovely person." Midnight paused, searching for the right words. "She was special."

A cloud crossed Midnight's face and his body stiffened. He remembered the man she was with – the cruel and violent man – the man who used to hurt her. The man who, on one occasion, he had very nearly killed with his own bare hands.

"Why don't you go and look for her?" Bishop John asked with calculated but totally dishonest innocence. "Why don't you try to find her? Why don't you go and look for Lady Jane?"

11

AMY BROWN started her methadone script with determination – faithfully taking the prescribed dosage, keeping her appointments at the day clinic, jumping through those hoops necessary in the agonising battle against heroin addiction. And for the first eight days she stuck religiously to the new and difficult routine.

Lady Jane, who hardly let her friend out of her sight, recognised the signs only too well. Wild and hungry eyes, the animal cunning, pained grimaces, the shaking, the inappropriate bursts of laughter, the coughing fits, the vomiting, the tension in both body and mind. Lady recognised the signs because she had displayed them herself ten years ago.

Amy was having a bad time because, for six days, she had been hoarding her methadone medication and was going through the agonies of 'cold turkey.' Lady had her suspicions but her friend's denials were vehement, although the vehemence did nothing to allay the older woman's fears. Amy was hoarding the tablets in order to sell them to buy heroin. It was a familiar course of action.

The two women were sitting on a bench in the tiny play area close to the refuge. They were watching Emily on the mini-seesaw with two boys of similar age. She was behaving in a bossy manner, instructing the lads to follow her and scolding them if they failed to keep up. A typical little girl, despite the abnormality of her circumstances. Amy was leaning forwards, twisting her hands in her lap, eyes fixed, unseeing, on a red-and-blue Thomas The Tank Engine rocking horse.

"I need to go to the shops," she said with a sudden jerk. "I've started my period, I need some Tampax." The smile she flashed Lady was quick and desperate and unconvincing. "Would you look after Emily … please. I won't be long." Amy sprang to her feet, a pleading yet stubborn expression on her face. "I'll see you both back home."

Lady said and did nothing; she stared ahead and then closed her eyes, while Amy hurried from the play area, forgetting to say goodbye to her daughter. Lady took Emily home, cooked her sausages, beans and chips, gave her a bath and put her to bed – her own bed, of course – and read her a story. She stroked the little girl's forehead until she went to sleep and then she kissed the child on both cheeks before creeping from the bedroom. She left the door ajar and a side-light on. She made herself a mug of instant coffee, snuggled into a corner of the sofa in the living room with a magazine and waited. Lady Jane fell asleep at two o'clock in the morning; the magazine slipped from her fingers onto the carpet and her fourth mug of coffee, half-consumed, went cold.

She awoke with a start, her heart thumping. Pale grey dawn was sneaking through a gap in the curtains. Before she looked at the clock on the wall, before she collected her thoughts, before she wondered what had happened to Amy, she darted out of the chair and into the bedroom to check on Emily. And she was fine, still asleep, lying on her back, diagonally across the bed, her favourite teddy bear (the one which Lady had bought for her) close by her side. Lady Jane sighed with relief, sat on the edge of the bed and rearranged the duvet to cover the child. She squeezed the tiny feet and winced guiltily because they were cold. She rubbed each one in turn between her hands. Emily stirred, blinked open her eyes, gazed wide-eyed at the ceiling for several seconds and then across at Lady Jane. She grinned, rubbed her eyes, yanked the teddy bear to her side and sat up.

"Where's mummy?" she asked without concern. Lady felt a cold wave of panic. She had no idea where Amy was; she might have returned to the refuge during the night, but then again she might not have.

"She's asleep, poppet. She's very tired and she asked me to look after you for a bit. You'll have to make do with your Aunty Jane."

Emily accepted the explanation without question: "Can I have some orange juice? Can I have it in my Cinderella mug, Aunty?"

Lady nodded, patted Emily on the head, tried to remember where the Cinderella mug was, raised a forefinger with sudden recall and hurried out of the flat, across the corridor and into Amy's room. There was no sign of the young mother. Lady Jane returned with the mug to find Emily jumping, feet together, up and down on the bed as if it were a trampoline.

"I'm jumping, Aunty Jane," she said breathlessly. "Let's all jump up and down." Lady proffered the Cinderella mug, half-full of orange juice, and Emily stopped in mid-jump. She reached for the mug with both hands.

"Is mummy not very well again?" She asked, orange juice dribbling from each corner of her mouth.

"No poppet, she's not very well at the moment ... but she'll be better soon."

"Can I stay with you until mummy gets better, Aunty Jane?" Emily asked, suddenly remembering her teddy bear and yanking him up by the right leg.

"Come here, poppet. Come and give your Aunty Jane a great big hug."

****

Lady telephoned the local police station, Bradford police headquarters and a number of Bradford hospitals – all in vain – before she decided to call Chris Sellwood. It was a Sunday morning – a time she knew was precious to the detective – but she could think of nothing else to do. She was frantic with worry.

Sellwood, his wife, seven-year-old daughter and five-year-old son were sitting around the breakfast table tucking into a selection of bacon and eggs, scrambled eggs on toast, boiled eggs and bread 'soldiers,' corn flakes, fresh fruit salad, orange juice, tea or coffee. Sunday mornings were indeed very special, one of the few times when the little family could sit down together and catch up. Chris was listening closely to Daisy patiently explaining to her rather backward father the difference between a dress and a skirt when his mobile phone rang. He let it switch over to Voicemail and waited until Daisy transferred her attention to helping Danny cut up his bacon before he checked the screen: 'Lady Jane.' He stepped into the hallway, closed the door gently and called her back.

"Chris?" the voice was soft but anxious. "Oh Chris, I'm so sorry to ring you today, a Sunday of all days, I really am, but I don't know what else to do …"

"That's okay, Jane, what's the matter?"

"It's Amy ... she hasn't been back all night. I don't know where she is and I'm worried sick. I've tried the police and the hospitals ..."

The policeman scratched the side of his head, thinking quickly, instantly the professional, no longer the family man.

"Where and when did you see her last?" he began, his tone flat and precise.

"Yesterday afternoon. She suddenly upped and went. We were in that little kiddies play area just off Parliament Street, around the corner from here."

"Can you remember the time she went off ... the exact time?"

"Half-past three ... no, it was closer to four ... quarter to four I think or maybe ten to."

"And you've got the little girl?" But it was more of a statement than a question.

"Of course," Lady said, "she's with me."

The detective smiled at the proprietorial tone in her voice before bombarding her with questions: what was Amy wearing, did she have any money and how much, was she carrying anything, in which direction did she go, did Lady know any of her dealers, where did she usually get her stuff, what was the name of her doctor, had she taken her methadone ...?

Clear of alcohol and focussed on the well-being of her friend and of her friend's daughter, Lady came up with a surprising number of accurate answers. Sellwood was impressed.

"Stay with Emily, Jane. Don't go looking for Amy yourself. Leave that to me. I'll ring you the moment I get some news. And keep your mobile phone by you and keep it turned on."

"Okay Chris ... oh, and Chris ..." Lady's eyes were warm with gratitude. The policeman waited for her to continue. "Thanks, Chris. You're a star."

"No problem. Is your phone charged?"

"It's been on charge all night."

Chris Sellwood smiled again and then he went to work. It was the end of his much-cherished family Sunday and the time was not yet ten o'clock in the morning.

****

The detective found Amy at around 5.45pm that evening. She was lying face down on the floor of a dreary bedsit in the attic of a rundown, four-storey, multi-occupancy DHSS house adjacent to the Goat and Bicycle, a notorious drugs and pick-up pub in down-town Bradford. The young mother was wearing a skimpy, purple bra and pants and a pair of black, fishnet stockings. Her handbag lay beside her, its contents, including an empty syringe, were scattered across the carpetless floor, along with two used condoms. She was breathing fitfully, groaning faintly and squirming her legs.

When Sellwood turned her over, she looked up at him with dull and vacant eyes and tried to smile. It was a ghastly attempt. Her lipstick was smudged and her mascara had run, forming two black streaks down both cheeks.

"Where are your clothes?" Sellwood shook Amy's shoulders and stared into her eyes, willing her to rally. She flopped her head to one side, nodded to a corner of the room and waved an arm in the same direction.

The detective helped the teenager get dressed, sat her on an unmade bed, boiled a kettle and made her a mug of strong, black coffee, which he had brought with him for that very purpose, along with a handful of sugar cubes. He sat beside her on the bed and coaxed her into drinking the coffee. She obeyed, clutching the mug and blowing weakly onto the surface. She took tiny but desperate sips and Sellwood waited for the coffee to kick in: it was half an hour and three mugs later before Amy turned and looked at him: "Don't I know you?" she slurred, her head lolling pathetically onto her shoulder. "I've seen you somewhere before … I think you're nice … if you like, it's okay, it's £20 if you want to …" She rested her hand on his thigh and gave him a lewd and curiously repugnant leer. He removed her hand firmly and put his arm around her shoulders.

"I know you and Jane from the refuge," he spoke carefully, allowing the words to sink in. "I'm a copper, Amy. Chris Sellwood. Detective Sergeant Chris Sellwood. Remember?"

"I've done nothing wrong. Honest. I've done nothing wrong." Amy's voice shook with sudden panic and she tried to break free from the policeman's hold.

"Amy, just listen to me. I'm not here to arrest you, I'm here to take you home. Your daughter, Amy. What about your daughter? What about little Emily?"

"Oh Christ … oh fuckin' hell," Amy broke away from Sellwood's hold with unexpected strength and staggered to her feet, head in hands. "Is she all right? Where is she? What's happened to her?"

"She's okay, Amy, she's okay. Jane is looking after her. She's in good hands."

Amy fought hard and successfully for control, brushed herself down, looked around the disgusting room as if for the first time, shuddered and said quickly: "Can I go home please? Can you take me home? I want to see Emily, I want to see my daughter."

The detective scooped up Amy's belongings (minus the syringes) and stuffed them into her handbag; he extended a hand, which she took timidly, and allowed him to lead her down the four flights of stairs. He ushered her into his unmarked police car which was parked outside the pub.

The landlord – a man well known to the police – peered out from behind a pair of net curtains and breathed a sigh of relief. Sellwood had burst into the Goat and Bicycle an hour previously and had made himself abundantly clear: "Tell me where she is and take me there *now* or tomorrow morning you will be hit by the biggest drugs raid you can imagine. The warrant's already made out and it only takes my say-so to execute it. Your feet won't touch the fucking ground and I'll close you down. Now … where is she?" Sellwood was being economical with the truth but it did the trick.

Amy started to cry in the car on their way back to the refuge. Tears rolled down her cheeks as she gazed, unseeing, out of the passenger window. She did not make a sound and Chris respected her sorrow and said nothing. There was nothing he could say, in any case.

Lady Jane was waiting on the doorstep of the refuge. Chris had already telephoned ahead. She did not make a huge fuss of the teenage mum – she merely cradled an elbow and kissed her young friend lightly on the cheek – but the look she gave Chris would have melted granite. Words of gratitude were unnecessary. Her eyes said it all.

Over the next few days, Lady Jane became more like a mother to the 19-year-old than a friend, escorting her to the doctor's surgery to collect her prescription and then to the pharmacy to pick up the medication and then sitting on the edge of Amy's bed in the refuge to ensure she took the methadone. Lady was leaving nothing to chance this time. And, to be fair, Amy was beginning to give it her best shot. She handed over her benefit money to Jane every week and followed the older woman around like a lamb. They went everywhere together.

Three weeks after her wobble, Amy decided to tell Lady Jane what had been on her mind for several days. Amy, Lady and Emily were sitting in a corner café one afternoon, when the young mum gripped Jane's arm and whispered: "I'm going to make a will, Janey. I haven't got any money or anything like that, of course, but I want to make sure that Emily is all right if – well, you know – if anything happens to me." She lowered her voice so that it was barely audible, but Emily was far too preoccupied blowing bubbles through the straw in her bottle of Pepsi to pay any attention.

Amy closed her eyes for a second before continuing: "Would you look after her – would you be her guardian, all official like – if I died?" She mouthed the last word silently. "I know it's a lot to ask, but I don't know what else to do."

Lady shushed her friend with a forefinger to the lips and pulled a funny face at Emily, who had looked up suddenly. "You know the answer to that, babe. Of course I would. But don't you ever worry about things like that. Don't be so morbid. You're only 19 and you're doing well with Doctor Badat. He's really pleased with you. Nothing is going to happen to you. You're going to be a great mum, honey, a great mum. You've just got to hang on in there. And I'll be around to see that you do."

Amy shrugged and looked out of the café window, which streamed with early April rain. Her pale and weary face bore the physical and mental marks of a middle-aged woman. When she turned back to Lady she wore a gay expression but there was despair in her smile which Lady recognised only too well. "I know ... I'll be fine."

"So what is it that you want to do ... with this will thing?" Jane asked. "I presume you want it all official, get papers drawn up, see a solicitor, that sort of thing ... Is that what you want babe?"

Amy nodded, her eyes wide but looking inwardly at the tragedy and confusion of her brief life. But she nodded with genuine relief.

"Can I have another Pepsi, Aunty Jane?" Emily asked as soon as she could blow no more bubbles in the first bottle.

"Have you ever known a good man? I mean a really good man. You know, kind and gentle ... and good." Amy asked the question inconsequentially, but passionately. And Jane followed the subtle sequence, as one woman to another.

"I had a boyfriend once, when I was a lot younger, younger than you actually." She smiled down into her cup of coffee and gave it a slow stir. "He was lovely. He had the most beautiful hands, I remember. Long and tapered and artistic, like a concert pianist."

"What was his name?"

Lady shook her head: "I don't know. I can't remember. All I can remember is his beautiful hands."

Amy smiled and took rare control for a second: "So what happened to him? Why didn't you get married, have lots of kids and live happily ever after?"

"You know what happened, Amy, you know why ..." Lady Jane trailed sadly. There was a pause in the conversation, a comfortable pause. Emily began to chatter about nursery school (Lady had organised that a week ago) and Amy smiled at her daughter.

"Has there ever been anybody else? I mean, were there any other nice guys in your life?" Amy wanted to know. She had never known a nice guy; she had never known a man with the hands of a concert pianist.

"Have I ever told you about Midnight Sam?" Lady Jane asked, a faraway look in her eyes. "Now there was a good man ..."

12

BOB Cooper put down the telephone, pursed his lips and leaned back in his faded green leather chair. He was still unsure of the word *his*. The chair belonged to his predecessor, Old Hoskins, for a huge number of years and it had refused to be replaced. Not that Cooper would have contemplated replacing it anyway, despite the fact that it squeaked at the slightest movement and listed stubbornly to the left … and was uncomfortable.

The only change about the editor's room was the plaque on the door: *Bob Cooper, Editor.* After all, surely he had waited long enough? He felt it was his due. Fifteen years on the Evening News, moving steadily and deservedly up through the ranks – senior reporter, news editor, deputy editor and finally the number one slot itself. At 54, had he not earned his journalistic spurs?

Cooper had always been a damn good journalist, but he also turned out to be a damn good editor, a hands-on editor who could and would (often to the frustrated admiration of his staff) roll up his sleeves and get stuck in. And who would invariably make a better job of it – whatever *it* was – from planning the Splash to rewriting the Splash to penning an emotional and compelling comment piece. At the thrice-daily editorial conferences his news editor, features editor, chief sub-editor, picture editor and sports editor would often grimace at the man's consummate ability. "That bastard is never wrong, it drives me mad," the news editor – a competent and ambitious young buck – had complained bitterly on a number of occasions.

Cooper stared at the telephone, scratched the side of his nose and rubbed his forehead. He was thinking about what Bishop John had said to him earlier that day. It was only the third time he had ever spoken to the man: the first was regarding the unforgettable sponsored walk by the city's homeless the previous summer and the second was to arrange coverage of The Professor's funeral. All the softly-spoken cleric had said was: "Do you mind if I come and see you, Mr Cooper? There is something you might be interested in. It's about Midnight Sam." A pause and then an apologetic question: "You do remember Midnight Sam, don't you?"

Remember Midnight Sam? How on earth could the editor forget him? It had been a great story: the homeless raising money for the homeless and in the most incredible fancy dress. And all the brainchild of one of the most popular if inauspicious citizens of the city. The fancy dress walk had been unforgettable. Scots Robby in a kilt, a pair of Manchester United football socks, a First World War army helmet and a Confederate army jacket from the American Civil War; Splodge and Nobby opting for a 'vicars and tarts' theme – an interesting mix of gymslip, fishnet stockings, red lipstick, St Trinian's school tie, dog's collar and, for some reason, a Draculean cloak; poor Paddy Maguire sweltering in a gorilla outfit minus the head, endeavouring to strum a stringless guitar; and Midnight Sam. Well …

Midnight had chosen his outfit with infinite care. After all, he was the organiser and surely all eyes would be on him? He need not have worried on that score. He had taken more than an hour and a half to prepare himself and the result was unforgettable: leopard-skin loincloth, a North American Sioux Indian chief's headdress, a pair of green Wellington boots and a Winnie The Pooh scarf. Ruby red warpaint on forehead, cheeks and chin completed the ensemble. And what a photograph it made! The story, thanks to a local freelance agency, went national. Inside page leads in The Sun and The Daily Mirror, a glowing feature in The Big Issue magazine and a respectable thirty seconds slot on BBC television national news, not to mention the lead item in the regional bulletin.

The following day Bishop John kept his appointment with the editor; he was five minutes early, but Cooper had given instructions that he was to be shown straight into his office. The editor was not a man to play games and the bishop, a quiet but supremely intuitive man, appreciated that.

"Do you mind if I come straight to the point, Mr Cooper?" the bishop asked as soon as he had draped his lanky and awkward frame onto a chair which faced the editor's cluttered desk, the clutter including four mugs of cold, black coffee and an overflowing ashtray. (The smoking ban had not reached the editor's office).

Cooper smiled and shrugged his shoulders: of course he didn't mind. He was a hard-nosed, dyed-in-the-wool journalist and getting to the point straightaway was etched on his soul.

Bishop John crossed his lengthy legs, patted his jacket pocket and pulled out his pipe. "Oh dear," his hand flew to his mouth, "I forgot for a moment. It's no-smoking, I take it." Cooper raised his eyebrows and nodded down at the ashtray, his eyes twinkling. He pulled a packet of Marlborough Lights from his pocket with a grin: "If you don't tell, then neither shall I." The two men lit up, the bishop's operation taking longer than the editor's.

"So what has the lovable rogue been up to this time?" Cooper leaned back in his chair, the cigarette dangling from the corner of his mouth. "Wrong time of year for one of his famous Christmas parties. (Bishop John winced: he remembered the fight and the subsequent story in the Evening News) Not another sponsored walk, is it?"

"No, no Mr Cooper, it really is nothing like that …," the bishop said, pretending to fuss with his pipe, which had gone out, but he was in fact suffering from an unexpected bout of embarrassment. He coughed to clear his throat, lost for words. Cooper came to the rescue.

"I'm intrigued," the editor leaned forwards, both elbows on the desk, resting his jaw in the palms of his hands. The chair squeaked viciously.

"Well, Midnight Sam has not been himself these days," the cleric began, thrusting the pipe back into his jacket pocket and immediately pulling it out again to ensure that it was not still alight. "No, he's not been at all himself. At first I put it down to The Professor's death – they were very close, as I'm sure you know – but then something else began to niggle away at me". Bishop John rearranged himself in the chair, picking up on the fact that the editor was far from bored with the conversation. "You probably don't remember Lady Jane – she was a latecomer to the group – but I got to meet her on a number of occasions. Vulnerable, lost soul, but she was a gentle and utterly charming young lady. She was very sweet. Well, Midnight Sam and The Professor and Lady Jane were always together until one day, completely out of the blue, only a few weeks before The Professor died, she disappeared. She and that rather unpleasant man she was with – they simply upped and left town. To be honest, at the time, her disappearance was somewhat eclipsed by The Professor's death, as I'm sure you remember?"

Bob Cooper nodded sadly: he certainly did remember. And, to his credit, after the funeral, he had run an emotional and hard-hitting story about the tragic and "unjust" circumstances that led to the once high-flying public school teacher's dramatic fall from grace. It had won him no favours with the Chief Constable or with his own Board of Directors. Cooper had accused the 'establishment' of destroying an innocent man.

"The thing is, Mr Cooper ... and this is why I am here ... well, the thing is that Midnight Sam misses Lady Jane and misses her a great deal, far more than he realises himself. I know I'm an interfering old busybody and you'll probably tell me to go away and mind my own business, but I think something should be done about it ... I really do."

Cooper rubbed his chin: "You say that Lady Jane – great name, by the way – you say that Lady Jane disappeared. Have you any idea where she went or, more to the point, why she went away?"

"As I said, there was this man she was with, an extremely unpleasant creature. He was, from what I've heard, a violent and very jealous man. He didn't approve of Lady Jane having friends, especially male friends. He didn't approve of that at all ..."

"And you have no idea where she went?"

Bishop John shook his head.

"And you want me to run a story in the Evening News about these two unlikely lovebirds? You want me to help get these two lovable down-and-outs together? You want me to play cupid to a couple of homeless and hopeless street-drinkers ...?"

"They may be homeless, Mr Cooper, and they may be street-drinkers, but they are not without hope. None of us is without hope, Mr Cooper. And they are most definitely not, as you say, down-and-outs."

Mildly chastised, Cooper, ever the consummate journalist with an eye for the unusual, prised the fingers of both hands together and smiled mischievously: "Okay, Bishop John, you've got yourself a deal."

13

MARCUS Webster poked his head through the swing doors of The Mitre, eyes darting about with curiosity, before he ventured inside. The scruffy old boozer down the lower end of South Street was not the sort of place he normally frequented. With a judge for a father, a consultant paediatrician for a mother and with all the resultant trappings of privilege and affluence, Marcus had moved in fairly grand circles since birth. His pedigree was predictable: preparatory school, public school, university and a 'gap' year penning indifferent but passionate poetry in his parents' holiday cottage in County Cork. He had returned to England unpublished but determined to become a journalist and, after studying for a year on the National Council for the Training of Journalists course in Cardiff, he had landed a job as a junior reporter on the Evening News. The pay was a pittance, but then money was never going to be a problem for him. His editor, Bob Cooper, had a nose for talent and Marcus Webster, despite the accent and the silver spoon, was one of those rare journalistic finds: a natural.

The 22-year-old had edged cautiously up to the swing doors of The Mitre, not because he didn't want to be there but because he wasn't sure he'd got the right pub. He noticed the name of the public house etched into the frosted glass panel, nodded with satisfaction and walked in, notebook in one hand, the other thrust into a trouser pocket. The smile on his face was neither flashy nor false; it was eager and friendly.

Bobby looked up and gave his new customer a cursory appraisal: faded light brown corduroy trousers, faded brown leather jacket, long woolly scarf wrapped twice around the neck and black brogues much in need of a polish. But Marcus always looked a cut above, whatever he wore, and the only concession to his class was an immaculate haircut and an ever-present, very expensive neck-tie, knot loosened along with the top button of his shirt.

"Could I have a pint of beer, please?" he asked, placing his notebook on the bar. Bobby picked up the notebook, swabbed a puddle of something on the bar, carefully wiped the back of the book and replaced it. Marcus took no notice and paid for his drink.

"That's jolly good," he said convincingly, smacked his lips and put the less-than-sparkling glass back on the bar. The landlord straightened his rounded shoulders a fraction and grunted. "I'm trying to track down somebody by the name of Midnight Sam. Apparently he's one of your regulars …"

Bobby stiffened, as did Midnight Sam, who was sitting in the alcove with Mickey the Mouth and Tattoo Terry. The words 'trying to track down' or such like immediately closed doors, brought blinds down and guards up and created an invisible but invariably impenetrable wall of wariness. Spectres of authority, the police, the council, 'them,' … trouble for the likes of Midnight and his mates.

Marcus was sensitive to the mood change and he continued hurriedly before the landlord could say anything: "I'm from the Evening News. My boss was having a word with Bishop John the other day. They want to do a piece about Midnight Sam and somebody by the name of Lady Janet, I think it was … ?" A clever query and a clever, intentional mistake over the name.

"You mean Lady Jane," Midnight piped up from behind the young man.

The reporter turned and raised his glass in acknowledgement: "Sorry, that's right. Lady Jane."

"What sort of … piece?" Midnight asked.

"Oh nothing at all sinister, just about life on the streets, the camaraderie, the highs and lows. You know the sort of thing …"

Midnight had no idea, but he nodded cautiously.

"We call it a colour piece," Marcus added importantly and Midnight bristled.

"What d'you mean 'a colour piece'? I'm not getting involved in all that racial stuf. Last time your paper wrote about racial tension there was a bloody riot in East Street. Someone chucked a brick through the mosque window and all hell broke loose." Midnight shook his head and retreated behind his glass of Olde English.

Marcus Webster gathered up his pint and strolled over to the alcove where he stood comfortably, intuitively not sitting down until asked. "No, no it's nothing like that. A colour piece is a newspaper expression for a descriptive story as opposed to what we call 'hard news.' Nothing at all to do with racial issues. Bishop John thought it might be a good idea for us to write about …," he paused and rubbed the side of his nose, "… the gentlemen of the road." The young man smiled and extended his hand: "You must be Midnight Sam. My name is Webster, Marcus Webster."

"Marcus," Mickey the Mouth savoured the word with a low chuckle. "Marcus Webster," he mimicked the posh English accent and prepared for banter, but Midnight gave the Irishman 'the look' and Mickey fell silent, although his fierce little eyes twinkled with mischief. Marcus and Midnight shook hands and the street-drinker nodded at the vacant stool. The ex-public schoolboy sat down.

Bob Cooper's brief to his junior reporter had been clear: Midnight Sam was to be given the impression that the interview was about homelessness in general and not about him and Lady Jane. So Marcus went to work, with journalistic acumen far beyond his tender years. He asked about the street culture, about alcoholism, about life out in the cold, about being homeless, about the dangers. But every so often he would casually drop in a question about Midnight and Lady Jane: what was she like? how did the others get on with her? what did he think of her? where did she go? why did she go? would it be nice to have her back? would it be nice to see her again? would he like to look for her?

The reporter did well – he got his story – but he made one mistake. Fifteen minutes into the interview and with four empty glasses on the table in front of them, he stood up and offered to buy a round of drinks, adding, fatally: "Don't worry, I'm on expenses, my editor told me to look after you."

Midnight, Tatts and The Mouth exchanged almost spiritual glances and the landlord, who had been listening, visibly flinched and prepared for the street-drinkers' regular afternoon session to stretch well into the evening, which it did.

They left The Mitre at eight o'clock. Midnight Sam, Tattoo Terry and Mickey the Mouth unsteady on their feet but focussed on reaching the night shelter before the 8.30pm watershed, while Marcus Webster, equally unsteady on his feet, was far from focussed. He dropped his notebook three times on a circuitous route to the swing doors. But

looking for lady

the young man was in such a wonderful, ethereal mood that he hardly noticed. He felt close to God. He told Bobby that The Mitre was the best public house in England; he pumped Midnight's hand and declared him to be a 'lesson to us all' and 'a living institution,' he swore undying allegiance to the IRA and told Tattoo Terry that he was determined to have a spider's web tattooed on his own right elbow. However when Tatts tried to persuade Marcus to make an appointment with Bert Finch Midnight felt obliged to intervene. He treated Terry to a withering stare. He had not forgotten the state of Tattoo Terry's nose after a session on the narrowboat, even if Tatts had.

The young reporter zig-zagged his way up South Street, fearlessly but tunelessly whistling Molly Malone and apologetically bumping into several people. It was fortunate that Cooper did not need the story for the next edition (he had tentatively pencilled it in as a possible 'splash' for Saturday, a traditionally 'soft' news day). For as soon as Marcus found his way back to his flat, he collapsed into a deep sleep, from which he did not emerge until eleven o'clock the following morning. When he eventually turned up for work (half a day late) he was roundly bollocked by his news editor and then suffered the sarcastic edge of his editor's razor-sharp tongue. But he made an excellent job of the story.

****

Midnight Sam was sitting on a park bench in the Cathedral Gardens, munching a cold pasty and sipping cider from a can which he had wrapped in a brown paper bag. Life had been so much easier before he had decided to cut down his drinking. One three-litre bottle of White Lightning or Tesco's Strong Cider or whatever, secreted in a carrier bag, would have seen him through the afternoon. But now he had limited himself to small cans of cider, the operation had become

dennis apperly

arduous and time-consuming. Also a carrier bag bulging with cans was less easy to conceal and made more noise.

It was one of those bright and fretful early spring days: nervous, cotton wool clouds scurrying across a pale blue sky and a cold but kindly sun bathing the city in a gay light.

Midnight was upending the brown paper bag to his lips when a tall, upright man in his early sixties stopped in front of him. Midnight Sam finished the can, wiped his mouth with the back of his hand and squinted up at the man, who was silhouetted against the rays of the sun.

"I recognise you," said the older man, hands clasped behind his back in a military manner. "You must be Midnight Sam."

Midnight put the brown paper bag back on the bench – it clanked – pulled a face and thrust both arms in front of him in feigned supplication: "I suppose I must be."

Commander Eric Pankhurst MBE, headmaster of King's College, sat down stiffly on the bench, next to the brown paper bag: "You don't mind if I sit here?" Midnight shrugged and gave the headmaster more room.

"Who are *you*, then?" Midnight asked, feebly fighting the slur in his speech. It had been a long lunchtime.

"Name's Pankhurst. Just came out for a breath of fresh air and to get a paper," he waved a folded copy of the Evening News.

"You one of those solicitors from the court?" the words rolled into one monotone, with 'solicitors' giving Midnight particular trouble.

"No, no, I'm a teacher … over at King's," Pankhurst said with a smile. "I'm the head, actually … for my sins."

Midnight sobered up a fraction: "Friend of mine was a teacher at your school. Best teacher you ever had, he was, best teacher in the whole wide world, he was …"

"Yes, I know," the headmaster said quietly. "He was a damn fine teacher, a damn fine chap all round actually."

A frown clouded Midnight's face and he shot the headmaster a sideways glance, a not altogether friendly glance: "Pity you lot didn't stand by him. Bloody shame. Good bloke, The Prof, best bloke I've ever known, apart from my dad, of course. We had some good times we did. Me, The Prof and Lady Jane. Some bloody good times …," Midnight looked away, overcome with melancholy, his eyes moist.

Commander Pankhurst stared at the ground, his mind reeling from the sudden stirring of those dark and muddy waters. It was like a physical blow, an unexpected and deadly assault on his conscience.

"It is indeed a pity, a great pity," the headmaster spoke after several seconds, "and, do you know, I don't think a day passes without me thinking about it and regretting it. Not a single day."

Midnight Sam looked puzzled: "How d'you know my name?" The beginning of their conversation suddenly registered.

The headmaster unrolled his newspaper and handed it to Midnight.

"You're famous Midnight Sam and so is your lady … and I wish you both all the happiness in the world," Pankhurst said brightly, but his voice was hoarse. He got up sharply and marched off down the path which wound its way around the Cathedral, without a backward glance. Midnight watched the retreating back of the headmaster until he disappeared around a corner. He then peered down at the front page of the newspaper on his lap.

His own face, grinning and streaked with warpaint, stared back at him, alongside a picture of Lady Jane. Both photographs had been taken at the street-drinkers' sponsored fancy dress walk nearly two years ago. The headline read: LOOKING FOR LADY.

14

GORDON BLACKLOCK waited in the doorway of a funeral parlour opposite the women's refuge in Bradford where Lady Jane lived. It was 8.30pm and Lady would be leaving at any minute: her shift at the nearby Indian takeaway began at 9pm and she was never late. She had been working there for three weeks and had become popular with customers, colleagues and with her boss, a chubby, sharp-tongued, middle-aged Asian woman with a heart of gold. Jane worked from 9pm until one in the morning, which suited her new responsibilities: she would always be on hand during the day, either to keep a close eye on Amy or to look after Emily should the young mother succumb to temptation, and it gave Amy some quality time with her daughter. The refuge had Chris Sellwood's telephone number, only to be used in extreme circumstances, and Lady Jane's mobile number too, to be used if necessary, whatever the circumstances.

Jane hurried down the path to the front gate, huddled beneath a large, golfing umbrella. The rain was bouncing off the pavement and Lady fumbled with the latch, dropping the umbrella during the operation and cursing to herself. Blacklock stepped out from the doorway opposite, took a few paces across the road, his steps muffled by the rain, until he was standing in the gutter a matter of feet from the refuge gate. He watched her struggling with the umbrella.

"How you doing, Janey?" his soft but cold voice froze Lady Jane. Her shoulders slumped but then raised again and she straightened and turned to face him. He was wearing that dangerous smile she knew only too well and the rain had plastered heavy locks of his thick, black hair to his forehead. Large raindrops dangled from his nose and chin. Lady returned his stare and fought to prevent her hands from shaking. "It's been a long time, my girl, too long."

Lady Jane inspected her watch and smiled weakly, apologetically at the man who had tormented her for five years. She looked at him, without saying a word, for several seconds and then something strange happened inside her. Her immediate reaction of resignation and fear faded and she realised, with astonishment, that she was no longer afraid of the man. A quizzical furrow creased her forehead and she bent down to pick up her umbrella. She noticed that her hands were no longer shaking.

Blacklock was taken aback; he felt restless under her calm and cool appraisal. So he resorted to type: he stepped up onto the pavement with a menacing jerk, the cruelty back in his eyes and in his body language. But, to his surprise, Lady held her ground, not challengingly but with mild patience. Blacklock was confused. The usual pattern, after he had overstepped the mark, was for him to apologise, grovel a bit, make a joke of the incident and escort her back to his domain. Lady would be quiet for an hour or so, but, with the help of a bottle or three of strong cider, he would soon have her back under his control, back where he believed she belonged. But this was different: she was looking directly at him (something she never did) and there did not appear to be fear in those eyes.

"I wondered how long it would be," she said. "I'm a bit surprised it's taken you so …"

"For fuck sake, come on back to me," Blacklock cut in impatiently. "Look, I'm sorry, I'm really sorry. I've had a lot of time to think – two months – and I promise you, on my dead mother's grave, I'll never raise a hand to you again." He continued in a falsely light and intimate tone: "You and I belong together, Janey, we always did. Do you remember when I rescued you from that scuzzy squat you were living in? Beat up a bloke for you, I did, beat the fuckin' shit out of him, I did. That's what I think of you, Janey. Think the fuckin' world of you, I do. And … come on, Janey … I know you feel the same about me."

Lady Jane hung her head for a few seconds and gazed passed Blacklock into the rain-drenched street. It was as if she was seeing him for the first time and Blacklock felt a cold wash of uncertainty, bordering on fear, so he employed the only tactics he understood. He broadened his shoulders and squared up to 'his woman,' his bulging chest a couple of inches from her chin, his small black eyes burning with violence, his massive fists clenching and unclenching.

"You're coming back with me now, you fuckin' bitch, you're coming back to where you belong," he snarled, his thin, cold lips curling to expose his teeth. But Lady did not flinch (she could hardly believe it herself) and she did not take a backward step. Instead, she gave her umbrella a little twirl, placed one hand on a hip and smiled. She had no idea where the strength was coming from – no more idea than Blacklock had – but no way was she going to let it go.

"I have to go now, Gordon," she said simply. She sidestepped the man, splashed through a puddle in the gutter and walked off, down the middle of the road. After a dozen paces she stopped, raised a forefinger and turned around: "By the way Gordon, I'm not a 'fuckin' bitch' and I'm not coming back with you and this (she pointed her umbrella back at the women's refuge) is where I belong. Goodbye Gordon … have a great life."

Lady Jane marched down the road, head held high, but her heart was thumping against her chest and her body was shaking with emotion. Blacklock scowled but he made no effort to follow her. He brushed the straggled hair from his eyes and walked off, very slowly, in the opposite direction. He had lost battles with Janey before, but he had never, ever lost the war. And he was never going to, the bitch! It was only a matter of time. She had held out in the past – a couple of days, a week, even a month – but she had always come running back to him in the end. However this time there was something different, something which Blacklock could not put his finger on and it disturbed him. As he splashed his way through the puddles to the Rose and Crown – a grim and loveless pub on the corner of an equally grim and loveless street of terraced houses – he could not rid himself of the expression in her eyes. She had never looked at him that way before.

****

Bretherton Elgoods was a good, well-established firm of solicitors; although specialising in criminal law (which is how Chris Sellwood had first encountered them) they dealt in most legal matters. Sellwood was friends with one of the junior partners, Richard Elgood, who handled conveyancing and probate; they played golf together most Sunday mornings.

looking for lady

Lady Jane and Amy kept an appointment which the detective had made with the young lawyer on their behalf and the older woman explained the situation, Amy nodding vigorously whenever her opinion was asked. They both listened attentively, Lady taking his words in more than Amy. They signed various documents and shook hands. Amy had made her will and she had stipulated that she wished Lady Jane to have sole custody of her daughter Emily in the event of her death.

"How much do we owe you?" Lady asked as the lawyer rose to his feet to usher them from his office. She fumbled inside her handbag and extracted her purse. She had hoarded £50 from her wages over the past three weeks and hoped that it would be enough. Elgood shook his head with a warm smile: "Don't you worry about that, it's been taken care of."

Lady frowned: "No, I must pay you … for your time … really I must."

"There's no charge. As I said, it's been taken care of." But Lady Jane pulled out two twenty pound notes and a ten pound note and thrust the money under the lawyer's nose. Elgood slumped his shoulders, waved the money aside and stroked his nose. "Your friend and mine – although I'm not entirely sure I still regard him as my friend anymore – thrashed the pants off me on the golf course last weekend and the wager, if I lost, was to sort out your affairs."

The frown remained on Lady Jane's face, but it softened: "And if you'd won?"

"I've been playing golf with Chris Sellwood most Sundays for the past eighteen months and I have never beaten the damn man … not once," the solicitor replied with genuine annoyance.

Lady and Amy left the office and walked down the street, arm in arm, towards the bus-stop. They shared a feeling of relief. Whatever happened in the future now, Emily would be looked after, Emily would be safe, Emily would be okay. The knowledge gave Amy huge comfort and it gave Lady peace of mind and strength and a rare sense of purpose, of destiny. For the first time since her younger brother Julian had died she felt a need to survive, a reason to be. She felt she had a place in the world, at last.

Blacklock was standing by the front gate to the refuge, when the two women walked down Parliament Street. He had been waiting for two-and-a-half hours, skulking in the doorway of the funeral parlour opposite. He was now wearing a second-hand suit, shiny and ill-fitting, and cheap new shoes. He had also had a haircut and had shaved off his beard. He could, however, do nothing about the expression on his face or the cruelty in his eyes.

"Who's that man?" Amy asked and gripped Lady's arm tightly.

"That's the bloke I've been telling you about. Gordon Blacklock. He came around the other day. But don't worry, Amy, he's wasting his time. It's over and I would never, ever go back to him. Don't you worry, Amy. He can't hurt us."

But Amy was not reassured: she knew men like Gordon Blacklock, she had known them all her life. Even from a distance, even before the man spoke, Amy instantly recognised the type and it made her tremble, it made her want to run away.

"What are you doing here, Gordon?" Lady Jane asked, her voice steady, steadier than the confusion inside – the battle between the old and new emotions, the old weakness and the new strength. Blacklock wore a pained, sorrowful expression; Jane noticed a recent bruise high up on his left cheek.

"Come to see you, Janey, come to see how you are."

"I'm fine, Gordon, just fine. You're looking very smart … cut your beard off as well. I thought you'd never do that." She suppressed the smile which tried to creep onto her face and waited. Amy Brown cowered at her side and coughed nervously.

"We need to talk, Janey," Blacklock looked at the ground, shuffling from foot to foot, his broad, square-cut shoulders sagging, his massive hands thrust deep into his trouser pockets. Janey took a closer look at the suit. It was too long in the leg and too small across the chest. "Let's go for a drink. I know a little boozer not far from here. Sort of pub you'd like." He flashed a ghastly smile and went to take Lady Jane's arm but she pulled back. Amy's grip on her arm tightened.

"I suppose you mean The Rose and Crown," Lady said. "No thanks, Gordon … and anyway I don't go to pubs these days, I don't drink any more."

"You don't *drink* any more?" Blacklock said incredulously. He raised his head back and chuckled nastily. "Don't give me that crap, Janey. You're a fuckin' alkie, always have been, always will be. Like me, Janey. You're an alkie, you'll never give up the fuckin' booze."

Lady shrugged, sidestepped Blacklock and opened the gate. She ushered Amy through first and then she followed, closing the gate behind her. She turned to face him: "It's no good you keep turning up here, Gordon. I'm not coming back. This is where I live now. It's over between you and me and I don't want to see you again. Not ever."

"It's her, isn't it," Blacklock growled, nodding his head towards Amy. It's that girl, isn't it. I've seen you with her, down at the kiddies playground with that little brat of hers."

"She's not a brat," Amy spoke for the first time, her voice shaking with a mixture of fear and indignation.

Blacklock looked over Jane's shoulder at the teenage mother, his eyes cruel, all pretence at humility and penitence gone. Jane recognised the expression only too well, as she did the sudden, dangerous mood swing. She turned around, nodded to Amy to do the same, and followed her friend up the path, bracing herself for the inevitable torrent of abuse (or worse.)

"You're a dyke, that's what you are. Can't get a man – and I'm not surprised the way you fuckin' look, half your fuckin' teeth missing – so all you can do is get it off with that little tart." He raised his voice to a bellow, his face white with rage, but he made no attempt to open the gate.

"You're a lesbian fuckin' dyke," he roared, turning on his heel and striding off down the middle of the road.

****

After Blacklock's fourth outburst outside the women's refuge, Lady Jane telephoned Chris Sellwood. But it wasn't simply the ugly scenes outside the refuge, often in front of Amy and on one occasion when Emily was present, which had prompted Lady to contact the detective. Blacklock had begun to follow them to the play area, to the shops and even to the doctors' surgery. He always kept his distance, said and did nothing, but he maintained a frequent presence, a disturbing presence. A dark and menacing cloud, never far away. His new tactics merely unsettled Lady Jane, but they terrified Amy. And even Emily became aware of "that nasty man who's always following us."

Sellwood picked up Lady an hour after she telephoned him. They drove north to a country pub the detective knew on the road to Ilkley, on the edge of the moor. Lady had masochistically insisted on going to a pub. It was a test she had been determined to take.

"It's a text-book case of harassment," said the policeman. "With corroborating evidence from Amy and from staff at the refuge, he wouldn't have a leg to stand on. Court would make an injunction preventing him from contacting you or from following you and if he took no notice of that he'd find himself behind bars before he damn well knew it."

"I want to leave the refuge, Chris," Lady said, "injunction or no injunction. I want to take Amy and Emily away, I want us to leave the refuge and set up home somewhere together, somewhere he won't find us." She sipped an orange juice and closed her eyes for a second. "As long as he knows where I am, even if he never comes round, I will never feel safe. And it's not just me I'm thinking about, Chris – it's Amy and Emily now. They're both terrified of Gordon and I feel responsible for that. It's my fault and I couldn't bear to think of …"

The detective shushed her with a finger to his lips, half-turned to gaze through the leaded-light windows of the pub across the ranging moor and worried a fingernail while he concentrated.

"I know someone in the city council housing department," he said, after half a minute's silence. He reached for his glass of red wine and continued: "Amy and Emily, I am sure, would be classed as having 'priority need,' especially given the current situation. That plus your own status as a carer for them both, in all but name, would put you pretty high up on the waiting list. I could make some discreet enquiries on your behalf, if you like."

Lady toyed with her glass of orange juice: "Why do you do all this for us?" she asked quietly. "I ring you on your days off, even on a Sunday, I cry on your shoulder. I must be a complete pain in the bum, but you never complain. You're always here for us … and there's nothing in it for you. You amaze me. I really don't know what we'd have done without you, Chris. Why?"

The policeman shifted awkwardly in his chair and scratched the back of his neck: "You must be about the same age as my wife. Late twenties, early thirties? You come from a nice, stable, fairly middleclass background, just like Sheila does. But there the similarities end. Sheila married a man who loves her very much and she gave him two beautiful children. We live in a comfortable home on a bland but safe housing estate. Of course there are the inevitable ups and downs, but by and large we are happy ... and we have things to look forward to, we have a future.

"And that could so easily have been you, Jane, if it hadn't have been for that lowlife who introduced you to heroin all those years ago. It could so easily have been you. And what about my wife? If the tables were turned, what would have been her story? Possibly the same as yours.

"D'you know, when I walk down the stairs in the morning, sit down in the dining room, eat my bacon and eggs, play with my kids, kiss my wife on the cheek and go to work ... I feel guilty. I feel that I don't deserve to be *that* happy."

Jane leaned forwards and patted Sellwood's arm: "Why guilty, Chris? For God's sake why? You've worked hard for what you've got and you damn well deserve it. You're a good man, Chris and fair play to you."

"So what about you? What about Amy Brown? What about little Emily?" Chris Sellwood sat up in his chair, challenge in his voice. He twirled the stem of his wine glass between his fingers. "You're living in a women's refuge, living in fear of a violent brute of a man, while I'm ..."

Lady interrupted: "You say that you love your wife very much and I'm sure she loves you very much too. *That's* where you're both very lucky."

"So what about you?" the policeman asked.

"I haven't got anybody," she replied. "I haven't got anybody to love, not a man anyway. I love Amy and Emily ... (a pause) ... and my mum and dad of course. But I haven't got a man and I don't suppose I ever will."

Sellwood frowned: "How do you know that? What about that bloke you're always on about – the mixed race guy from your days down south? Can't remember his name. You often talk about him."

"Midnight Sam, you mean?"

Sellwood nodded.

"He's a lovely man, gentle and good and kind …," Lady trailed, lost in some memory. "But he doesn't love me or anything like that. He's just Midnight Sam."

15

THE UNDERPASS was empty and quiet and Midnight Sam was content to share his hideaway with a Tesco's trolley, an abandoned and half-consumed takeaway burger and chips and an empty bottle of Blackthorn Dry Cider.

Midnight was a troubled man, troubled and disturbed. He had hated all the publicity. The local radio and television stations had followed up the story in the Evening News, as had the Big Issue and two of the 'red tops.' He had endured a week of unwanted exposure, which, more than anything else, had interrupted his drinking routine. But now he had had enough. He could not understand what all the fuss was about anyway. Oh yes, he liked Lady Jane, of course he did; he was very fond of her and he missed her. But all this palaver about 'two unlikely lovebirds' and 'Looking for Lady' … What the hell was that about?

Midnight stood at the entrance to the underpass and looked up into the clear night sky. Not a cloud and, away from the bright lights of the city, a dome of stars pulsed with silent, infinite mystery. He was overwhelmed by a deep sense of relief: whatever happened here, here on the ground, on the wasteground or wherever, whatever happened on the whole damn planet … what did it really matter? The sheer, unadulterated insignificance of his own existence gave him a huge feeling of comfort. The stars reached down and touched his soul and, for a trice of time, he became part of the universe.

Midnight cracked open his fifth can of Strongbow, toasted the gods and took a long, indulgent drink. Since the publicity about him and Lady Jane, he had kept a low profile, avoiding most of his usual haunts and leading an unaccustomed solitary existence. Besides feeling deeply embarrassed and ridiculous, he felt let down by the people he trusted and respected most … by Bishop John and Brian Davies, in particular. Midnight guessed that they must have played a major part in the subterfuge. The young Evening News reporter was merely doing his job – Midnight did not blame him for that – and the editor of the newspaper, he too was just doing his job. But the bishop and the night shelter manager were not just doing their jobs; they were interfering in Midnight's life and not being entirely honest about it.

Midnight arranged his sleeping bag amidst a supermarket trolley, a rusty bicycle frame and a pile of six-month-old free newspapers some bored delivery boy or girl had thrown away. They were miraculously dry, which was a bonus for Midnight, who never felt truly complete unless he had a fire going nearby. So he made home in the neglected and rarely used subway three-quarters of a mile out of town underneath the western bypass. And there he remained for the next three weeks, barring furtive trips to the post office on Thursdays to pick up his benefit money and to the One-Stop Shop most nights to replenish his stock of cider and cold pasties. He stopped selling the Big Issue and sought no company but his own. Once a colourful, welcome and ubiquitous character around town, he was hardly ever seen and when he was, he would scuttle away, head down, refusing to speak.

Brian Davies missed him. Midnight was such a calming influence at the potentially volatile night shelter. The other homeless street-drinkers missed him too. His warmth and constant good humour helped them through the long, bleak days. Bobby missed him on both personal and commercial grounds (the alcove in The Mitre was never the same without the lovable down-and-out) and Bishop John missed him. Midnight's regular visits to the Bishops' Palace always brought a breath of fresh air, a slice of reality to the formal and austere inner sanctum of the Christian faith. It was, in fact, the Man of God who finally broke the impasse and coaxed his errant lamb back into the fold.

The bishop got caught in a brief but ferocious shower on his way to the underpass. His ankle-length raincoat was black with rainwater, a shapeless deerstalker sagged over his over-sized ears and his huge, brown brogues splashed through the inky black puddles which had formed in the domed entrance.

Midnight was squatting on a stool he had 'found' in Wilkinsons, warming his hands in front of a small, fierce and cheerful fire, a can of Strongbow by his side, when he saw the veteran cleric out of the corner of an eye. He heard Bishop John clear his throat tactfully, but he did not acknowledge the older man's presence. The bishop picked his way through the detritus and turned the shopping trolley onto it's side and sat down, legs dangling between the wheels. He undid the buttons of his raincoat and loosened the belt. He removed the deerstalker, ran his long, bony fingers through his unruly, snow-white hair and extended both hands to the flickering flames of the fire.

"How are you, Midnight?"

The street-drinker's shoulders were set stubbornly and there was a sullen sadness about his demeanour, a dullness in the normally warm and twinkling eyes. Midnight Sam shrugged and pulled a face, his mouth down-turned.

"I've missed you, I've missed our little chats …," the bishop persevered, a small puddle of rainwater forming between his feet. He drew out his pipe from an inside jacket pocket, filled the bowl with tobacco and fussed clumsily with several matches before he got it going. Suddenly remembering something, he patted a pocket of his raincoat and produced a packet of Benson and Hedges. He leaned forward and dropped the cigarettes into Midnight's lap.

Midnight shifted his position and picked up the packet: "Thanks for the cigarettes, your honour." His voice was small and flat. They both relapsed into silence, smoking and occasionally coughing. After five minutes, it was Midnight Sam who spoke.

"I didn't want all that stuff in the paper," he said sadly. "I didn't want everyone to read about me and Lady Jane … it was private. Just between Lady Jane and me. Not that there was anything between us," he added hastily.

"I'm sorry, Sam," said Bishop John with genuine remorse. "I'm really sorry. Best intentions, I assure you. We just wanted you and Lady Jane, wherever she is, to be happy."

"Made me a laughing stock, your worship. Everyone's laughing at me." Midnight stared into the flames and tilted a can of cider to his lips.

"Still cutting down?" Bishop John asked solemnly and Midnight nodded with equal solemnity.

"I don't seem to be saving any money, though," he said. "In fact, since I've cut down to half pints, it's been costing me more. I can't understand it."

"Nobody is laughing at you, Sam," the bishop stretched out an arm and patted Midnight reassuringly on the knee.

"Mickey the Mouth seemed to think it was funny."

Bishop John shook his head dismissively and blew a cloud of tobacco smoke to the ceiling of the underpass: "Nobody takes much notice of Mickey, Sam. He's always laughing at someone. Nice enough chap, I shouldn't wonder, but full of the old Irish blarney. No Sam, rest assured, you are most certainly not a laughing stock. And, anyway, as they say in the newspaper business, it's yesterday's news … tomorrow's fish-and-chip paper. Everyone's forgotten about it now."

Midnight looked up sharply, eagerly: "D'you think so, bish – I mean your honour – do you really think so?" Bishop John nodded, took the pipe from his mouth and inspected the old briar with a scowl: it had gone out.

"Would you like a can of cider?" Midnight rummaged around in the black plastic bin liner at his feet.

"Do you know, Sam, I don't mind if I do," said the bishop. He took the can, examined it with a bewildered expression on his face and tentatively handed it back to Midnight Sam. "But would you mind awfully opening it for me. It looks a mite complicated and my good lady wife is forever reminding me how clumsy I am." Midnight opened the can and handed it back to the bishop. "Can't remember when I last tasted cider," the bishop rubbed his chin reflectively. "I think it must have been at a harvest festival down in Taunton many, many years ago …"

Some things have to be seen first-hand and not simply read about, to be truly appreciated. The writer can do his or her best to tell the story, paint the picture, convey the atmosphere. But the written word will always be second-hand and therefore marginally second-rate. The reader must rely on imagination. So, try to imagine the scene …

An elderly bishop, dripping rainwater, sitting astride an overturned Tescos shopping trolley in a deserted, rubbish-strewn underpass on the outskirts of his city, drinking Strongbow cider from a can in front of a little fire. And, squatting opposite, on a stool recently stolen from a local superstore, also drinking cider from a can, a ragged street-drinker by the name of Midnight Sam.

****

Three days later, Midnight collected his benefit money from the post office and walked down the centre of pedestrianised South Street towards The Mitre, his head held higher than it had been for quite a while. Nobody was laughing at him – the bishop had said so – and nobody was. Instead they smiled and that was because they were pleased to see him.

Bobby's chest heaved with relief when he saw Midnight push open the swing doors to his pub. Forgetting that his errant regular was 'cutting down,' he poured a pint of Olde English before Midnight reached the bar.

"Thanks Bobby, but I only drink halves these days – don't you remember?"

The landlord pursed his lips and made to retrieve the pint, but Midnight (who was eccentric but not insane) quickly picked up the glass: "Wouldn't like to see it go to waste." He demolished half a pint in one go, wiped his mouth with the sleeve of his donkey jacket and looked around the pub to re-familiarise himself with the place. He pulled out a brown envelope from a trouser pocket – his benefit money – and inspected the contents.

"It's on the house, Sam," Bobby mumbled almost beneath his breath and added gruffly, "good to have you back."

Midnight smiled – the warmth was back too – and he turned to acknowledge Mickey the Mouth, Tattoo Terry and the nervous, taciturn youngster with a terrible stutter and bad teeth, who had latched onto the trio a couple of months ago.

"Come and sit yourself down, Midnight," Mickey pushed a stool out from underneath the table in the alcove and Tatts sprang to his feet, beaming with pleasure. The nervous youngster smiled nervously.

"I've got a new tattoo, a real beauty," Tattoo Terry bristled with enthusiasm. "You'll never guess where it is."

Midnight stroked his chin, revelling in the crazy intimacy of his drinking pals and shook his head: "You're right there, Tatts, I've no idea."

"I think we'd better pop into the gents – I can show you there. A bit more private." Tatts scanned the bar secretively, from left to right.

Midnight shook his head: "I don't think so, Terry. Why don't you just tell me where it is – and what it is?"

"Well, the other day I had this idea, so I went down to see Bert Finch in his barge and …"

"Don't tell me you went back there, not after what he did to your nose?" Midnight was aghast. "Good God Tatts, you must be out of your mind."

Mickey the Mouth came to the rescue, bored to distraction with the topic of Tattoo Terry's latest work of art, which had dominated the conversation for ten seemingly endless days. With a stroke of genius, he volunteered to buy a round of drinks and it wasn't even his turn. No announcement was more guaranteed to change the course of any conversation.

"I've been thinking about this 'Looking for Lady' stuff over the past few weeks and I've made a decision," Midnight said, while the other three sipped their cider in unison. Three glasses were returned to the table with a combined, orchestral clink and Midnight scrutinised his little audience, searching for the merest hint of mockery and finding none. "I think I would like to find her. Find out how she is, nothing more than that. She was a friend to me and The Professor, a bloody good friend, and I would like to know that she's okay and I …," Midnight stopped himself and picked up his glass.

"And what, Sam?" Mickey leaned across the table, his shoulders hunched. "And what?"

Midnight Sam frowned at the Irishman: "And nothing, Mickey. As I said, she's an old friend and I'm worried about her. I just want to know that she is all right, that nothing bad has happened to her. That's all Mickey. Nothing more than that."

Mickey shrugged and brought out his harmonica. He blew noisily through the frets, wiped the tiny instrument with a tissue and raised his eyebrows to the landlord, who nodded. Mickey's unshaven mouth clasped the harmonica, his eyes closed, the crows' feet spread out across most of his pale and weathered face and the veins on his temples bulged. The pub fell silent and Bobby placed the glass he had been polishing back on the bar without a sound. When he had finished, Mickey blinked the tears from his own eyes, wiped his mouth organ dry and put it back into the pocket of his threadbare jacket.

"Where d'you learn that, Mickey?" asked Tatts quietly and the Irishman shrugged.

"Moonlight Sonata, Ludwig van Beethoven … and beautifully played," mused Midnight Sam and Mickey the Mouth darted him a curious look.

16

THE time had come for Amy Brown and her daughter to venture out together on their own. The young mother had been on a methadone script for the past four weeks and was beginning to display a cautious determination to succeed, rather than her previous lack-lustre obedience and eagerness to please Lady Jane. Jane was nervous about the experiment. Nevertheless she forced herself to make light of the situation.

"Isn't Aunty Jane coming with us, mummy?" Emily asked as Amy struggled with her daughter's tiny shoes.

"No babe," Lady chipped in gaily. "I've got a bit of a headache. Mummy is going to take you to the swings today."

Emily frowned: "But mummy might get ill again, Aunty Jane."

Lady was firm: "No she won't Emily. Mummy is a lot better now. Now you two get along and have a good time. I'll see you both later."

Lady Jane pulled the net curtains apart to watch Amy, hand-in-hand with her daughter, walk down the path, open the gate, head off down the pavement to the playground and brave the world. Her heart surged out to her young and vulnerable friend and her friend's even younger and more vulnerable charge, but there was nothing she could do about it: the experiment had to be tried.

The air was sweet and bright with the advent of spring. Mild-mannered May brought a brush of new greenery to the trees and water-coloured the cloudless sky the palest blue. Amy shook her head with an air of involuntary freedom and raised her pale face to the gentle sunshine. Emily looked up at her mother and shivered with pleasure. Neither noticed Gordon Blacklock, skulking in the doorway of the funeral parlour opposite the refuge.

Amy settled on to a park bench, lit a cigarette and watched Emily race from one piece of play equipment to another, following an older boy whose face was solemn with importance. After she drew on her cigarette she inspected the backs of her hands and noticed, with mild surprise, that they were hardly shaking at all.

The past few weeks had been a colossal uphill struggle for the young woman and she didn't know how she would have coped without Lady Jane. Although she felt she owed everything to her older friend, Lady had been adamant that the only person who could truly help a heroin addict get clean was the heroin addict. And Amy was sticking scrupulously to her reducing methadone script and the craving – the unbearable, all-consuming, mind-bending craving – was getting duller by the day. She had bad times of course but Lady helped her through those, sometimes hurrying back to the refuge midway through her shift at the takeaway to sit with her friend and wait for the monster to go away. For the first time during her 19 years in the world, Amy was tentatively experiencing an alien but heart-warming concept: hope.

She was done with prostitution, she was done with heroin, she was putting on weight, she was feeling fitter physically and mentally and Emily had stopped wetting the bed and had stopped suffering those appalling nightmares.

The three of them were shortly due to move into a pleasant, two-bedroomed, ground floor flat in a housing association development in Queensbury, three miles west of Bradford. It had a fully-fitted kitchen, a new bathroom and was sparsely but adequately furnished courtesy of three homeless charities who had been approached by Chris Sellwood and also courtesy of the detective's wife, who pretended that she needed 'a sort-out.'

Amy finished her cigarette, stubbed it out on top of a rubbish bin and waved to Emily, who was serving the little boy with imaginary goodies from the play shop.

"You want to give up them cancer sticks," a voice with a strong Newcastle accent made her start. "Stick to the brown lassie, won't do you as much harm as them cancer sticks."

Blacklock stepped out from behind Amy and sat down on the bench next to her. He pulled a quarter bottle of cheap whisky from an anorak pocket, took a generous swig and belched loudly. Amy inched to the far end of the bench, staring at the man with wide and apprehensive eyes and saying nothing.

"You still shaggin' my woman?" Blacklock asked, moving closer to Amy. The young mother clasped her hands together in her lap and fought to find some courage.

"It's not like that," she whispered finally, not looking at Blacklock. "It's nothing like that. She's my friend, my best friend, the best friend I've ever had."

Blacklock scratched the back of his head and then rubbed his chin – he was growing his beard back again and the black stubble was patchy: "Tell me lassie, what do you dykes get up to? Who does what? Seen it in the porno mags of course, but I never really understood what you get out of it. Why don't you get yourself a bloke and have a proper fuckin' shag?"

Amy felt herself begin to shake all over and a sickness crawled from the pit of her stomach. She tried to light another cigarette but she dropped the lighter. Blacklock bent down and picked it up. He offered the lighter back to her but when she went to take it he grabbed her wrist with his other hand and squeezed, a cold, thin smile on his lips. Amy gasped and tried to wrench her hand free and the mother of the small boy who was playing with Emily on the other side of the play area stood up uncertainly, conscious that something was wrong. Emily suddenly stopped playing and peered across at her mum. "It's that nasty man again," she told the boy, who shrugged and launched himself at the climbing frame.

Blacklock thrust his head forward from his hunched shoulders until his face was almost touching Amy's and hissed with extraordinary venom: "She's my woman, you fuckin' dyke, and I'm going to get her back where she belongs – with me. If I were you I'd take that little brat of yours and fuck off for good before something happens – to the fuckin' pair of you."

Amy lashed out with her free hand and scratched Blacklock on his left cheek. Blood oozed from two vertical wounds. He winced with pain, dabbed his cheek and inspected the blood on his fingers. He looked back at Amy, his eyes dull and lifeless, and cuffed her hard with a cupped hand across the side of her head. She tumbled off the bench on to the ground and both Emily and the mother of the boy ran across the playground to where Amy lay. Blacklock ran off heavily and vanished around a corner of the street.

Emily screamed and burst into tears and the other mother knelt down by Amy and draped an arm around her shoulders.

"Shall I call an ambulance? I think we should call the police." The woman searched for her mobile phone but Amy shook her head from side to side.

"No, no, please don't, I'm okay," she said, touching her cheekbone which was beginning to redden. "No damage done … you musn't call the police."

"But you've just been assaulted, you really ought to get the police, you know."

Amy scrambled to her feet and flopped back onto the park bench, breathing deeply, and extended an arm for Emily. Her daughter shuffled closer, her chest heaving and tears trickling down both cheeks.

"No," she said, mustering her strength. "Please don't call the police. Look, I'm sorry … and thank you … but I've got my reasons."

"Well if you're sure," said the other woman uncertainly, "if you're sure you're all right …"

Amy smiled weakly: "I'll be okay … and thanks again." The woman raised her eyebrows and shook her head. She called her son and the pair left the playground, the little boy glancing over his shoulder as they went.

On their way back to the refuge, Amy swore her daughter to secrecy: "You musn't tell Aunty Jane about that nasty man, Emily; you musn't say a word about what happened. Do you hear me? Not a word. If you do, then Aunty Jane will go away and you'll never see her again." Emily's eyes widened with horror and fresh tears glistened. "I wish Aunty Jane was here, mummy. Everything is all right if Aunty Jane is here."

Amy's heart sank: however hard she tried it was never going to be enough; however much she loved her daughter it was not going to be enough. She felt for Emily's hand as they walked down the road but her daughter kept her distance and followed, two steps behind, scuffing her feet and staring at the ground.

****

On the following Saturday, Lady Jane, Amy and Emily moved out of the women's refuge and into the two-bedroom flat in Queensbury. It was a fretful, blustery day, indecisive and with outbreaks of glorious sunshine hot on the heels of petulant flurries of rain. But for the odd little family it was a day of optimism, a day of hope.

Chris Sellwood loaded his car with their meagre possessions, plus two large cardboard boxes of various foodstuffs (his wife had been busy) and drove them to their new home.

"What's all this?" Lady surveyed the light and airy living room with amazement. There were flowers everywhere: vases of lilies, roses, gladioli and daffodils on the window sills, on the second-hand pine dresser and on the square, glass-topped coffee table in the middle of the room.

"Susan's idea," Sellwood said gruffly. "A sort-of 'welcome to your new home' thing. Brightens up the place though, don't you think?"

Amy sniffed at the roses on the coffee table and her daughter dutifully followed suit. But then Emily spotted the rocking horse in a corner of the room and she lost all interest in the flowers.

"And where did that come from?" Lady frowned at the detective and inspected the rocking horse. It was made out of solid wood and it was new. Emily stood by the lovely thing and stroked the mane of real horse hair. Her eyes were wide with wonder. The policeman shrugged.

That Monday Lady registered with the nearest medical centre and organised Amy's methadone script. She also made a decision one morning, while she was looking at her reflection in the bathroom mirror. The four missing teeth – thanks to Blacklock – would always make her look ugly. So she sought out the nearest National Health dental practice and added her name to the waiting list, which would give her time to save up. And in the same week she managed to find herself a part-time job, five mornings a week, working in a town centre café, at first as a waitress but soon doubling up as a breakfast chef. She was efficient and reliable and the Turkish family who ran the café took to her straightaway.

Amy did not tell Lady about her confrontation with Blacklock until they had been living in the flat for three months and even then she did not tell the whole story.

"You should have told me, Amy. I could have got Chris to sort things out."

"I wanted to wait until I could be sure that we'd managed to get away from him," Amy replied. "I don't know why I felt that way really; I was confused and scared. But he doesn't have a clue where we are, Jane, does he? He's gone for good now, hasn't he? Out of our lives forever?" Lady nodded.

"Are you sure he didn't hit you or touch you or anything like that …?" Lady trailed. Amy shook her head and Lady left it at that. She wasn't convinced her friend had told her everything but it was a long time ago and Blacklock had not reappeared on the scene.

Emily experienced her first birthday party on August 15th, when she was four years old. Six of her friends from nursery, three young families from the same block of flats, Chris Sellwood, his wife and their two children were invited. They all came. Chris organised a Bouncy Castle and he took responsibility for the barbecue in the communal gardens. The weather was kind and Emily was beside herself with excitement. To avoid the excitement transforming into a tantrum, Chris engineered the birthday girl's victory in pass-the-parcel … several times.

It was the first and last birthday party Emily spent with her mother.

17

NOBODY could ever recall who suggested the car boot sale. Some thought it was Midnight Sam, others pointed the finger at Mickey the Mouth or Tattoo Terry and there were those who laid the blame squarely on the shoulders of Brian Davies or even, believe it or not, Bishop John. But nobody really knew for sure. Not that it mattered: the idea gained momentum at such a fantastic pace that its origin soon became irrelevant.

However what is undisputed (and a matter of record) is that the majority of the planning took place in The Mitre, on Thursday afternoons, over several pints of Bobby's finest (and only) draft cider.

Since Midnight's return to the fold and since his reluctant admission that, yes, he did miss Lady Jane and that, yes, he would like to see her again, the original generic sentimentality became a serious business. Looking for Lady assumed near-military status; it had become a tactical operation and would, in future, be treated as such. And, as with all military manoeuvres, there had to be a nerve centre, an 'Ops Room,' and that's where the alcove at The Mitre came in. Mickey the Mouth was in his element, back to his glory days planning and fighting for the Republican cause.

"You're going to have to go out dere and find her – she won't come to you," said the Irishman. "It's no good farting about here, saying how much you miss her. You're going to have to get up off your big fat fuckin' arse and look for her." Mickey slammed his glass of Guinness on the table and glared at Midnight, his Irish eyes twinkling. Not waiting for an answer, The Mouth continued: "And dat, my Sambo African matey, is going to cost money. And dat is why we are going to organise d'car boot sale to beat all car boot sales. To raise money for d'Looking for Lady fund."

The next two weeks saw a flurry of activity that involved virtually everyone who knew Midnight Sam. For the likes of Brian Davies, Bishop John and Bobby (or more accurately the landlord's wife) that entailed scrabbling around in attics and soforth to unearth unwanted but saleable items; it also meant unearthing wanted items that the womenfolk altruistically pretended were in need of replacement. But for the likes of Tattoo Terry, Mickey the Mouth, Midnight Sam and the rest of the motley crew who drifted in and out of the night shelter and the day centre, the activity naturally gravitated towards the illegal. Mickey, who was accustomed to raising money for somewhat different operations, slotted comfortably into the role of fundraiser-in-chief. Campaign meetings were held in The Mitre and the landlord obligingly turned a blind eye to the proceedings. After all, such important discussions required lubrication and Bobby, like most people, needed to make a living.

"I've always found charity shops to be pretty good," Midnight mused one afternoon, fondly recalling how he had kitted out The Prof and himself for their memorable day trip to Weston-super-Mare. "And the way I see it, it's sort-of recycling, cutting out the middle man ..."

No sooner said than done: the word was out and within days Help the Aged, Save the Children, the Heart Foundation, Sue Ryder, Oxfam and Cancer Research experienced a sudden and, to them, inexplicable reduction in donations. Volunteer shop assistants would arrive for work in the mornings, puzzled at the dirth of donated goods which normally cluttered their shop doorways. The first task of the day had traditionally been to clear a pathway to the door so that they could open up for business, but not any more.

Soon a major problem arose: where to store all the goods until the day of the sale. The day centre and the night shelter were most definitely out: Brian Davies had anticipated the inevitable request and had said 'no' with a passion that disappointed but impressed Midnight Sam.

Bobby was initially reluctant but he caved in when six down-and-outs, struggling with black plastic bin liners bulging with clothes, staggered into The Mitre one Tuesday afternoon. They drank seven pints of cider apiece and two of the more hardened drinkers downed three brandy chasers each. Doubles. The session boosted the landlord's average Tuesday afternoon takings by just over 830%. And very soon the redundant skittle alley became the car boot sale storeroom, floor to ceiling with an amazing assortment of items.

The initial intention of visiting other car boot sales had been to glean a flavour of what goods were normally sold at such events, a perfectly laudable exercise of market research. But Mickey the Mouth saw things differently. During the following two-and-a-half weeks, which involved six car boot sales in and around the city, only two of Mickey's Merry Men were caught. Impressive odds, seeing that 236 items found their way into Bobby's skittle alley.

"When did you say the sale was?" Midnight, who had taken a back seat throughout the arrangements, asked one Thursday afternoon.

"Dis weekend, Midnight, Sunday morning, nine o'clock sharp," the Irishman replied. "And Sam, honest to God, by Jesus, we are going to make a fortune." Mickey shook his head and attacked his first pint of the day with a vengeance. "A fuckin' fortune," he added reverently.

"How are we going to get the stuff down to the car park?" Tattoo Terry asked innocently, but his words had the effect of napalm. Nobody spoke for several seconds. Tatts broke the silence, not too sure what the trouble was and inadvertently rubbed salt into the wound: "And what are we going to put all the stuff on, when we get it down there?"

Mickey tightened his lips into a straight line and concentrated hard: he was back on the streets of Belfast or Londonderry at the dead of night, English soldiers on every corner. He was thinking on the hoof, just like the old days: "I can get hold of a van ... and half a dozen trestle tables should do the trick. No problem Tatts, no fuckin' problem at all."

"There's a sale at Wilkinsons," Midnight ventured. "I was around there the other day getting some kindling. Something like 20% off ... and I saw a stack of trestle tables in one of the window displays." It was a paradoxical but touching testament to the deep-seated but diverted honesty of the man that the words 'sale' and '20% off' could be uttered with such innocent conviction, when the transaction would undoubtedly be completed without a solitary penny passing hands.

"How about the van?" Tatts persisted, oblivious of the effect his persistence was having on the Irishman.

Red-faced and eyes blazing, Tatts growled: "What d'fuck d'you mean 'how about d'fuckin' van?' Didn't I just tell you dat dere's no fuckin' problem wid d'van. Just leave d'fuckin' van to me!"

looking for lady

Which they did and, true to his word, on Saturday morning, a day before the car boot sale, a triumphant Mickey the Mouth drove a rusty, white Ford Transit into the tiny car-park at the rear of The Mitre. Bobby took one look at the vehicle and at the sly expression on Mickey's face and quietly but firmly threatened the Irishman with serious violence if he did not immediately drive the vehicle elsewhere.

The van was minus registration plates, front and rear, and carried a tax disc which was three-and-a-half years out of date. Also both front tyres were as smooth as a baby's bottom and the exhaust pipe, despite a sling adapted from a wire coat hanger, scraped the ground.

Mickey and his van received similar receptions at the day centre and at the Bishop's Palace, but eventually a deal of sorts was struck. Mickey could take the vehicle to the car park behind The Mitre when it was dark and, with the help of Tatts, Midnight and several other willing street-drinkers, load up and drive immediately down to the wasteground, a mile-and-a-half south of the city centre. And wait until dawn.

By 6.45am on Sunday morning, the Ford Transit was a different colour. Mickey had got hold of a five-litre can of black gloss (interior) paint and had spent most of the previous night treating the stolen vehicle to a facelift. The Irishman's enthusiasm outweighed his decorating skills and the result was interesting. Nevertheless the van looked nothing like it had done the previous day, which was the general intention.

Three trestle tables were stacked against the back wall of the pub, alongside a Flymo mower in a battered presentation box and an aquarium, complete with lights but, thankfully, minus fish.

Midnight, Tatts and The Mouth took two hours to pack the stock into the back of the van and by the time they had finished there was only room for the driver. Midnight and Tatts would have to walk to the site of the car boot sale, a park and ride car park a mile-and-a-quarter out of town.

The regular 'car-booters' had never encountered anything quite like it. Not only had they not seen this particular trio on the car boot circuit before but they had never witnessed self-publicity on such a scale. Mickey had erected a Republican flag, Midnight Sam had acquired a large Gambian flag which flew alongside and Tattoo Terry graced the proceedings with a cherished six-foot by three-foot poster of the World's Most Tattoed Woman. Lucille – a gargantuan, swarthy, middle-aged lady from downtown Marseilles – naked astride a Harley Davidson motorcycle.

Words – even for seasoned scribes – are inadequate on occasions like these ...

As was to be expected, other car-booters sent out their scouts to sound out the new kids on the block and the initial reports back almost caused a riot. "D'you remember that set of silver-plated cutlery some bastard nicked from last Wednesday's sale?" a youngster, breathless with excited indignation, told his boss. The older man, large and craggy with a broken nose and a tired sheepskin jacket, folded his arms and listened.

Many similar reports reached the ears of the stallholders during the early hours of the day's trading but it was tricky for them to know how best to respond. An obvious course of action would have been to report the discovery to the police. But there were two important reasons why this was unadvisable. Take the set of silver-plated cutlery, for example. Firstly, the initial theft from the stallholder's stand the previous Wednesday had not been reported to the police and secondly, the stallholder himself had purchased the set from a 19-year-old burglar with a known crack cocaine habit, who was in a desperate hurry to make the transaction. And physical violence was out of the question.

At worst, dodgy car-booters were opportunists after a fast buck, but they would not hurt anybody. But honour had to be satisfied and Sheepskin Jacket weaved his way to where the three Wilkinson's trestle tables sagged beneath the weight of a wide range of goods, including the set of silver-plated cutlery.

"Nice cutlery set you've got there," the big man growled and Mickey, instantly recognising the expression on his face, stopped playing his mouth organ and stepped swiftly behind one of the tables.

"Genuine silver-plate, it is, to be sure. Beautiful craftsmanship. My great grand-mother's as a matter of fact …" Mickey trailed wistfully, but his eyes were alert. Sheepskin nodded gravely and looked deep into the Irishman's eyes: "Well now, that's a funny coincidence. My great grand-mother had a set the same as yours, *exactly* the same." He let the words hang in the air before he turned around and wended his way slowly back to his pitch.

Luck was on the side of the street-drinkers that day. The plain-clothed detective, who had drawn the short straw and had to spend his valued Sunday trudging around the cluttered car-park in search of stolen goods, was nursing a king-size hangover from a stag party the night before and was not his usual vigilant self. He did however notice the recently-gloss-painted Ford Transit van without registration plates but boasting a valid tax disc 'borrowed' from an ailing Vauxhall Astra.

The prospect of interviewing Mickey the Mouth, who he knew professionally, and the subsequent mountain of paperwork was too daunting for him so he had a quiet word instead: "I don't ever want to see that heap of junk again. I don't care what you do with it but get it out of town and make it disappear. Do you understand?"

To be fair to Mickey, he did exactly as he was told. He drove the Ford Transit, complete with a smattering of unsold items and a can of recently-acquired petrol, down South Street, out of the city, along a narrow lane and onto the unmade track which led to the wasteground. There, he doused the vehicle with the petrol, struck a match and tossed it through the open back door of the van.

Back at command headquarters (the alcove at The Mitre) a jubilant Midnight Sam and Tattoo Terry were busy calculating the takings. The table in front of them was festooned with tiny towers of coins and piles of creased, wrinkled bank-notes. Bobby was watching with more than his customary nosiness: the landlord reckoned (quite rightly) that not all of the money on the table would be spent on searching for Midnight's lost love.

Mickey the Mouth, his hands and arms smeared with oil and minus his eyebrows, pushed open the swing doors and strode triumphantly into the pub, just as the car boot sale tally was reached. A strong smell of petrol followed him.

"Fuckin' 'ell," gasped Tatts and Midnight repeated the figure, lingering over the words for effect.

"Four hundred and ninety four pounds and fifty-six pence … and we've still got the cutlery set," he whispered reverently. "I think that calls for a drink. Same all round, Bobby and get yourself one."

18

GORDON Blacklock kept a low profile after the ugly incident in the playground. He moved out of his squalid bedsit and on to a lumpy sofa in an equally squalid flat belonging to one of his drinking cronies from The Rose and Crown. Consequently he missed Lady Jane's hasty exodus from the refuge and had no idea where she was. He guessed that Amy Brown and 'the brat' had gone with 'his woman' and the realisation put him in a thunderous mood.

"Pint of Guinness," he snapped at the barmaid. The peroxide redhead, heavy with makeup and fighting a losing battle with being the wrong side of forty, poured his drink badly and without a word. She knew how to pour a pint of Guinness but she didn't like Blacklock.

"How you doing, Blackie?" The question came from the direction of the fruit machine, where a bald-headed weasel of a man stood, one foot hooked behind the other.

"This Guinness is fuckin' flat," Blacklock lifted the glass and inspected its contents with a sneer. And he was right. But the barmaid shrugged her shoulders and minced off down the bar to where the bloke she fancied was drinking from a bottle of Mexican beer. Blacklock picked up his glass and joined the weasel at the fruit machine.

The weasel, who was called Freddy, cursed: "Fuckin' thing's fixed, ain't paid out for the past three days. Fixed, I tell you … fuckin' fixed." Nevertheless, this did not stop him from continuing to feed the machine with a seemingly endless supply of pound coins. "You found that bird of yours?" Freddy asked without looking away from the machine. Blacklock did not answer. "How long's it been, now?"

Blacklock frowned: "Three, four weeks, I suppose, maybe longer. Fuckin' bitch. She'll come running back soon enough, don't you worry on that fuckin' score. She'll come crawling back, tail between 'er fuckin' legs."

Freddy shot Blacklock a quick look, shrugged sceptically and turned back to the fruit machine. There was a tinkle of coins – a modest payout – and he grunted with mild satisfaction.

Blacklock, who had been waiting to 'bump into' Freddy Grimshaw for the past week, moved closer: "Reckon you can find 'er for me?"

"Probably, but why the fuck should I?"

"How about a oner?"

The weasel relaxed his grip on the fruit machine and looked over his shoulder at Blacklock: "And where the fuck are you going to get your hands on a hundred notes?"

Blacklock looked triumphant: he had been hoping for that reaction. He casually put his hand into his jacket pocket and pulled out a handful of ten pound notes. He fanned them out theatrically and Freddy counted the money with his eyes. The weasel made to take the money but Blacklock withdrew his hand with a crooked smile and a throaty chuckle.

"Not so fast, Freddy." The tone in his voice reflected the switch in power. Blacklock was now in control and that was where he liked to be. "I'd do it myself but everyone around here knows about me and that bitch and that includes the pigs."

"So what's the score, Blackie?"

"Like I said, find 'er for me, just find out where she's living. She won't 'ave gone far. She'll be around 'ere somewhere. She'll 'ave that fuckin' dyke and 'er brat with 'er. She won't 'ave gone far."

Frowning with feigned concentration at the fruit machine, Freddy Grimshaw said: "Fifty now and fifty when I find her?" He took a step back from the machine, hands on hips and looked at the ground: "She was staying at that women's refuge place, wasn't she?"

Blacklock nodded.

"Didn't she have a job somewhere?"

Blacklock nodded again: "She worked at the Indian takeaway on the corner of King Street – you know the one?"

Grimshaw rubbed his chin and held out a hand for the money. Blacklock peeled off five £10 notes and passed them over reluctantly. "See you back here in a week, then." There was threat in his voice. He finished his pint of Guinness and recoiled: "Fuckin' aweful shite, flat as a fuckin' pancake."

****

Freddy Grimshaw, at the age of 47, was a hardened, small-time crook. His speciality was house burglary but he was also an inspired conman. Not on a grand scale, but on the level of levering modest sums of money from vulnerable pensioners. He had only been caught twice and had never seen the inside of a prison cell.

Thanks to an impressive interview and unchecked references, some years ago he had managed to get a job as a postman. He soon developed a talent for recognising envelopes which contained credit cards, which he pocketed, registering the time and address and patiently awaiting the inevitable follow-up delivery of the PIN numbers. Grimshaw made a lucrative living for four months before his luck ran out. He narrowly escaped a custodial sentence after furnishing his defence lawyer with impressive mitigation fodder. A bitter marriage breakdown, the tragic death of an alcoholic father, the parlous plight in which that left his cancer-ridden mother and the clinical depression he suffered. It helped steer the magistrates towards a pre-sentence report which led to a community rehabilitation order and 200 hours of unpaid work.

In the confusion and embarrassment surrounding his dismissal from the Post Office, Grimshaw walked away with his uniform, post bag and the regulation red-and-black bicycle. It served him well on a number of occasions and was brought back into service for the job he had agreed to do for Gordon Blacklock.

Two days after their meeting in the Rose and Crown, Grimshaw trimmed his lanky hair, donned the postman's uniform, swung the postman's bag over a shoulder, climbed onto the red-and-black bicycle and pedalled around to the takeaway where Lady Jane had worked.

"Got some mail here for someone called Jane Hicks," he said, frowning at an envelope. He then lowered his voice dutifully and continued: "Women's refuge returned it 'gone away' but they advised us to try here. Just give me a forwarding address and we can send it on to her – it looks quite important, something from social services …"

"Just a minute, I'll call my supervisor," came the expected response and a minute later a large and sour-faced woman in her early forties appeared from the kitchens.

"I've got a letter here for Jane Hicks," Grimshaw repeated breezily, waving a brown envelope in the air. "You got a forwarding address?" The manageress shook her head but, suddenly remembering something, she barged back through the beaded curtains and returned seconds later, brandishing a scrap of paper.

"Don't know where she lives now but she's got a job at a café in Queensway, place called The Marmaris. Don't know the exact address though …," she trailed.

"No problem, luv, that'll do fine. We can get the address easy enough. Ta very much." Grimshaw flashed the manageress a broad smile, tipped his postman's hat and sauntered out of the takeaway, whistling tunelessly.

****

Amy Brown successfully completed her course of methadone and walked out of the doctor's consulting room late one September afternoon with mixed emotions: elation at having kicked the heroin habit which had blighted her life for so long, but trepidation at what the future might hold. But there was a third emotion – a sweet, yet alien one – which crept into her head as she headed for the bus-stop, holding Emily's hand. She was not alone anymore. Besides her beautiful daughter, she had Lady Jane.

A bright foretaste of autumn sparkled the air and Amy shuddered with pleasure. For perhaps the first time in her life, she noticed and enjoyed the season, and also for perhaps the first time in her life she felt in control of Emily. And Emily responded: she started to ask her mother questions, proper questions, and she listened to the answers. She sought physical contact, squeezing her mother's hand, and walked a little straighter, a little prouder, a little closer. By the time they reached the bus-stop and caught a single-decker bus to their apartment block the long overdue beginnings of a filial bond were drawing mother and daughter together. Nothing was said, no words were spoken and yet the difference in their relationship was enormous.

During the following weeks Amy's confidence grew. She began to take a real interest in her daughter's progress at nursery; she struck up a relationship with the vacuum cleaner, the washing machine and the floor mop (much to Lady Jane's relief) and she started to talk about the world, the world beyond the next fix. She was becoming a functioning human being. And the struggling, brave little household became a happy one.

While Lady Jane was serving up kebabs at The Marmaris and while Emily was running merry riot in the nursery, Amy had plenty of time to herself, at first a daunting concept: she felt vulnerable and susceptible to temptation. But she quickly came to realise that the monster which used to sink its claws into her soul and steer her to self-destruction had relaxed its grip. She began to take a pride in the flat and in the housework which had previously been a tiresome chore, a duty, a pay-back to Lady. She began to vacuum, to clean and to polish for an entirely different reason. She wanted their home – and home was a word she was beginning to understand for the first time – to be tidy, to be clean, to be *nice*.

But something else lovely was happening to Amy Brown: she was developing an urge to leave the hitherto safe and secure confines of the flat, to go walking, to explore. On the mornings when Lady Jane was working at The Marmaris and Emily was at nursery, Amy, once her chores were done, would venture out to a nearby golf course. It was a public course and so long as people respected the players and didn't set up barbecues on the greens there was a fairly relaxed attitude to non-golfers. These solitary walks had a beneficial effect on the young reformed heroin addict. The dark and debilitating shackles of her 19 years eased from her shoulders; she breathed in the fresh early autumn air; she looked up at the sky; she felt the soft, springy turf beneath her feet; she tasted the countryside; she joined the world into which she had been born. She became a person in her own right; she became Amy Brown.

"Do you think I could get a job?" Amy asked Lady one evening, after they had eaten and she had cleared away the plates. Emily was watching Shrek The Third on video – she had been allowed half an hour before her bedtime – and the two women were still sitting at the dining table. Lady looked up: "What kind of job, babe?"

"Down at the golf club?" she gave Lady an anxious look, shaking her head in anticipation of rejection. "They need someone to do the cleaning there, five evenings a week. A friend told me …"

"A friend?" Lady asked and Amy's shoulders sagged. "Well no, not a friend …," she paused. "I haven't got any friends, apart from you. Well, anyway, I just heard there was a job going."

Lady leaned across the table and grabbed Amy's forearms with both hands: "That's fantastic babe. You go for it."

A week later Amy Brown started her first proper job.

****

Gordon Blacklock caught a bus to Queensway one cold and grey October morning. It was trying to rain and the wind was gusting. Blacklock was unfamiliar with the town but he was familiar with the name of a particular café. He should be: it had cost him £100. When he arrived at the bus station he asked a taxi driver to take him to The Marmaris: "Drop me around the corner from the café, matey, I want to give someone who works there a surprise."

The Marmaris was situated in a small shopping arcade, sandwiched between Woolworths and a betting shop. Blacklock stepped into the bookies, picked up a copy of The Sporting Life and perched on a stool by the window, from where he could see the entrance to the café. He pretended to study the form and resigned himself to a long wait. Which was just as well: it was Lady Jane's morning off.

Paradoxically for such a quick-tempered man, Blacklock was capable of infinite patience and when the café closed at six o'clock with no sign of Jane he left the betting shop, which was also on the point of closing, and caught a bus back to Bradford. He returned the following day but on this occasion he placed a couple of bets to avoid suspicion. He won £12 on an each-way outsider in one race and lost £10 on the favourite in another.

At 1.15pm his patience was rewarded. Lady Jane emerged from the café, deep in conversation with a middle-aged Turkish woman, who kissed her lightly on the cheek and walked off in the opposite direction. Jane hurried passed the betting shop window, inspecting her watch. Blacklock slid from the stool, wiped the corners of his mouth with a thumb and forefinger, screwed up the losing betting slip into a tight ball and let it fall to the floor.

Two days later, Blacklock returned to the Rose and Crown having arranged another meeting with Freddy Grimshaw. As usual the weasel was late – three-quarters of an hour late – and Blacklock was not amused.

"Where the fuck have you been? I said one o'clock and it's a quarter to fuckin' two."

Grimshaw's face broke into a crooked grin and he shrugged his narrow shoulders: "Are you buying, Blackie?"

Blacklock grunted and tapped a coin on the bar to attract attention.

"I'll have a large house whisky, then," said Grimshaw. The two men picked up their drinks and found an empty table near a sign for the toilets. They sat down facing each other.

"There's something else I want you to do for me – and you'll get paid," Blacklock glowered across the table, his broad shoulders hunched, clasping his pint of Guinness with both hands and sniffing irritably. He had the beginnings of a cold. He darted his head from right to left to make sure that nobody else was in earshot. Grimshaw downed his whisky in one gulp and stared back across the table at Blacklock.

"What is it this time?"

Blacklock leaned across the table and whispered: "Can you get hold of some heroin … and a syringe?"

The weasel staightened in his chair, genuinely taken aback, picked up his empty glass and held it out: "Same again please, mate." Blacklock froze, waiting for an answer.

"Of course I can, but it'll cost you." A frown and a pause and then: "Didn't know you was into that stuff."

"I'm not," said Blacklock, gazing over Grimshaw's shoulder, unseeing, at the opposite wall. "But I know someone who is."

19

THE SUMMER season was at an end. The glitzy amusement arcades flashed their lights to a dwindling audience; the Grand Pier, recently rebuilt, was closed; a myriad blue-and-white, striped deckchairs were piled in stacks near the sea wall or had already been locked away; and only a few people, mainly locals, braved the beach, but with their coats on. The distant waters of the Bristol Channel were grey, cold and unfriendly and a bitter wind whipped in from the south-west. October in Weston-super-Mare. But Midnight Sam, hugging himself into his navy blue donkey jacket, sat on a lone deckchair, a warm and beautiful smile upon his face (the result of nostalgia, Blackthorn cider and red wine). He was reliving his previous visit to the seaside resort.

The trip to Weston by Midnight Sam, Mickey the Mouth and Tattoo Terry was the first step in the mission to find Lady Jane and it was Midnight's idea. Brian Davies, who had been appointed custodian of campaign funds, had gently tried to dissuade Midnight, but to no avail. Midnight was determined to go.

"That's where we went, Brian – don't you remember? – and you saw us off at the bus station," Midnight Sam said. "The Professor, me and Lady Jane. That's where we went for that day trip, only a matter of months before Lady did a runner and The Prof 'shuffled off this mortal coil.'"

Brian Davies looked up sharply, recognising the quotation but not expecting to hear it from the lips of Midnight Sam: "Beg your pardon?"

"Shakespeare, Hamlet," Midnight shrugged and continued: "Anyway, we had such a good day – the three of us – that I've got this sort-of hunch Lady might have found her way back there. Can't explain why, but I've got this feeling. She loved the sea," he added wistfully.

"It's been well over a year, Sam," Brian began cautiously and kindly. "What makes you think that Jane would have gone back there? I mean, why not simply come back here? Much easier."

But it was hopeless. The expression on Midnight's face was deep and wise and unassailable; his eyes were bright with some unfathomable insight, some secret wisdom; and he had the unswerving support of Mickey and Tatts, whose motives for spending a couple of days in Weston-super-Mare, all expenses paid, were not quite the same as Midnight's.

Coach D of the Virgin Inter-City to Weston was conveniently situated next to the train shop. Mickey the Mouth and Tatts Terry sat opposite Midnight and nobody else came near them throughout the journey. An invisible force-field (which they were accustomed to whenever they found themselves in contact with that other world) gave them both space and privacy. And it suited them. The three street-drinkers reached their destination after six cans of Strongbow apiece, a feat of relative restraint considering that the journey lasted an hour-and-a-half.

In homage to the memory of The Professor, who had spent a majority of the legendary day trip drinking himself into oblivion on a deck-chair while Midnight Sam and Lady Jane had gone off to explore, Midnight followed The Prof's example while Tatts and The Mouth, armed with photographs of Lady, trawled the numerous bars along the front. Unsuccessful but in good spirits, they returned to 'headquarters' just as it was getting dark to find Midnight snoring peacefully amidst a clutter of empty cider cans.

After a vague debrief, Midnight and Tatts wandered along the beach towards the dunes in search of a quiet spot where they could curl up in their sleeping bags and spend the night. Mickey the Mouth had arranged to meet them both by the Grand Pier in the morning. He fancied a couple more pubs before turning in for the night. They didn't see him again for eight days, when he crept sheepishly into The Mitre at 4.30pm on a Thursday, with a bad limp and his right arm in plaster.

"No joy then?" Bobby addressed the alcove in general and three heads shook.

"One thing's for sure, though," Midnight pursed his lips and reached for his cider. "Lady Jane has not gone back to Weston-super-Mare."

Mickey nodded solemnly: "I don't think we missed many pubs. If she was there, then we'd have found her."

"You didn't miss a single pub," Tatts corrected the Irishman. "You can't have done, you were there for over a week."

Mickey sipped his drink and gazed through the frosted pub window: the memory was still painful, it was still raw. Everything had been going pretty well on the first night – he hadn't had to buy a drink, his mouth organ earning him numerous pints of cider – until the Irishman decided to change his repertoire. It was the wrong time and the wrong place for him to play (and sing) A Nation Once Again – yet again. The wrong time because a group of well-built, teenage Neandertals were drowning their sorrows in a corner of the pub after England had lost to some lowly team in a European Cup tie. And the wrong place because the sour-faced landlord had suffered a far more serious loss ten years ago: his own 18-year-old soldier son in an ambush on the outskirts of Londonderry. It was indeed not a wise choice of music.

A comfortable silence descended on the alcove and the serious business of drinking assumed centre stage. The landlord broke the silence with a question which was on everyone's mind: "So where are you going to go next, Midnight?"

Midnight Sam was quick to answer: "Lady Jane was born and bred in a place called Padstow, in Norfolk, I think it is …"

"North Cornwall," Tattoo Terry corrected.

"What?" asked Midnight.

"North Cornwall," Tatts repeated. "Padstow is in north Cornwall, it's not in Norfolk. Other side of the country, mate."

Midnight raised his eyebrows and shrugged: "Whatever. Anyway, I reckon there's a damn good chance Lady will have gone back to her roots and that means Padstow. And that's where I'm going to go next." He looked across the table at Mickey's right arm, encased in a plastercast, and added: "I think it would be best if I went alone this time."

The Irishman looked uncomfortable and hurt but he said nothing. Tatts, on the other hand, leapt to his own defence: "Seeing as you were headed in the opposite direction, I think somebody should go along with you and I think that somebody should be me." Midnight was taken aback by the determination in Tattoo Terry's voice. "I'm an old seadog, Midnight, been around the frigging world four times. I reckon I could get us both down to Padstow."

****

Brain Davies was less sceptical about destination number two, although he secretly thought it was still probably a waste of time. Nevertheless he had to concede there was an outside chance Lady might have returned to her home town.

However finances had to be discussed: the £494.56p from the car boot sale had already been whittled down to £168. This was partly due to the obligatory celebration drink after the sale and partly to the abortive but equally liquid trip to Weston-super-Mare.

"If you're really serious about this Sam you're going to have to raise more money," Brian said and immediately wished that he hadn't. Lights sparked in Midnight's eyes and Brian could almost hear the cogs in the man's brain whirr into action. Why the hell did he have to say that? Why the hell didn't he simply leave the whole ridiculous business to run out of steam on its own accord? But it was too late.

Brian and Midnight were sitting on a faded, liberally stained and well-worn sofa in the reception lounge of the day centre in South Street. Brian was sipping from a mug of tea and Midnight was trying to roll a cigarette. The street-drinker never drank tea. It was a strange muddy colour and hot and he had no inclination to give it a go, despite numerous invitations over the years.

"When are you planning to go to Padstow?" Brian asked quickly, keen to deflect Midnight from further fund-raising ideas. It had taken all his powers of persuasion to placate the local Constabulary after the car boot sale.

"I'm off next weekend, Brian," Midnight replied dreamily. He popped the cigarette into his mouth, frowned, took it out and nipped off an inch-long strand of wayward tobacco before lighting up. "When's Bonfire Night?" he asked.

Brian Davies closed his eyes.

20

AMY BROWN was settling into a routine that owed nothing to heroin. She was a mother and not only was she becoming proud of the fact at last but she was becoming quite good at it too. And her greatest fan was Lady Jane, who encouraged her and praised her every step of the way.

Lady increased her shifts at The Marmaris and Amy was now working part-time at the golf club. They both juggled their hours to accommodate Emily, who was thriving at nursery school. The little girl had proper friends at last and was even betrothed to a *much* older boy (he was four-and-a-half) called Leo. Emily found it difficult to utter a sentence without the word 'Leo' in it somewhere.

Walking across the golf course to work had whetted Amy's appetite for 'Nature'. She had only ever known the concrete jungle of a big and rambling city and the discovery of fields and trees and streams had a profound effect on her. The countryside was quiet, it was peaceful, it was kind and it was, above all, undemanding. Amy walked and walked, shuffling off the destructive restraints of her former life and exploring the free and creative freedoms of a new one.

But her walks in the countryside had not gone unnoticed. Gordon Blacklock had been watching, from a discreet distance, for several weeks, until he knew the young mother's routine as well as she did.

It was a Thursday afternoon, late October, and a north-easterly wind whipped banks of grey clouds low across the fields. The sky was overcast and gloomy and rain spat in the air. But Amy could not have cared less: the weather played no part in her new routine. She walked quite jauntily down a narrow lane which twisted between a couple of farms. She held her head high, enjoying the wind which flustered her hair and she fastened the top button of her anorak against the cold.

Winter was on its way, she thought, and that meant Christmas. *Christmas.* She could hardly believe the beauty of the word, a word which had meant nothing to her before. She clambered over a style and followed a footpath which ran diagonally across a ploughed field to an isolated copse of pine trees, a place where she always stopped, whatever the weather. She leaned back against the trunk of a tree and lit a Marlborough Light, taking in the panoramic view of distant Queensbury surrounded by grey and lonely fields. She shivered with a mixture of pleasure and the cold … but then her stomach turned to ice.

Amy heard his voice before she saw him; it came from behind, very close, and although she had only heard it a couple of times before she recognised the strong Newcastle accent immediately. She knew who it was.

"Fancy meeting you here," Blacklock said, leaning against a tree only a few feet behind Amy. She tried to marshal her thoughts, to work out how to react, how to behave, what to do, but the hard and scornful tone in the man's voice catapulted her back to a world she had been so valiantly trying to escape.

"What do you want?" she managed to ask, but her voice was shaky and Blacklock instantly recognised the weakness, the defeatism and he knew he was in control. He straightened and stepped away from the tree, forcing her to turn around with the intimidating power of his presence.

"I want you to keep away from my woman," he growled. "She's my fuckin' woman and not yours. I don't know what you two get up to – turned my missus into a fuckin' dyke you have – but I'm telling you it's got to stop and it's got to stop now."

"There's nothing to stop. I don't know what you're talking about. Jane and me are good friends, that's all. She's been very good to me … there's nothing like that. We're just good friends." Amy's eyes were wide with fear and she began to hyperventilate, pressing a hand to her chest. "Why are you doing this?" she asked with sudden desperation. "Why?"

Blacklock sidestepped to face her, shoulders hunched, fists clenched and eyes black with anger. He had waited a long time for this moment: "Because, you fuckin' bitch … (he let the insult hang in the air) … because she is my woman, as I've just told you. And you, you're just a fuckin' junkie whore and a fuckin' junkie dyke. That's what you fuckin' are. Do you understand?" His voice had risen to a scream.

Amy was shaking, hugging her knees and rocking to and fro. Blacklock crouched down in front of her and repeated, quieter but more menacing: "Do you understand?" But the terrified mother stared into her hands, which she was kneading furiously, and said nothing. So Blacklock stretched out his left arm and cupped a hand underneath her jaw, lifting her head so that she was forced to look at him. Her eyes flicked from left to right, desperately trying to avoid his brutal stare.

"Look at me when I'm talking to you, you bitch," he said with soft venom, tightening his grip on her jaw until she gasped. And then, after glancing quickly around to ensure they were still alone, Blacklock bunched his right hand into a fist and delivered a short, heavy blow to the middle of Amy's forehead. Her head snapped back and she slumped soundlessly into a heap.

And then Blacklock went to work. He fumbled in the pockets of his black, three-quarter length overcoat and pulled out a length of thick cord, a syringe and a phial of brown liquid. He ripped off Amy's anorak, swept the left sleeve of her polo neck jumper up above the elbow and tied the cord into a tourniquet around her upper arm. Following Grimshaw's instructions, he filled the syringe from the phial, tested it for trapped air, located and tapped a vein and then carefully injected the unconscious woman with a massive dose of heroin. Amy squirmed faintly and whimpered.

Blacklock put the syringe and phial back in his coat pocket, untied the tourniquet and pulled the sleeve of Amy's jumper down to her wrist. He clambered to his feet, looked around again, grunted and made off at a half-run down the footpath, across the ploughed field to the style, breathing heavily.

****

Chris Sellwood found Amy Brown in the fifth public house he visited. She had been missing for three days. It was half past ten at night and the young mother, clearly drunk, was talking to a man at the end of the bar. Chris flashed his police identity card and the man slipped from the bar stool and left the pub in a hurry. The detective sat down on a stool and rested a hand firmly on Amy's shoulder when she tried to get up. He took out his mobile phone and rang Lady Jane.

"How is she?" Lady asked urgently.

"Not too good, but she's in one piece … ," the policeman paused and continued, turning away from Amy and lowering his voice, "I'm afraid she's been using, Jane. Her eyes are all over the place. Can't get any sense out of her at the moment. I'm going to bring her home and you're going to have to get her to bed. And Jane …"

Lady interrupted: "I know, Chris, I know. Lock the doors and sleep in with her."

Sellwood smiled thinly into the mobile phone and added, loudly, for Amy's sake: "Is Emily all right?"

"No, not really. Keeps on asking if mummy's not well again. And you know Chris, she knows her mum is not well again. I can see it in her eyes. Poor little love looks a hundred years old sometimes … ," Lady's voice broke and she fought for control.

"Jane, I'm really sorry … it'll be okay," he said without conviction.

"She was doing so well, Chris, she was doing so bloody well. What in God's name happened?"

"I'll bring her home," the policeman said flatly.

When Lady Jane confronted Amy – gently but directly – the teenage mum was sullen and uncommunicative. She denied that she had been using and snapped at Lady Jane: "For Chrissake I got pissed, that's all. Pissed. What the fucking hell's so wrong with that? I went out and had a bloody good drink. I got *pissed*."

Lady had heard it all before (in the past from her own lips many times) and she was angry with her friend: "You got pissed, as you say, for three days, Amy. *Three days*. When I got home on the first day one of the nursery staff was standing outside the flat with your daughter. They had been waiting for over an hour … in the rain."

Amy whirled on Lady Jane: "I'm sorry, okay, I'm fucking sorry." She checked herself, chewed her lower lip and hung her head: "I'm sorry, it won't happen again. I promise. Too much wine … one thing led to another … it won't happen again." A pause and then, in a barely audible whisper: "Is Emily okay?"

Lady sighed: "Yes, Emily is okay. Leo's mum has been brilliant. She's been helping out. I even think Emily and Leo have been making wedding plans …"

Lady smiled and Amy forced a thin smile and the two women looked at each other. A sad and forlorn and tragic look.

The first thing to go was Amy's job, not because she failed to turn up for work (although that had happened on a number of occasions) but because items started to go missing from the locker rooms and small amounts of money from the bar till. The thefts were not particularly subtle and the golf club steward, who liked Amy, was a saddened and disappointed man. He had known about her past (or rather a sanitised version of it from Chris Sellwood) but he had given her a chance. And, for the first couple of months, his trust had been rewarded. She had turned out to be a dependable and diligent worker and to be entirely trustworthy. But suddenly something had gone badly wrong: Amy had become unreliable, agitated and incompetent and worse, she had begun to steal. The club steward had taken her aside and warned her, firmly but kindly, that unless things improved he would be left with no alternative. But it made no difference and Amy lost the first and last proper job she had ever had.

The second thing to go was the new-found relationship with her daughter. The familiar pattern returned: broken promises, outbursts of unreasonable temper, unexplained disappearances, uninterest in Emily or her friends, uninterest in the little girl's aspirations, feelings, questions. And Emily reacted quite naturally, out of an instinctive sense of survival: she turned to her Aunty Jane. Dependable, even-tempered, reliable and ever-caring Aunty Jane. But the perfectly understandable switch in allegiance merely drove Amy deeper and deeper into self-destruct.

The third thing to go was Amy's self-respect. She had begun to discover the unfamiliar sensation after a lifetime of abuse, neglect, prostitution, drug addiction and violence; she had begun to realise she was a human being, a person of worth, a person with qualities of her own, with dreams, with (dare she think it) a future. She had begun to bond with her daughter; she had begun to take a pride in herself, in her appearance, both outward and inward; she had begun to live; she had begun to be Amy Brown. But no longer.

Lady Jane was in despair. She had seen it all before, from the inside, and she knew there was nothing she could do apart from to wait and to hope and to be there. But it was not just for the sake of her friend, it was for the sake of a four-year-old girl. Lady had to be strong for Emily.

The nights were the worst. Lady hardly slept. She would lie awake, staring at the ceiling, shoulders tensed, listening and jerking at the smallest sound. Her only solace was to look across the room to where she had brought Emily's bed and to watch the little child asleep, cuddled up to the giant pink Teddy Bear which Chris Sellwood's wife had given her on her fourth birthday.

A heroin addict is a cunning, utterly single-minded creature (as Lady knew only too well). Whatever she did to try to contain Amy, whatever ploy she adopted to foil the young mother's plans, it was never going to be enough. Amy would find a way of slipping through the net and every time she slipped through the net, she would sink deeper into the mire.

It wasn't long before Amy stopped pretending. She could no longer be bothered to make excuses. Her obsession, her addiction revisited (and revisited with a vengeance) began to exclude all subtlety, all subterfuge. She no longer bothered to lie.

****

Lady Jane heard the front door slam – no longer the secretive click – and she immediately flung back the duvet, leapt out of bed and scuttled to the window. It was eleven-thirty. She looked out and saw a figure. Huddled against the cold, hurrying away through the rain, head bowed.

"Amy, for God's sake, where are you going?" she called, her voice a hoarse and urgent whisper. She did not want to wake Emily. But her friend did not even turn around; she did not answer; she checked her progress for half a second but that was all. She then broke into a trot and vanished into the night. Lady closed the window carefully and turned around to find Emily sitting bolt upright in the single bed, rubbing her eyes with her fists and drawing short, rasping breaths. She had brought herself out of a deep sleep by an instinct that something was wrong.

"What are you doing, Aunty Jane?" the child asked, her voice gulping, very close to tears. Lady went over to the bed, open-armed, and 'mother-henned' Emily back to her pillow. Emily drew the duvet to her chin and stared, wide-eyed, at the ceiling. The eyes of a wise and sad old woman, not those of a fresh and innocent little girl.

"Is mummy not very well again?" she whispered finally, knowing what the answer would be, still staring at the ceiling. She pulled the pink Teddy Bear close to her chest and turned onto her side, away from Lady Jane. Lady gazed down at Emily for a long time, stroking her long, wavy, nut-brown hair.

Lady's mobile rang at twelve minutes passed four in the morning. She had not been asleep – dozing and jerking awake with heart-thumping starts whenever she felt her eyes closing – so she managed to answer the call before it woke Emily. She whispered into the phone and flustered silently out of the room. She stood, breathing heavily, in the tiny hallway and bent over her mobile phone, brow knitted in concentration and rubbed her forehead as Chris Sellwood told her what had happened.

****

With money she had stolen from her daughter's piggy bank – a pink, china monstrosity with big black spots – Amy had taken a taxi into Bradford and headed for Manningham's red light district. Underneath an ankle-length, cream mackintosh she wore a tight black mini-skirt, red fishnet holdups, a black see-through blouse and a skimpy black bra. Dressed for business.

The middleaged, bespectacled man who picked her up in his six-month-old BMW was quite specific about what he wanted and what he wanted did not involve the use of condoms. But Amy could not have cared less. She was technically on the pill although she could not remember when she had last taken one and sexually transmitted diseases were vague things that happened to other people. And £75 was £75.

She met with Gordon Blacklock in the Rose and Crown an hour later. She squirmed onto a bar stool next to where he was standing, revealing the fleshy gap between the top of her hold-ups and her G-string pants. Blacklock leered at her and chuckled darkly.

"Have you got it?" she asked, looking straight ahead, her voice an urgent whisper.

"'Course I fuckin' have. Have you? Sixty quid. That's what I want. Six little bags, tenner a bag. Sixty quid."

Amy took three £20 notes from her handbag and waved them in Blacklock's face. He instinctively reached for the money but checked himself and Amy pulled her hand back. She gave him a crooked smile. Her bright red lipstick was smudged and her mascara looked as if it had been applied with a trowel.

"For fuck's sake, not in here, woman," Blacklock growled. "I'll see you out the back, in the yard. You go to the bog first and I'll follow in five minutes."

Amy pulled a face, slipped off the bar stool and tottered tartily across the room to the door marked 'Ladies.' Blacklock finished his pint of Guinness, winked at the landlord and left the room by a back door which led to a small, concrete yard. Amy was leaning against a stack of beer crates and barrels, smoking a cigarette.

The relationship between Blacklock and Amy Brown, which had delevoped over the past month, was cruel and cold. In Blacklock's case sadistic and in Amy's masochistic. He regularly abused her, mentally and physically, used her for sex whenever it took his fancy and kept her supplied with heroin. Although his underlying motive was to destroy the young mother so that she would never again get between him and Jane, he was enjoying the situation; it was where he liked to be: in complete control. Here was a drugged-up dyke who had taken his woman away from him, selling her pathetic body to anybody who had the price of her next fix. By the time he was through with her, Jane would wish she had never clapped eyes on the tart and she would come running back to him, like she always did. But what Blacklock had not considered was the bond which had formed between 'his woman' and the 'drugged-up dyke's' daughter. He had not factored Emily into the equation and that was to prove to be his big mistake.

Once Amy had been forced back down to the squalid twilight world she had been struggling so valiantly to escape, she gave up the fight altogether. Nobody falls further or more irretrievably than a reformed heroin addict who starts using again. When the gossamer safety net of hope and help is wrenched apart there is nothing to stop the plunge, nothing to prevent the helter-skelter spiral downwards to the abyss. Everything had gone: her new-found self-respect, her hopes, her dreams, her discovery of the joys of motherhood, Lady Jane, her life. And in its place was a cruel brute of a man, a man who supplied her with heroin, who supplied her with 'clients,' who supplied her with random outbursts of violence which she masochistically craved.

Ten minutes after Blacklock and Amy had completed their business transaction by the beer barrels and overflowing dustbins in the back yard of the Rose and Crown, the police raided the pub. Amy had already injected and she lurched back into the bar, out of control and in an agitated state. (The heroin she had taken had been cut with crack cocaine – Blacklock's idea of a joke). The northerner had of course already left.

****

"Amy's been arrested," Chris Sellwood said wearily. "Not a lot I can do about it, I'm afraid, Jane. She kicked one police officer on the shins and bit another on the hand. She also spat at them. She had to be sprayed with CS gas and handcuffed."

"Oh my God," Jane whispered, "where is she?"

"Bradford south police station in Nelson Street," the detective replied. Jane could hear another voice – a female voice, presumably Sellwood's wife – muffled in the background. "They're going to have to keep her in until she's fit enough to be interviewed. She'll get bail and I'll arrange to pick her up and bring her over."

"She won't come home, Chris," Lady said quietly.

"Of course she will," the policeman said shortly, puzzled by his friend's comment. "I'll collect her and bring her home. Desk sergeant will let me know."

"She won't come home," Lady repeated.

And she was right.

21

BRIAN Davies swept a pile of files and correspondence from a chair in front of his cluttered desk onto the floor and nodded for Midnight Sam to sit down, which he did awkwardly and self-consciously. He had not been in the centre manager's office before and he felt out of place. To mask his embarrassment he concentrated on trying to make a roll-up. One or two things went wrong with the operation and Midnight Sam ended up smoking a three-quarter length Malborough Light which had been lodged behind his right ear. Brian made a half-hearted attempt at tidying his desk while Midnight tussled with the tobacco. Besides papers, letters and reference books, were several mugs of cold, black coffee and an overflowing ashtray. Not Brian's – he was an avid non-smoker – but testament to the constant stream of clients who asked him for advice.

"So what's the problem, Sam?"

Midnight shifted his position in the chair: "Well Welshie, it's like this. All this bollocks about 'Looking For Lady' … I never really liked it, you know. To be honest, it makes me feel bloody stupid. I mean, what the bloody hell is it all about?" He paused and shook his head. " Okay, I went to Weston-super-Mare and she wasn't there. Tatts and Mickey went round every friggin' pub …"

"Yes, I heard about that," said Brian.

"I'm lost," Midnight said, staring down at his feet. "I don't know what to do and I don't know why I'm doing it … if you get what I mean," he added, puzzled.

Brian got it all right: "Sam, let's stop messing about. Do you want to see Lady Jane again?"

Midnight straightened and looked taken aback: "Of course I do. We got on real well, you know. Not just me and her, you understand, but with The Professor too. It was always with The Prof. We were a team, the three of us, a great team." Midnight's face turned suddenly sad and he added wistfully: "Until The Prof went and died, that is. We were such a great team …"

"So, what's the matter?" There was irritation in Brian's voice.

"I don't know, I just don't know."

"Well I do," Brian snapped, irritation turning to anger, "I bloody well do." But the centre manager had no idea what he was going to say to back up such a bold statement and he was relieved when Midnight Sam came, unwittingly, to the rescue.

"I guess I'm a bit scared, to tell you the truth," Midnight began, staring over Brian's shoulder, through the open office door into the bustling room beyond. "But a bit sad too. Sad that Lady Jane has gone and I don't think I'll ever find her, but scared because I don't know what the hell I would say to her if I did … find her."

"You drew a blank in Weston," Brian said without a trace of irony, keeping a straight face. "So what are you going to do now? Where are you going to go next?"

"Okay, okay," Midnight held out both hands in mild supplication. "I know it was a stupid idea, but I had to start somewhere, I had to …," he shook his head and chewed a fingernail. "I'll be really honest with you, Welshie. This is crazy: what the hell would Lady Jane want with a useless, homeless drunk like me? Come on, be honest." He laughed harshly.

Brian Davies paused for a couple of seconds before he replied in a slow and measured tone: "I think there's something you ought to know. A couple of weeks before he died, The Professor had a long chat with Lady Jane. It was Lady's birthday and they decided to have a little celebration dinner party for two in The Parlour. Afterwards, The Prof took me aside and said that you two ought to get together. He was serious Sam … he was really serious."

Midnight Sam's mouth fell open and his eyes were misty.

"You see, he knew that he didn't have very long to live … and well, he loved you both. And he really did, Midnight, because he told me. He loved you both and he said that you were right for each other."

"But I'm a washed-out alcoholic tramp and Lady … well, Lady Jane … what the bloody hell would she want with the likes of me?"

"Do you respect The Professor's opinion?" Brian asked, playing his trump card.

Midnight bristled with indignation: "Of course I do, more than anybody else in the world. Of course I respect his opinion."

"Well then, there you are. If The Prof said you and Lady should get together, he must have been right. No argument." Sam was puzzled and pleased at the same time. Brian continued: "So my friend, I think you have got something of an Odyssey on your hands. What I mean is …"

But Midnight Sam cut in gently: "I'm not too sure that I'll make a very convincing Ulysses, but I'll give it a go."

Brian's jaw dropped and he gave Midnight a curious, sideways stare: "Bloody hell Sam, you're a dark horse, you're a bloody dark horse all right." His eyes twinkled from beneath his wayward, bushy black eyebrows.

Midnight Sam shambled to his feet, patted the cans of Blackthorn cider in the pockets of his donkey jacket and made for the open door. He stopped in the doorway and turned, rubbing his chin: "By the way, I've been thinking about Bonfire Night …"

Enough was enough. The day centre manager could stand no more surprises. Homer was sufficient for one day without bringing Guy Fawkes into the equation. "No Sam, I'm sorry, but not now. I'm sure your proposals for November the Fifth are interesting and original – I'm sure they are – but at this precise point in time I fear they would send me over the edge."

Midnight Sam slumped his shoulders and sighed. He was thrilled with his plans and wanted to share them. However, being a kindly and understanding man, he was quite content to leave things be, for the time being.

****

Midnight Sam met up with Tattoo Terry and Mickey the Mouth for their once-weekly session in The Mitre. Tatts and The Mouth were already ensconced in the alcove when Midnight strolled through the swing doors, wearing a sea captain's hat. (Padstow, on the north Cornish coast, where Lady Jane had grown up, was his next destination). Bobby raised an eyebrow but said nothing. It was the second time he had raised an eyebrow that afternoon. The first had been when the Irishman had scuttled into the pub, half an hour beforehand, an igloo tent under his arm and an expression of defiance on his face. The dark green canvas bag which contained tent, poles and pegs sported a sticky label bearing the words 'HALF PRICE SALE,' a slash mark through the 'original' price of £79.99p and the new price of £40 in red ink.

"What a bargain!" Mickey exclaimed to the landlord and heaved the tent on to the bar. "State-of-the-bloody-art two-man tent wid all mod cons – half bloody price. Only forty quid. What a bargain!"

Bobby knew that Mickey the Mouth had not parted with any money; Mickey knew that he hadn't parted with any money; and Mickey also knew that Bobby knew. But it was important to keep up appearances. Nevertheless The Mitre was Bobby's pub and he had a reputation to defend.

"Get that thing off the bar," he growled, "and put it underneath the table, over there, in the alcove. And do it now."

The Irishman was crestfallen but he did as he was told. After all, he was gasping for a drink. He treated the landlord to a winsome smile, picked up his pint of Olde English with one hand, tent with the other and staggered to the alcove.

"I bet you haven't given a thought to where you're going to stay in Padstow, once you get down there," Tattoo Terry said, bristling with triumph. *He* obviously had.

Midnight gulped at his half pint and licked his lips: "Nope, I haven't given it a thought. You're quite right."

"Well I have," Tatts drew the words out slowly. "I lived in Plymouth for a while when I was in the merchant navy. I know Devon and Cornwall pretty damn well."

"Ever been to Padstow?" Midnight asked, finishing his drink and getting up for a refill. His efforts to cut down his drinking had initially caused some complications with the trio's 'round' system, complications which had soon been solved by Midnight downing two halves to his mates' pints. Although sometimes it ran to three …

"Yep," said Tatts assertively, rolling up the left sleeve of his jumper and thrusting a forearm under Midnight's nose: "Got that one done in Wadebridge, mile or two from Padstow, six, seven years ago."

"The mermaid or the anchor?" Mickey craned forwards and squinted at Tattoo Terry's arm.

"The mermaid … had the anchor done in Freetown. That's a port town in … ,"

"Sierra Leone," Midnight Sam interrupted. The other two looked at him sharply.

"How d'fuck d'you know dat?" asked the Irishman, frowning. Midnight shrugged and waited for Tatts to continue.

"As you're going to be spending two or three days down there you might as well be comfortable," said Tatts, "so we got you this."

Mickey coughed indignantly and put his hands on his hips: "Excuse me, Tatts, but what's all dis 'we' business? If I remember correctly it was I, Mickey the bleedin' Mouth, who purchased dis here tent."

"Purchased?" Tatts countered.

"Acquired," said Mickey suavely, faking an English accent.

Tattoo Terry continued: "There's a camp-site just outside town. Place called Dennis Cove. It's ideal."

"Will it be open, this time of the year?" Midnight asked.

Tattoo pulled a face: "Does it matter?"

****

Midnight Sam caught the early morning train to Bodmin Parkway and, out of a sense of decency, he waited until 8.45am before he cracked open his first can of Strongbow. Several other passengers flashed disapproving looks but the train manager decided against challenging him as to the source of the alcohol. The retail shop in Coach D was not due to open until 10am but the manager had been up since 5.30am and he was in no mood for an argument.

Tatts and The Mouth were hurt and offended when Midnight insisted on embarking on his next quest on his own, but their friend was adamant. And when Midnight Sam made up his mind there was no room for manoeuvre.

Strange things were happening to Midnight, things deep down inside his head, and he felt both nervous and excited. It was as if a fog was beginning to lift, a fog which had protected him from the real world for many years. The hazy comfort of his squalid, alcoholic existence – an existence based solely on getting through each day at a time – was beginning to clear and he had no idea what was going to take its place.

Admittedly nothing had been the same since The Professor had died – Midnight had gone downhill, in fact – but now that Lady Jane had somehow become an issue, his mind was thrown into turmoil. But, he had to admit, it was not an unpleasant turmoil.

The barrier which he had erected after his father's death was beginning to crumble and this disturbed him. The barrier had been there for a reason, a very good reason: it had protected him from himself, almost certainly saved him from suicide. Without it, he would not have coped, he would not have survived.

Midnight gazed out of the train window at the rolling green meadows, bathed in white-gold autumn sunlight. He smiled at the grazing cattle and the lone, dumb horses and he felt a warmth in his heart. He closed his eyes and allowed the memory of his childhood, of his homeland, of his father to flood his mind.

Bodmin Parkway is a quaint, old-fashioned, ramshackle station, really no more than a halt, surrounded by trees and without a house in sight. First impressions are that one has been dumped in the middle of nowhere. Midnight stood self-consciously on the tiny platform, tent under one arm, clutching his holdall with the other, captain's hat askew on the back of his head and he froze with panic. What now? Where to now?

"Where are you headed, mate?" asked a friendly back-packer, aware of the aura of bewilderment which surrounded Midnight Sam.

"Padstow," Midnight replied in a small, nervous voice.

"Bus for Bodmin will be along in a few minutes," said the young man. "You can get another bus from there, takes you right into Padstow. Might have a bit of a wait though. They don't run too often."

Midnight Sam's 'bit of a wait' lasted for two-and-a-half days and it had nothing to do with the infrequency of the local bus service. It had more to do with the three good-natured down-and-outs he chanced upon in a backstreet boozer behind Bodmin's bus station. He had only gone in for a swift half, just to settle his nerves, and he had no intention of getting involved.

When he came to, around 60 hours since the backpacker at the railway station had spoken to him, his mind was a muddle of disjointed recollections: a volatile game of spoof, an overturned table, broken glasses, an indignant landlord, the linoleum on the floor of a darkened room, the purring of a cat, a churchyard, two police officers and the park bench which he realised he was still sitting on …

Midnight suddenly thrust his hands into the pockets of his donkey jacket and, with relief, pulled out a fistful of crumpled bank notes. He thumbed through the money: to his amazement he was only £20 out of pocket. And the tent and holdall were still there, on the bench beside him, along with an unopened, three-litre bottle of strong supermarket cider. They must have been a great bunch of boys, he thought fondly, tentatively tapping his throbbing forehead.

Midnight Sam took Tattoo Terry's advice and walked the 16 miles to Padstow, along the Camel Trail, the former railway route that followed Camel River from Bodmin through Wadebridge and on to the seaside resort. Less than a mile from Padstow he came across a sign for Dennis Cove Camping, which sported a sticker 'Closed until April 21'. He shrugged mentally, tossed his tent and holdall over the padlocked gates and clambered after them. He crept up the driveway, keeping to the shadows afforded by a row of dark pine trees, until he reached a large house with a Swiss-style chalet attached. From his vast experience (Midnight Sam had dossed in more empty, abandoned or closed-up buildings than he cared to remember) he knew instinctively that nobody would be at home. And also that nobody had been at home for quite some time.

Considering that Midnight had never pitched a tent before, that he was still severely hung-over and that he was mildly drunk again, it was a valiant effort. The result bore little resemblance to the diagram but he managed to worm his way inside and lie on his back, hands clasped behind his head, and gaze contentedly at the material which sagged 18 inches above his head, at an odd angle.

After a pleasant doze, Midnight awoke ravenously hungry, slithered from the tent and headed for town. The tide was out and scores of marooned sailing boats leaned in the soft and glistening mud. Isolated pools of seawater and the narrow snake of a river meandering down the middle of the estuary. Midnight stopped for a moment and breathed in the sharp, briny air, almost tasting it. The smell of the sea made him shiver and his eyes widened with some childhood memory.

The lights of Padstow twinkled as night descended and Midnight stopped at the first eating establishment he encountered, opposite a couple of warehouses. His needs were simple: fish and chips. Nothing fancy. Plain, good, old-fashioned greasy fish and greasy chips, preferably in a greasy paper bag.

"I'm very sorry, sir," the middle-aged and kindly *maitre d'* shook his head apologetically, without a trace of condescension, but blocking the entrance to the restaurant with infinite grace. It was almost as if the head waiter had not noticed the liberally-stained donkey jacket with a bottle of cider poking out from one of the pockets, the unzipped flies on Midnight's trousers and the sea captain's hat which still boasted its price tag.

"But I only want some fish and chips – to take away – I've got the money," Midnight protested gently.

"I'm sorry, sir, but we don't do takeaways. There's a nice chippy a few hundred yards down the road, in the centre of town."

"Oh come on, mate. Just one bag of fish and chips won't harm you. Plenty of salt and vinegar. I'm bloody starving."

The *maitre d'* was genuinely sorry – he liked Midnight Sam – and if it had been down to him he would probably have obliged. But it wasn't down to him: it was down to the owner of the fish restaurant, a man by the name of Rik Stein.

****

Midnight spent three days in Padstow and, despite the blip in Bodmin, he made progress in his quest. Of the three banks in town he struck gold at bank number two, thanks to a severely-dressed but good-natured, middleaged cashier with a seriously-Seventies perm: "Yes, I know who you mean. Derek Hicks was the manager here five, six years ago, maybe more, before Mister Overill. Bit before my time, but I've heard the name."

"Any idea where he is now?"

The cashier chewed her lower lip, raised a finger, closed her till drawer and rolled back on her chair: "I don't know, but I'll go and have a word with Mr Overill." She got up, turned, checked herself and asked: "And who shall I say would like to know?"

"My name is Samuel Midaka. I'm a friend of Mr Hicks' daughter. Her parents haven't seen her for a long time and I have some information for them."

The cashier scratched her nose, glanced down at the floor, nodded and scuttled through a back door. Five minutes later the bank manager emerged from a side door into the main banking hall.

"Mister Midaka?" he said politely, taken aback by Midnight's appearance but hiding it well. He extended a hand and Midnight Sam shook it firmly.

"I'm trying to find Lady Jane?" he asked. Overill looked puzzled and Midnight explained: "Sorry sir, that's a nickname. I'm trying to find Jane Hicks. She's a good friend of mine and I'm worried about her. And I know that her parents are too."

"It was all regrettable, most regrettable," the bank manager mused sadly, shaking his head. Midnight nodded sympathetically and waited. "Derek got a transfer to one of our branches in Oxfordshire. Witney, I think it was." He paused and rubbed his chin. "Yes, yes, it was definitely Witney. Assistant manager only – bit of a step down for him, I'm afraid, to be honest – but at least it meant they could get their daughter away from here. Not that there's anything wrong with Padstow, you understand. Fine place to …"

"I know the reason, Mister Overill," Midnight Sam interrupted politely.

22

AMY BROWN appeared before Bradford magistrates at 2pm on a Friday afternoon. She had been remanded in custody, having breached her bail conditions twice, and she looked terrible. Pale and gaunt, wide-eyed and jumpy.

Lady Jane sat stiffly and awkwardly in the public gallery, Chris Sellwood by her side. The detective had booked a rest day to lend his friend moral support. Lady raised a hand tentatively at Amy but there was no response. The young mother stared straight ahead without expression.

The magistrates retired to read the pre-sentence report which had been prepared by the probation service and filed back into court twenty minutes later. The chairman of the bench – a middle-aged woman with a tight perm and tight lips – pronounced sentence: two months in prison.

Amy gasped and croaked: "What about my baby?"

Lady Jane closed her eyes and Sellwood squeezed her hand reassuringly. "Don't worry, Lady, it'll be okay," he whispered.

Lady felt numb and frightened as she sat in the car on their way home. Her second-hand responsibility for Emily had become a first-hand one.

"What am I going to do, Chris?" she asked, her voice wavering and tears brimming in her eyes. "What in God's name am I going to do?"

Sellwood's face was stern and he waited for several minutes before he replied: "You know what you are going to do. You are going to look after Emily, end of story. And you know damn well that I'll be here to help out – well, me *and* the missus, actually."

Lady started to say something but Sellwood stayed her with an irritable wave of his left hand: "Just call this my good deed, Jane, just let me indulge myself, make up for all the bad things I've done in my life …"

"I've said this before, Chris, and I'll say it again: by Christ, you are one hell of a bloke."

"Bugger off," the policeman snapped, concentrating hard on the road ahead.

****

Freddy Grimshaw met Blacklock in the Rose and Crown at midday. Blacklock was clutching a pint of Guinness with both hands and scowling at a young man (a black man with impressive dreadlocks) who was playing the fruit machine.

"Think they own the fuckin' place," he said nastily, but in a low voice. "Come over here, live off the fuckin' state and cocky as fuck they are too."

"You're on benefit, Blackie, so am I for that matter," Grimshaw pointed out.

"But it's my fuckin' country," Blacklock grumbled, curling his upper lip. "I was fuckin' born here."

"He probably was too, Blackie. I don't like it either but they've got as much right to be here as you and me."

"Oh fuck off," Blacklock closed the discussion and reached for his Guinness. He swallowed half the contents of his pint glass in one go, slammed it down on to the bar and wiped the froth from his beard with the back of his hand.

"Have you got the stuff?" he asked, his voice low, looking straight ahead.

"Of course I have. Hundred per cent bloody pure it is too. Zonk out a bleedin' elephant. But it's going to cost you, matey, I can tell you."

Blacklock's face darkened and he swivelled on his bar stool to face Grimshaw: "Twenty-five quid, you said. Twenty-five quid for some really good stuff. That's what you said. You'll not get a fuckin' penny more."

Grimshaw shrugged: "Fifty, Blackie. That's the price, matey. Fifty quid. Look … the stuff I've got in my pocket would put half of Bradford to sleep. You said you wanted the best. Well that's what I've got for you, matey, the bloody best. But the best don't come cheap."

Blacklock scowled, nodded, finished his Guinness, slid from the bar stool and headed for the toilets. Grimshaw smiled at the barmaid who had been trying to listen to their conversation, toyed with his drink, lit a cigarette, inhaled indulgently, made a fuss of stubbing it out when an indignant landlord approached and then followed Blacklock.

****

Lady Jane sat Emily down and tried to explain the situation as honestly as she could, but it was not easy. She emphasised that Amy was a "good person" who loved her daughter very much but had "got ill" again and had to go away to get better. "When she comes home, it'll be fine, my darling, it'll all be fine." But disbelief and distrust burned in the four-year-old's eyes. She was not convinced; she had seen and heard it before. She got up from the kitchen chair, marched into the living room, sought out her pink teddy bear and sat on the floor, immediately engrossed in a private game. Lady Jane followed her into the room, a helpless look on her face.

"I don't want mummy to come home again, Aunty Jane," she said softly, quite matter-of-fact, without looking up. "I want *you* to be my mummy."

Lady juggled her hours at The Marmaris and befriended a single mother in the same block of flats, who helped out with baby-sitting duties. And, despite protestations from the surrogate mother, Chris Sellwood (or more accurately, Chris Sellwood's wife) made regular donations of food, clothes and treats for Emily.

Amy was two weeks into her prison sentence – in theory just two weeks away from release on licence – when the detective telephoned Lady one evening. "She's going to have to serve the full two months, I'm afraid," he said. Lady closed her eyes and waited for the detective to continue. "She got hold of some heroin from somewhere. They found her unconscious in the prison toilets. She was in a bad way and spent two days in the prison hospital. She's bloody lucky not to have died. Christ knows where she got the stuff from. She also assaulted a prison visitor."

"What in God's name is going to happen when she gets out, Chris? It scares the shit out of me, I can tell you." Lady grasped the hair on the top of her head with both hands. Sellwood fell silent; there really wasn't anything useful he could say.

****

Three days later Gordon Blacklock – clean-shaven and kitted out in a cheap suit from Oxfam, cheap shoes, shirt and tie – knocked on the door of the apartment he knew Lady Jane occupied. It was a Thursday morning and Emily would normally have been at nursery, but on that particular Thursday the little girl was home with a chest infection. And Jane was looking after her.

"I wondered how long it would be," she said with a weary sigh. "What do you want, Gordon? And before you say anything, I'm not coming back. You're wasting your time. It's all over between us, well and truly over. I'm getting on with my life … why don't you get on with yours?"

But Blacklock was not going to be that easily deterred. He had spent a lot of time, effort and money to reclaim the woman he felt belonged to him.

"We're a team, Janey … you and me … a team," he began sheepishly, but Lady knew the conciliatory tone, she knew it of old: it meant nothing. It was inevitably the calm before the storm. "I know we've had our ups and downs, Janey, but we're good together, we belong together. You and me."

"Why have you come here … now?" Lady asked, narrowing her eyes with sudden suspicion. "Why now, Gordon?" She tightened her mouth and held his stare. "This is your doing, isn't it. Amy getting back on drugs. It's somehow your doing." She had raised her voice and her face was white with anger, but she remained very much in control. There was real hatred in her eyes and Blacklock was visibly shaken by the power of the woman he had terrorised for years.

"Don't know what you're on about, Janey," he whined, suppressing the anger which was welling up inside him. "I've never spoken to the girl, I don't know anything about her. I don't know what you're talking about."

But Lady Jane knew, from past experience, when Blacklock was lying. She recognised the defensive bristling of the shoulders, the head held back and to one side, the thick fingers scratching the chin and the averting of those black, lifeless and dangerous eyes.

"What have you done?" she asked darkly and took a step towards him. Blacklock held his ground in the doorway as his anger took control but Lady, although she recognised the signs, did not back down. "What have you done?" She repeated the question with such power, with such incisiveness that Blacklock was forced to answer and to answer truthfully.

"She's a fuckin' whore, Janey, nothing but a useless, fuckin' junkie whore. She picks up blokes in the Rose and Crown … every fuckin' night. She's nothing …"

"That's your pub, Gordon. That's where you drink."

"Okay, it's where I drink. So fuckin' what?"

"You bastard," she growled, her eyes wide with fury, her chest heaving. She pushed him in the chest with both hands and snarled, her voice a scream: "You fucking bastard."

Emily, clutching her teddy bear, came running from her bedroom, flushed with infection, her face startled. She hugged Lady Jane's legs and looked up fearfully at Blacklock, who now wore a cold and deadly smile.

"You're coming with me, lassie," he said, puffing out his chest and clenching his fists. "And I suggest that you put that snivelling little brat in care, where she belongs."

"Get out," Lady placed a protective arm around Emily's shoulders. "Get out of here now, get out of my life … just get out."

Blacklock grabbed Lady around the neck and pulled her towards him. She let go of Emily and punched him in the chest. He laughed and swung her away from the girl. Emily, sobbing, flung herself at Blacklock and rained ineffective blows on his legs. He looked down at her quite dispassionately and struck her in the face with a carefully-measured, back-handed blow. Emily collapsed in a heap and Lady wrenched herself free of Blacklock and knelt down beside the child, who was curled up on her side and drawing short and shallow breaths. Emily sat up suddenly, both hands covering her nose, and let out a piercing scream. Blood seeped through her fingers and Blacklock backed off. Doors opened, curtains twitched and neighbours crept tentatively from their homes.

Somebody called an ambulance and somebody called the police, while Lady Jane cradled Emily in her arms. Blacklock had run off. The paramedics arrived on the scene first and took Emily, along with Lady, to hospital. The police turned up a few minutes later and took one or two statements from neighbours who had not really seen very much but who had a lot to say.

After Emily was treated in the accident and emergency department of Bradford Royal and sedated in readiness for a general anaesthetic operation to set her nose, Lady Jane slipped out of the hospital and sat down on a bench in a small garden area. She telephoned Detective Sergeant Chris Sellwood and waited. The policeman arrived at the hospital half an hour later.

"He's broken her nose," Lady said, looking deep into Sellwood's eyes with a cold and terrible hatred. "How could he do such a thing … to a child? How could a man …"

"He's going down," Sellwood interrupted quietly. "GBH and against a four-year-old girl. With his record he'll get three or four years at the very least. I'm going to get the bastard for this, Lady Jane."

Lady smiled sadly and reached out to hold the detective's hand: "Thanks for coming, Chris. I couldn't think who else to phone. Only my knight in shining armour."

"Well you are a damsel in distress, aren't you," he returned her smile and squeezed her hand.

23

"IT'S a mobile phone, dat's all it is for Chrissake, a mobile fuckin' phone," Mickey the Mouth glared across the table in the alcove of The Mitre but Midnight Sam was not impressed. He picked up the second-hand Nokia with a forefinger and thumb and examined it with cursory distaste. He mentally wiped his fingers after he replaced the alien instrument on the table. For comfort he reached for his half pint glass of Olde English and polished it off in one go. Tattoo Terry, whose turn it was, struggled wearily to his feet and snatched Midnight's glass.

"How long is this going to go on for?" he muttered. "It's wearing us out, Midnight. Up and down, up and bleedin' down. Why the hell can't you drink pints like the rest of us? Wearing us out, it is."

"I'm cutting down my drinking," Midnight retorted imperiously. "I thought you knew that."

Tattoo Terry and The Irishman exchanged helpless glances and Bobby looked up with the faintest of smiles. But, in deference to Midnight's pride, nobody said a word.

"So what do I need a mobile phone for?" he asked, shaking his head. "Done okay without one so far."

"Communication, Sammy, for fuck's sake, communication. Keeping in contact." Mickey the Mouth spoke slowly and patiently, as if to a backward child. "Look here Sam, dis Looking for Lady business has got to be organised – organised like a military operation – and t'most important ting is for us here at base camp to be able to get in fuckin' touch wid you at any time."

"You sound like Scots Robby," Midnight said with a faraway look in his eyes. "Just the sort of thing Scots Robby would have said." There was a moment's respectful silence while they remembered their dear, departed friend. "So how do I use the bloody thing?"

Mickey the Mouth launched into a phrenetic diatribe which left all three of them impressed but with no desire for further explanation. Tattoo Terry lost interest half way through and meandered across to the fruit machine, but Midnight, ever the gentleman, nodded sagely and said: "Oh I see. I think I get it." Which he didn't.

****

Midnight caught the 10am National Express coach to Oxford. Tattoo Terry and Mickey the Mouth saw him off from the coach station. The Irishman was suffering from a monumental hangover: he had finally been allowed back into the Irish Club in King Charles Street. Sadly for Mick, it turned out to be a one-off experience. Tatts, on the other hand, oozed smugness. He had got drunk of course, but, apart from losing his left boot in the park, he had managed to get home in pretty good shape.

Mickey and Tatts felt uncomfortable in Midnight's presence that morning. Their friend had followed Brian Davies' advice to have a proper haircut and to generally tidy himself up. He had acquired a pair of jeans and a polo-neck sweater from Matalan and cheap but colourful trainers from Shoe Zone. But the centre manager encountered a brick wall when he broached the subject of the navy blue donkey jacket. That stayed.

Nevertheless, despite the partial makeover, Midnight Sam still, to the outside world, looked like a tramp and he knew it. But for the first time the thought niggled him. Nevertheless Midnight nodded, gave a thumbs-up to his mates, boarded the coach and shuffled down the aisle to the back seat.

He peered sightlessly through the window at the damp countryside as the coach wound its way through the kindly Cotswolds eastwards to Oxford. What a strange world. What strange twists of fate had brought him here, had transformed Samuel Midaka – a promising university student destined perhaps for great things – into Midnight Sam – a down-and-out, homeless and hopeless drunk, destined for anonymity and for an early death. What a strange, strange world, indeed.

Oh yes, he knew the *when*, to the exact moment, and he knew the catalyst. But, despite appearances, Midnight was far too intelligent a man to be satisfied with a mere catalyst. The death of his beloved father in a car accident had been that catalyst, a devastating catalyst. But there was something else, something long before his father's death. And as Midnight Sam watched the grey-green fields trundle by beneath a mean and melancholy and sunless sky he began to face the real reason why he had become what he had.

Midnight Sam always knew that his mother had never loved him – a condition which had haunted her as much as it had damaged him – but what he had not realised before was the devastating seed of self-destruction that lack of maternal love had sown. His very start in life had been an emotional wasteground. No wonder he ended up on the physical one.

Midnight swept a ragged semi-circle in the condensation on the window of the coach with the back of his hand and stared out at his life, his eyebrows bunched with concentration. And suddenly, instinctively and comfortingly his thoughts turned to Lady Jane. He could see her face, her sweet but street-ravaged face and that rare but beautiful smile, a smile which could light up the world. And those small and delicate hands. And that quiet aura of unrequited strength and goodness. And the way she had looked at him the day he confronted Gordon Blacklock.

Squirming into the corner of the back seat of the coach, watching the rain, Midnight Sam came to the most important conclusion of his life: Looking for Lady was the same as looking for Midnight Sam. Find one and you find the other …

****

"Mr Hicks is our assistant manager," said the young woman, eyeing Midnight Sam with reserve. "But he's on a day off today, should be in tomorrow. Can you call back then?"

It was the third bank Midnight had tried and he raised his eyebrows with relief: "Thank you, my lovely. I'll pop back tomorrow and have a word with him." He turned to walk away but suddenly remembered something: "Could you tell him that it's about his daughter?"

"What sort of time shall I say?"

"Around 11am," Midnight suggested, "oh and tell him that Midnight Sam called."

"Midnight Sam?"

"That's right, my dear," he confirmed with a broad smile and shambled out of the banking hall. He selected a couple of leaflets on the way: 'Make Your Money Work For You' and 'Fixed Mortgage Interest Rates For Five Years' read the titles.

Derek Hicks was waiting for Midnight Sam the following day, making a pretence of shuffling papers behind the three cashiers. It was just after eleven o'clock when Midnight walked in.

"Could I have a word with Mr Hicks?"

The cashier – a middleaged, plump and pleasant woman – nodded and glanced over her shoulder. Derek Hicks edged up to the counter: "Hullo. I'm Derek Hicks. You must be Midnight Sam?" Midnight nodded and took a backward step from the counter.

"Would you like to sit down over by that table next to the window? I'll be around in a tick." The assistant manager adjusted his glasses, straightened his suit jacket and tried to control the thumping of his heart against his chest, while Midnight walked across the banking hall and sat down.

"You have news of my daughter, Mr Sam?" he asked, chewing his lower lip nervously. "Have you heard something about Jane?"

Midnight shook his head: "I'm trying to find her, Mr Hicks. I'm a friend of hers and I want to find her."

Lady Jane's father sighed and his face fell: "Oh … oh dear … and I thought that you were going to tell me where she is." He closed his eyes for a second and rocked his head back with disappointment. "You see, we haven't seen our daughter for six years. Six years! And we are so worried, Mister Sam. We have no idea where she is, how she is … "

Midnight leaned forward: "Well, Mister Hicks, I saw her less than two years ago and she was fine then."

"Two years ago?" the older man repeated, his eyes widening. "Where was that? Was she well? What was she doing? How was she?" The words stumbled over one another.

Midnight told Lady's father most of what he knew, omitting the really bad bits, not mentioning Gordon Blacklock, and embellishing the few good bits, the bits about the special relationship the three of them had – Lady Jane, Midnight Sam and The Professor. He painted a picture of tentative hope and Derek Hicks felt happier, more optimistic than he had felt for the past six years.

"So why have you come to see me, Mister Sam? I mean, where do we go from here?"

"Does Lady ... I mean Jane ... does she keep in touch at all? A phone call, a letter, maybe a card ...?"

Derek Hicks shook his head sadly: "No phone calls, no letters ... but she does remember to send us a Christmas card every year." He paused and cleared his throat. He whipped off his glasses and polished them with the end of his tie. "And Martha – that's my wife – she always keeps them. It's our only contact with our daughter, you see. It's all we've got, I'm afraid. A little pile of Christmas cards ... oh, and the envelopes too. Martha keeps the envelopes as well."

"Have you checked the postmarks on the envelopes? You would know where she sent the cards from ... it would say so on the envelopes, wouldn't it?" Midnight shrugged his shoulders vaguely and the assistant manager rubbed his chin.

"Different places, Mister Sam, different places ...," he trailed then added, "but for the last two or three years they were from Blackpool or Bolton ... or was it Bradford? No, I think it was Bradford. Martha always contacts the police and the Missing Person's Helpline, but we've drawn a blank, I'm afraid. The police can't help unless they've got a previous address to go on and Missing Person's lost track of her four years ago. She obviously does not want to be found." Derek Hicks looked across at the warm eyes opposite him and experienced a wave of goodness.

"I'm going to find her for you, Mister Hicks," Midnight said and the words were measured and quietly-spoken but with extraordinary power.

"I hope that you do, Mister Sam," the middleaged man who looked ten years older than his half century made to get up but then changed his mind, a sudden impulse: "Would you like to come to my house this evening and meet my wife? I'm sure she would like to talk to you. I knock off at five o'clock. If you'd like to meet me outside the branch, we could go back together in my car. Would that be okay?"

Midnight recoiled and sprang to his feet, fastening the buttons of his donkey jacket: "I'd better not, Mister Hicks. I'm not too sure that your good lady wife would appreciate the likes of me in your house."

The older man shot to his feet and glared at Midnight: "The *likes* of you? What on earth do you mean by that? You appear to be a good man, Mister Sam. You looked after my daughter, you've been kind to her. The *likes* of you, indeed. Five o'clock sharp, outside the branch."

"Okay," Midnight relented, "if you're sure." They shook hands and Midnight Sam headed for the door. He stopped, half-turned and added: "My name is Samuel Midaka, by the way. Midnight Sam is a nickname. Just call me Sam."

****

Midnight stayed with Derek and Martha Hicks in their home in Long Hanborough, some ten miles from Witney, for two nights. Jane's parents would have liked the lovable tramp to have stayed longer but Midnight Sam was eager to get home. After all, Bonfire Night was just around the corner and the Looking For Lady campaign funds were getting low again.

But it had been a tender two days, during which Derek and Martha Hicks discovered what a fine and decent friend their prodigal daughter had stumbled upon; and during which Midnight discovered what good and loving parents Lady Jane had. It was also a very expensive couple of days for the couple, whose usual domestic bar bill ran to a bottle of French Chardonnay on Saturday evenings and an occasional couple of drinks at the local pub during the week. Derek's wife had soon assessed the situation and estimated that 32 half-litre cans of dry cider would be sufficient. It was inspired arithmetic as only two cans remained when Midnight checked out.

They lingered long over the two most recent Christmas cards from Lady – the franked postmarks were faded and barely legible – but they came to the same conclusion that the origin was Bradford.

Derek Hicks gave Midnight Sam a lift to the station and waited with him for the coach to swing into its allotted bay. There was a comfortable silence between the two men, suddenly broken by the assistant manager, who, although not a tactile man, ventured a hand onto Midnight's shoulder and made a rehearsed but clumsy little speech: "If you find her …"

Samuel Midaka interrupted: "*When* I find her."

"Okay Sam, *when* you find her." He paused, his eyes bright and moist. "When you find my daughter, apart from bringing her back to us, will you promise me one thing? Will you promise me that you'll never let her out of your sight again?"

24

THE CREDIT on her mobile phone had long run out, along with the battery, but nevertheless Amy Brown fumbled fitfully in the brown paper parcel which contained her meagre belongings, the parcel returned to her that morning, the morning of her release from prison. She finally found the battered old Samsung, frowned at the blank screen, shrugged and threw the phone across the pavement.

Amy tried to remember the prison officer's directions for the bus-stop. She stood perfectly still, her ankle-length, white mackintosh flapping in the late autumn wind, hands on hips. And then a flicker of decision entered those dull eyes and, in a flurry of activity, she fastened the buttons of her mackintosh and brushed her shoulder-length hair, now dyed blonde. Dyed by her ever-obliging cell-mate Sadie. A big, Afro-Carribean woman as hard as nails, but with a dangerously misleading soft and soothing voice. Sadie was doing two years for GBH and, at the age of 36, was a seasoned jailbird. She was also a seasoned lesbian, but this had not particularly bothered Amy, who had tried most things for money to fund her heroin habit.

Amy stood on the edge of the pavement and extended a thumb, thrusting her right knee from the folds of her mackintosh. After a quarter of an hour she got a lift into Bradford city centre. It cost her a hurried slide of the driver's hand up the inside of her thighs – she let her legs fall obligingly open – but there was nothing more. Not that she'd have cared if there had have been.

The landlord of The Rose and Crown was pleased to see her: she attracted a certain kind of customer to his pub and, in any event, he had no other use for the drab little room on the third floor.

"Has Gordon been in?" she asked. The landlord smiled nastily. He had a miserable morsel of gossip to impart and he was going to make the most of it.

"No, he fuckin' well hasn't and I don't think he will again, not if he's got any fuckin' sense," he began, pouring Amy a large gin and tonic. A look of panic swept across her face: "Why, what's he done?"

The landlord craned across the bar, savouring his malicious moment of ascendancy: "Well, you wouldn't have heard of course, not with you being inside, but your Gordon Blacklock is keeping his head down, right down, after what he did to that daughter of yours …"

Something stirred in Amy's soul. A muddled maternal panic crashed about in her head, a drug-dulled emotion struggled to swell her heart.

"What's he done to Emily?" she asked.

"He had a go at that friend of yours and he broke your daughter's nose in the process. He's a nasty piece of work, your Mister Blacklock, a nasty piece of work. Your little girl had to go to the hospital. Warrant out for his arrest, there is. He'd be looking at GBH and what with it being a kid and with his record, well, he'd be looking at three years, maybe four or five. Your mate's in the shit all right. Right up to his fuckin' armpits."

Amy sipped her drink cautiously, holding the glass with both hands, and stared unseeing at the wall behind the bar.

"Does Freddy Grimshaw still come in?" she asked and the landlord nodded. She breathed a small sigh of relief. "Any chance of that room again?"

"It's yours, but no stuff on the premises, and the usual fifty-fifty," the landlord said, folding his arms.

"Okay," Amy replied with false gaiety and drained her drink. " Can I have another gin?"

"If you've got the money, dearie."

"Can I have a tab?"

The landlord leaned forward, both hands on the bar, and whispered lasciviously: "Of course, you can, dearie. Same deal as before?"

Amy nodded.

****

Detective Inspector Chris Sellwood knew the exact date of Amy Brown's release. He had made it his business to know. He also guessed, correctly, where she was likely to go. Three days after her release from prison the policeman walked into The Rose and Crown at 8.30pm on a Saturday evening. The first person he saw was Amy.

Emily's mother was sitting at the bar, deep in conversation with a middle-aged Chinaman, who was fondling her knee. She wore a tight, red mini-skirt which left little to the imagination. Ruby red lip-stick had been unevenly applied and her eyes were heavy with black mascara. The expression on her face was bright and frivolous. The man was sipping a coke, she a large gin and tonic.

"Hello Amy," Sellwood said evenly, smiling coldly at the man. He slipped onto the bar stool next to the couple. Amy swivelled around, exposing a couple of inches of white flesh above the black, fishnet hold-ups she was wearing.

"Why, if it isn't Chief fuckin' Superintendent whatever your fuckin' name is," she said, her voice shrill and unpleasant. "Have you met my friend … ?," she paused and draped an arm around the Chinaman's shoulders: "Mister … Ching Chong Chinkie Chinaman." Amy Brown giggled and Chris Sellwood sighed. He suspected that he was wasting his time but he had to try for Lady's sake, for Emily's sake and, strangely enough, for his own sake.

"Your daughter is missing you, Amy. She wants you to come back home. And Jane misses you too. They both do. They want you home – more than anything else." He looked into a pair of wild but paradoxically dead eyes and felt a surge of despair.

The Chinaman withdrew his hand from Amy's knee; he sat back rigidly on the bar stool and inspected his watch. He looked over his shoulder at the door and began to squirm.

"Why don't you fuck off?" Amy suggested softly, staring wide-eyed into the policeman's face. "Can't you see that I'm busy. Just fuck off … please," she added with a false smile.

Sellwood slid from the bar stool and walked to the far end of the bar, taking his half pint of bitter with him. He would have left the pub altogether, but he had some unfinished business with the landlord. He repositioned himself and waited for the landlord to come within speaking distance. While he waited he saw, out of a corner of his eye, Amy and her client leave the bar arm-in-arm and disappear up the dimly-lit flight of stairs at the side of the pub.

"Can I have a word?" the detective asked, when the landlord came within earshot. "Official business, I'm afraid." Sellwood flashed his police identity card wearily, almost apologetically. The landlord eyed Sellwood with open dislike, his head held back, his eyes narrow. Sellwood was accustomed to the expression and, after many years as a front-line copper, he had developed a way of dealing with it: become what they expect, don't try to be chummy, don't try to win them over. Be a 'them' and somehow they end up giving you a degree of reluctant respect.

"As you are no doubt aware, we are looking for Gordon Blacklock, one of your regulars," he began evenly, the formal voice tinged with threat. "He is wanted in connection with an assault, a particularly unpleasant assault on a four-year-old girl …"

"Don't know nothin' about that," the landlord interrupted and made to walk away. Sellwood leaned forwards and stopped the publican in his tracks with the sheer force of his personality.

"Blacklock broke the girl's nose. He is facing a charge of grievous bodily harm and with his record he will go down for a long time. And anybody who protects him, anybody at all …," Sellwood stared directly into the landlord's eyes, " …will find themselves in the dock with him. Perverting the course of justice – that's what the charge would be, a very serious offence. Up to ten years behind bars, I believe. Ten years."

"I told you, I know nothing. I've no fuckin' idea where he is. I'd tell you if I did. He hasn't been in here for Christ knows how long."

"I'll tell you what we're going to do," Sellwood began pleasantly but with a deadly glint in his eyes. "You are going to tell me where Gordon Blacklock is living, which hole he has crawled into …"

"I don't fuckin' know. How many more times?"

"I don't care," Sellwood said evenly, the smile still on his face. "I really don't care what you say. I don't give a damn. If you really don't know where this low-life is living then you are going to have to find out. Up to you. Listen: don't fuck me about, please don't even *think* about fucking me about. I am an angry man. It doesn't happen very often, but when it does, when I get angry, then little pieces of shit like you tend to get squashed, and I mean seriously squashed."

The landlord recoiled, fought and failed to hold his own and feigned a sarcastic 'do-your fuckin' worst, copper' stance, hands on hips, an expression of child-like defiance on his face. But he knew he was foundering.

The detective pressed home his advantage: "I'll be back here in exactly one week, same time. And if you don't have an address for me, this shit-hole of yours is going to be raided and closed down before you, Sonny Jim, have time to break wind. What a mess we're going to make of The Rose and Crown and, who knows, what a mess we're going to make of you."

"I'll have you for police brutality," the landlord stammered feebly and Sellwood chuckled darkly.

"You would, of course, have to be alive first," he added with a black smile. He downed his drink, replaced the half-pint glass carefully on the bar and left the pub without a backward glance. The landlord watched him bleakly.

****

Lady Jane huddled for warmth on one of the benches surrounding the adventure playground in Queensbury and watched Emily embark upon a secret, complicated and important game with Leo, her best friend, the boy she had decided she was going to marry. The game was even a secret from the tousle-haired lad, although he tried hard to follow the ever-changing rules. It involved using all the playground facilities – roundabout, rocking horse, slide and toy dolphin – in a certain order before arriving at the counter of the toy shop, where Emily sold her young fiancé certain imaginary groceries. Only Leo kept getting things wrong – whizzing down the slide before scooting around on the roundabout or forgetting about the toy dolphin altogether. Little clouds of steam followed the two four-year-olds like chilly halos and Emily turned midway through admonishing Leo for some tiresome lapse in concentration to blow a kiss to Lady. The involuntary, inconsequential but instinctive act of a child. For no reason at all apart from a sudden wave of love which demanded instant demonstration. Lady blew a kiss back.

A sense of unease crept into Lady Jane's mind as she recalled the words of Chris Sellwood over coffee in her tiny kitchen a week ago. The words were kindly and gentle but they disturbed Lady Jane's equanimity, the burgeoning peace in her life, and they were intended to. They were talking about Gordon Blacklock.

Lady was worried: "What if they find him not guilty? He's a cruel and vindictive man. God knows what he would do to me or more importantly what he would do to Emily, if I take the stand. The bastard has already broken her nose."

Sellwood picked up his coffee cup, blew on to the steamy surface and looked across the table, his eyebrows raised: "Blacklock is going to jail, Jane, he's going to jail for a long time. Trust me. All you have to do is tell the truth, nothing more, nothing less. Don't make anything up. If you can't remember, if you're not sure of the answer to any question, then say so. It's not you on trial, although the defence lawyer will make you feel that it is. Gordon Blacklock is the one on trial … and he is the one who is going to go down."

"You haven't caught him yet."

Sellwood smiled: "We'll get him … I'll get him … don't worry about that. It's only a matter of time."

"But he could be anywhere, he could have left Bradford, he could have left the country, he could be anywhere …"

Sellwood laughed harshly: "Do you really believe that, do you think he would leave here when he knows you're still around? No, he can't leave without you and that will be his Achilles' Heel."

Lady slumped her shoulders and nodded: "No, you're right. He's still around – somewhere – I know he is. The only time he'd leave is if I went with him and, do you know, the incredible thing is that I think he believes I would. Despite everything he's done to me and to Emily, despite everything I've said to him. He really thinks I would go back to him." She shook her head.

The detective picked up a spoon and stirred his coffee thoughtfully. He stood up, stroking his chin, and walked across the room to the sink. He turned around, resting both hands behind him on the work surface and cocked his head to one side.

"I've got an idea and I want you to hear me out," he began slowly. He paused: "I think the time has come for you and Emily to get away from here. Completely away, I mean." Another pause. "Look Jane, whatever happens to Blacklock, however long he gets, you are never going to feel safe here and you are never going to feel that Emily is safe here either. The best thing for both of you would be to move away, turn your backs on Bradford, on Queensbury, give the whole Up North thing the bum's rush."

"You're fed up with us," Jane said petulantly, unfairly and immediately regretted her words. "I didn't mean that, Chris."

He shook his head – he knew she didn't mean 'that' – and continued: "You were born and bred by the sea, right? Cornwall, if I remember. Place called Padstow? Well," he braced his shoulders and raised his eyebrows, "how do you fancy going back down south, back to the sea, away from all this? A complete change of scenery, of environment, a complete change of life ..?"

"Oh dear," Lady sighed, "of course I do, Chris, of course I do. It sounds such a wonderful idea, but you must know how impossible it is. Surely? What about Amy?"

"Amy?" the policeman asked, shaking his head and closing his eyes. "Amy is beyond help, Jane. You didn't see her in the Rose and Crown, I did. She is beyond help, she really …"

Bristling with anger, Lady Jane interrupted: "How can you say that, Chris? How can you? You should have seen *me* a few years ago. Talk about 'beyond help.' Christ, I was that far, that far …," she pinched a forefinger and thumb together, tears welling up in her eyes.

Sellwood turned around, his back to Lady Jane, and stared out of the window, shoulders hunched with stubbornness. He had rehearsed his speech and he was damn well going to finish it.

"Have you heard of a place called Salcombe? It's on the south Devonshire coast, about 20 miles from Plymouth."

Jane nodded: "Yes I have, but so what? Look, I know you care – you are a good man, a really good man – but I am not going to abandon Amy. No way. It's as simple as that."

"So what about Emily, what about that little girl?" The cruel trump card. "Don't you think she deserves a good life, a better life, a safer life?" Chris Sellwood began to wish he had never started the conversation. Oh yes, he knew what he wanted to say – that Amy Brown was a beat-up, hopeless heroin addict who would do anything for her next fix, who would sell her body, probably her own daughter, who had sunk too low, far too low now, to ever be able to drag herself out of the mire. But he also knew the terrible dilemma Lady Jane was facing.

"Emily belongs with her mother … and with me," Lady retorted starchly. "And that means here."

25

MICKEY the Mouth was lost in his rendition of The Old Ragged Cross. His eyes were closed. The folds of skin on his eyelids overlapped and tiny blue veins spidered this way and that. He was playing the harmonica softly, lovingly and in perfect tune. A bright green woollen hat clung to the back of his head and pale ginger-grey wisps of hair curled down his forehead to the bridge of his nose, a pink and bulbous affair which bore testament to a lifetime dedication to alcohol.

The Irishman was sprawled in the alcove of The Mitre, his small and spare body swamped by a vastly over-sized, navy blue overcoat with no belt and only two buttons remaining, both near the top. The coat was a gift from Midnight Sam almost exactly two years ago, just after The Professor had died. Midnight reasoned that The Prof would not need the coat anymore and it might as well stay in 'the family.' The only thing missing from the dead schoolteacher's garment was the length of coarse string he used to wrap twice around his waist, a substitute for the long-gone belt. Nobody knew what had happened to it. Maybe it was still on the wasteground …

Tattoo Terry and Midnight Sam walked into the pub together, hunched from the cold, both rubbing their upper arms as the warmth of the room hit them. Midnight unfastened his donkey jacket and Tatts made a mess of unzipping his anorak, snagging the zip in the dark green woolly jumper he was wearing. From the looks of it, the jumper had been snagged before.

Bobby waited patiently but eagerly for the inevitable conversation to begin. This was always the best part. The anticipation, the delicious uncertainty, not-knowing what weird and wonderful subject would emerge from absolutely nowhere, to be bandied about with comfortable, sometimes aggressive, aimlessness for a majority of the afternoon. He did not have long to wait.

"It's only a week away, Sam," Mickey frowned and raised his eyebrows accusingly. "Next fuckin' Friday, to be precise. Eight days and we've done Sweet Fanny Adams, nothing at all, not a fuckin' ting …"

Midnight Sam looked hurt; he shook his head and sighed, his eyes closed: "That's why we're here today, Mickey. We're here to sort out the bonfire. I've made a list …," Midnight produced a scrap of paper.

"I thought we were here because it's a Thursday and we always come here on Thursday afternoons …" Tattoo Terry trailed and cleared his throat nervously.

"Remember, remember, the fifth of November, gunpowder, treason and plot," Midnight raised his voice theatrically and Bobby raised his head from the glass he was polishing. Tatts and Mickey frowned and eyed Midnight curiously.

"Fifth of November, 1603," Midnight began patiently. "Bunch of terrorists tried to blow up the House of Commons. That's what Bonfire

Night is all about. Bloke called Guy Fawkes was the main man. But they all got caught."

"Fuckin' pity," muttered the Irishman.

"Pity they tried to blow up the House of Commons?" asked Tatts, embarking upon the first and last political debate of his life.

"Pity dey didn't fuckin' pull it off," muttered Mickey bitterly.

****

Bishop John stood in the front row, a plastic beaker of Tesco's Strong Cider in one hand and a sparkler in the other. A baked potato, three sausages and a dollop of baked beans sat deep and warm on his stomach and his wispy, snow-white hair danced in the breeze. One hundred and eighty-six faces glowed orange in the dying embers of a truly magnificent bonfire. What a thing of beauty it had been, rising majestically from the wasteground, towering above the rusting bicycles, doorless fridges, evil cookers, myriad tyres, sad sofas and once-revered kitchen units which had been ripped out and abandoned by fickle, surburban families. Such a fine and symmetrical creation that it was with a degree of sadness it had to be set alight at all.

The annual council event, two miles away on the other side of town, had however been a less successful affair. When the tarpaulin was removed from the official city bonfire in front of 12,500 expectant onlookers, there was a mass silence loud enough to wake the dead. The skeletal pyramid frame of eight 15-foot wooden posts resembled a giant North American Indian wigwam in the early stages of construction. There was nothing inside; no wood, no boxes, no tyres, no leaves, no sacks, no cardboard boxes, no paper. Nothing.

Tattoo Terry, whose task it had been to collect materials for and to build the 'alternative' bonfire, had been busy. But he had not seen the sense in foraging far and wide for suitable combustible materials, when everything he could possibly need was already in one place. All that was needed was discretion, a borrowed panel van – white in colour, of course – and the cover of darkness.

Meanwhile, back on the wasteground, Tatts, who stood several feet closer to the glowing circle of fire than the others, watched the flickering flames fondly, occasionally braving the heat and poking the embers with a blackened broom handle. He nearly caught fire twice but Mickey broke ranks and yanked him out of harm's way.

Although an undeniable success, the celebrations had not gone entirely to plan. Mickey the Mouth and eight helpers had been entrusted with the task of letting off 36 four-foot rockets which encircled the bonfire as simultaneously as their legs would allow, while Midnight Sam declared he had devised a method of ensuring that the bonfire would burst into flames immediately.

Three of Mickey's helpers ran in the wrong direction and the ensuing collisions skewed some of the two-litre cider bottles containing the rockets. One Thunderdome corkscrewed inches from the heads of the crowd, while three others plunged into the base of the bonfire. Bishop John had a narrow escape when a Skyburst Special clipped the right sleeve of his overcoat on its journey towards a clump of blackberry brambles. The remaining rockets snaked off in various directions, all except one, another Thunderdome. It lay sullenly on its side, along with the empty bottle of GL which had been its intended launch pad.

Had the attention of the spectators not been distracted by Midnight Sam hurling a Molotov Cocktail into the bonfire somebody might have seen fit to warn Mickey the Mouth not to pick up the rocket.

Impressively (and incredibly) his was the only injury requiring hospital treatment. The Irishman was carted off to A&E with a badly-burned right hand and forearm by Brian Davies, who had, of course, turned up for the occasion.

The Cathedral bell was striking midnight when Bishop John gave Midnight Sam and Tattoo Terry a lift back into town. The rain, which had been considerate, conveniently returned to dampen the smouldering remains of the bonfire and the onlookers, leaving their empty cider bottles behind, had drifted off into the night.

"I hope Mickey is all right," Midnight broke the comfortable silence, while the bishop negotiated the wet and lumpy track on to the narrow lane which led to South Road, now deserted. He drove sedately into town.

"He'll be fine Sam," the bishop said, "although I'm not too sure he'll be able to wear The Professor's coat again."

****

Brian Davies breathed a sigh of relief. WHO STOLE OUR BONFIRE? screamed the front-page headline in the Evening News, but the only reference to the activities on the wasteground was an innocuous four-paragraph filler at the bottom of a double-page picture spread rounding up the night's festivities. Fortunately no connection had been made between the two events.

26

THE LANDLORD of the Rose and Crown feigned not to have seen Chris Sellwood, who had walked into his pub, as promised exactly one week since the detective's ultimatum. The publican nudged a barmaid in the policeman's direction and looked pointedly away.

"Half of bitter, please," Sellwood said with a cold smile, "oh and would you ask the landlord to spare me a minute?" The woman shrugged.

"I'm back," the policeman called over the shoulder of the barmaid.

"I've asked around, I've asked all over, I've put the word out …" the landlord gave a helpless, open-handed gesture with his hands. "God knows I've tried, but nobody knows where the bloody hell he is." The publican leaned forwards across the bar with a conspiratorial glance from left to right. "Between you and me I reckon old Blackie has gone and done a runner, buggered off. Could be the other side of the fuckin' country by now …"

Sellwood remained impassive and said nothing.

"Look here, I've kept my side of the bargain. I've pulled out all the stops, called in a few favours, made a bloody nuisance of myself, but your man simply ain't here. He's gone. Don't know where, don't know when, but he's gone and that's for sure. Buggered off." The landlord sighed and stood back from the bar, hands on hips. Sellwood nodded and got up.

"Within the next four days the drug squad is going to raid your pub," the policeman said evenly, leaning forwards. "And they are going to find various quantities of Class A drugs – heroin and crack cocaine – on your premises. In the toilets, behind the bar, up your arse, I shouldn't wonder. And they are also going to find evidence of prostitution."

The landlord squared his shoulders ready to protest but Sellwood raised a hand and continued: "And you, my friend, are going to be charged with conspiracy to supply Class A drugs and with running a brothel. You're going to be quite a celebrity when the judge sends you down."

The detective sipped his drink and winced: "And your beer is disgusting. I'd have you for that as well, if I could."

He pushed the glass across the bar with a forefinger, stood up and left the pub.

Sellwood was about a hundred metres down the road before the landlord caught up with him, wheezing with the effort. The policeman stopped and put his head to one side quizzically, while the landlord bent his body at right angles to the ground, chest heaving as he fought for breath.

Sellwood waited and pulled up the collar of his coat against the cold, his breath puffing out in small, frosty clouds. Finally the landlord beckoned Sellwood to follow him along the road for a couple of hundred metres and then into an unlit alleyway to the left.

"He's got a flat, above a Chinese takeaway, lives there with another bloke, don't know his name," the publican whispered.

"Whereabouts? What's the address?"

The landlord thrust his left hand into the pocket of his jeans, pulled out a scrap of paper, made to give it to the policeman but suddenly pulled his hand back: "No raids, no arrests – is that a deal?"

Sellwood nodded and took the piece of paper.

****

Gordon Blacklock was sitting on a sofa a couple of feet from a television set in the living room of a one-bedroomed flat above the Hong Kong Dragon takeaway on the corner of a dreary street. He was watching Eastenders and devouring a carton of spare ribs with egg fried rice. A can of Special Brew lager stood on the linoleum floor alongside an overflowing ashtray. A half-smoked cigarette, just about hanging on to an inch of ash, lay askew across a scatter of dogends. Blacklock reached for the smouldering cigarette, stuck it into the middle of his mouth, inhaled deeply and blew a funnel of smoke to the ceiling. He drained the can of lager and dropped it onto the floor.

It is difficult to identify and describe what was going through Blacklock's mind. Most of us have elements of good and bad, positives and negatives, plusses and minuses. Most of us yearn to be good and kind and happy but sometimes pride, fear, resentment, anger – sometimes simply life itself – gets in the way. We intend to do one thing – the 'right' thing – but something untoward occurs and we end up doing the wrong thing instead. And then, with righteous or plain defiant indignation, we try to justify our actions. Such is normal human nature.

But with Gordon Blacklock the initial intention was different from the norm. He did not understand the concepts of good and bad or of right and wrong. His only motivating factor was self, an unassailable determination to have his own way. He listened to no-one, cared for no-one, understood no-one, unless, of course, they were travelling in his direction.

He sprawled across the sofa, still wearing his black duffel coat, eating and drinking without pleasure and scheming, ever-scheming, to get 'his' woman back. The ungrateful bitch. Oh yes, she'd come running back to him in the end, tail between her fucking legs, begging him to take her back. That's what she always did. And he would – of course he would – but not before a fuckin' good row and a thump or two to remind her who was the fuckin' boss. He relished the cold anger rising in his chest, the sensual sensation of impending confrontation – a violent confrontation he knew he would always win. He yearned for that look of terror on her face, the backing-off, the hands outstretched in a vain attempt to ward him off. He missed the near-orgasmic pleasure which accompanied that first, measured blow; he missed the pleading to stop. He missed the hysterical protestations of undying love and fidelity. He missed the power he thought he still exerted over Lady Jane.

But because he was incapable of thinking beyond his own designs, because he was incapable of introspection, of self-examination, of self-criticism, because he was incapable of normal thought, Gordon Blacklock was unable to recognise the truth (unless it accidentally coincided with his own version.) He was therefore incapable of accepting that Jane had broken free from his tyrannous control. The thought had not, would not and could not enter his head. The ungrateful bitch belonged to him and to him alone and he was going to get her back. End of fuckin' story!

These thoughts were encircling Blacklock's mind when Detective Sergeant Chris Sellwood put a shoulder to the front door of his flat and burst into the darkened hallway.

Blacklock shot to his feet and crouched, apelike, his huge hands clenching and unclenching, his closely-set black eyes wide like a cornered animal. The two men faced each other and there was a silence, a palpable silence, apart from the policeman's heavy breathing and the muted soundtrack of the television soap opera.

"Gordon Blacklock ... I have a warrant for your arrest," Sellwood forced an official tone into his voice.

"On what fuckin' charge, copper?" Blacklock sneered, raising himself to his full height, which, at six foot one, was a good two inches taller than the detective. Sellwood smiled thinly, but his face was dangerously white with anger. The blood had drained from his lips and his eyes burned.

"I am arresting you on suspicion of assault occasioning grievous bodily harm. You do not have to say anything, but ..."

"Cut the crap copper and fuck off," Blacklock growled, sinking his head bullishly into his shoulders. "I've done nothing fuckin' wrong ... I've not assaulted nobody. You've got the wrong man."

"Is your name Gordon Blacklock?" Sellwood asked softly.

"What if it is?"

"Then you are under arrest," Sellwood repeated almost apologetically, not moving and staring levelly into Blacklock's eyes. "You will come with me to the police station." But there was little conviction in the detective's tone; he was going through the motions; he wanted Blacklock to make the next move. He made no further effort to administer the official caution, to take his charge by the arm in the time-honoured fashion, to apply the handcuffs, to escort his captive to the police car and thence to the police station and to the cells. Because Detective Sergeant Chris Sellwood was intentionally alone, alone and in a murderous mood, and the warrant was not due to be executed until the following day. He was alone with a terrible anger that had been festering inside him ever since the brute in front of him had broken Emily's nose. But maybe before that: perhaps an anger which had been growing over the years, years of watching violent thugs like Blacklock terrorise and hurt innocent and vulnerable people, year after year after year.

And when the self-control snapped inside the detective's head, it did so with a deadly calm. One moment Detective Sergeant Chris Sellwood, the police officer who did everything by the book, known and respected in the force and on the street for being fair, calm and honourable; but the next moment, Chris Sellwood, the man, the man who was standing in the same room as a piece of shit like Gordon Blacklock.

Blacklock hooked the toe of his right foot underneath the lip of the coffee table in the middle of the room and jerked it towards the policeman. The table cracked against Sellwood's shins and the policeman stumbled forwards. It gave Blacklock enough time to snatch his wallet from a sideboard, turn and lumber across the room into the kitchen. He yanked open the fire escape door and lunged for the metal steps, but he tripped and sat down heavily. By the time he had managed to stagger to his feet, Sellwood was there, fists clenched and eyes hooded. The two men, barely a foot apart, stared at each other.

With a glittering career behind him and a potentially even more glittering career ahead, Chris Sellwood took one swift step forward, drew his right arm back a fraction and whipped out a punch which landed smack in the middle of Blacklock's face. The policeman's little finger broke but he didn't feel the pain. Arms outstretched, Blacklock catapulted backwards down the fire escape steps, until he landed with a solid thump in a heap at the bottom. His head hit the concrete with a loud crack.

Blacklock lay perfectly still and Sellwood remained at the top of the steps for half a minute, gazing down at the inert body, before he descended wearily. He crouched over Blacklock's body and placed two fingers against the man's neck, in search of a pulse. He closed his eyes with relief when he felt the fluttering beat.

Sellwood sat down on the bottom step of the fire escape and thought hard. He didn't know how badly Blacklock was injured but he did know that the punch in the face coupled with his own broken finger could not be explained away by an 'accidental' fall down the flight of steps.

After a couple of minutes, Sellwood got to his feet and clambered back up the fire escape, taking the steps three at a time. He stood in the middle of the kitchen for a few seconds, before pacing across to the sink and rummaging about in the washing-up bowl until he found what he was looking for – a carving knife. Wrapping a tea towel around his right hand, he picked up the knife and hurried back down the fire escape steps. He rubbed the handle over the palm of Blacklock's right hand and tossed the knife several feet away. It pinged on the pavement.

Drawing a deep breath, the detective pulled out his mobile phone and called his control room. It was going to be a long and difficult night.

27

THE ambulance threaded through the Saturday morning people who thronged the pedestrianised city centre. No siren sounded and the blue lights flashed apologetically, as if an emergency could not possibly occur on the weekend before Christmas.

A circle of onlookers parted as two paramedics, one carrying an oxygen mask and cylinder and the other wheeling a stretcher, knelt either side of Midnight Sam. He lay motionless with his eyes open, wide and startled like an injured animal. His breathing was shallow but steady and there was fresh vomit on the lapels of his donkey jacket. His face was agleam with sweat and almost grey in colour. He had suffered a major heart attack – at the age of 34.

For 36 hours it was touch and go, but by 9pm on Sunday night Midnight Sam gazed through the forest of wires and tubes attached to his body, twitched his shoulders, yawned and cleared his throat. A nurse swivelled around and leaned over the bed.

"Where's my jacket?" he whispered, rolling his eyes. The nurse smiled, inspected the monitor, made a note on the chart at the bottom of the bed and waggled an admonishing but relieved forefinger: "Now don't you go worrying about a thing like that – you've been poorly, young man, very poorly."

"Have you got my jacket?" he repeated, louder this time and more insistent. His eyes focussed on the nurse, who nodded and then shook her head: "Of course we have, Samuel, of course we have. But you won't be needing it just yet."

"Samuel," he repeated, "nobody has called me Samuel for years, not for such a long time. Samuel …"

"You've been very ill. You need to lie still and to get as much sleep as possible. You've been very ill."

"What happened?" Midnight asked.

"The doctor will explain, Samuel. He'll be doing his rounds soon and he'll explain." The nurse examined the watch pinned to the breast pocket of her tunic. "In around five minutes, as a matter of fact. Just you lie nice and still until then."

Doctor Jonathan Jackson arrived on cue, inspected Midnight's chart, watched the monitor for half a minute and then turned to face his patient. Midnight Sam, sleepy and safe, raised his eyebrows and murmured mischievously: "Which tribe are you from, Doc?" The West Indian doctor frowned but his eyes twinkled: "I have no idea, Mister …," he consulted the chart again, "… Mister Midaka, I have absolutely no idea. Possibly the head-hunters of Walsall, because that's where I was born. How about you?"

Midnight chuckled: "I am one half Mandinka with a bit of Fula and an even smaller bit of Serahuli mixed in, and the other half of me is English."

"Right then, now that we've got that one out of the way, I expect you would like to know what happened."

Midnight waited.

"You have had a cardiac arrest, in layman's terms a heart attack. And a serious one. In fact you very nearly died …," Doctor Jackson paused for the information to sink in.

"Am I going to die?" Midnight asked.

"I haven't finished," the doctor frowned, "and no, you're not going to die, well not unless … but we'll come to that in a minute. Now you just listen to me and you listen carefully. Besides having had a major heart attack you are suffering from hypothermia and malnutrition. And also – and I'm sure this won't come as a surprise to you – the kidney and liver function tests we have carried out on you were not particularly encouraging."

"But I'm not going to die?" Midnight persisted. The doctor stepped back from the bed, hands on hips, stethoscope swinging from his neck, and glowered down at his patient.

" If you carry on the way you have been, well yes, you are going to die and very soon, but if you change your lifestyle, and change it drastically, then that's a different matter." The doctor softened and sat on the edge of Midnight Sam's bed: "You drink like a fish, you hardly ever eat and you sleep rough in all weathers. You are a relatively young man and you are physically strong. But you have a problem: you have a weak heart. If you carry on with your lifestyle, I would be surprised if you made it to 40. You were lucky on this occasion, the paramedics got to you in time. But you could have been anywhere, anywhere in the city – the Railway Triangle, the wasteground, the underpass …" Midnight looked up at the doctor sharply. "Yes Sam, I know where you hang out. I make it my business to know." Midnight Sam raised his eyebrows and nodded: he was impressed. "Sam, you do not have a strong heart and the next attack could prove to be fatal."

Midnight looked away from the doctor and grimaced. He tried to fold his arms but there were too many wires and tubes in the way.

"But I'm an alcoholic."

"Yes, I know you are, Sam."

"So how am I ever going to be able to stop drinking?"

Doctor Jackson looked up at the ceiling and sighed: "I don't have all the answers, Sam, and I'm not sure that's the only question you should be asking, although it's an important one. There are other issues."

"Other issues?"

"Your whole lifestyle, as I've said. You simply don't look after yourself ... not at all."

Midnight slumped back in the bed and turned his head obdurately to one side: "I do all right."

"Don't you ever listen? I've already told you that you are suffering from hypothermia and malnutrition and that your kidneys and liver are ...," the doctor searched for the right word.

"Fucked?" Midnight ventured, coming to the rescue.

"Yes, quite. Look, I'll be quite frank with you. You are 34 years old but you have the body and the constitution of a 60-year-old. And it's all self-inflicted, all of it. But you are not beyond help." Doctor Jackson smiled and reached out to touch Midnight's shoulder: "You don't really want to die, do you ... I mean, not yet?"

Midnight looked deep into the doctor's eyes before he replied and when he spoke it was in a measured tone: "No doc, I don't think I do. Didn't used to care. Only thing that kept me going was looking after The Professor and then ...," he paused, "... and then there was Lady Jane."

"Lady Jane?"

"I don't want to die, doc," Midnight said after a while. "I don't want to die. Not now, not ever."

"Who is this Lady Jane? And who is this Professor character?"

Midnight tut-tutted: "You can't have been around here long."

The doctor nodded in agreement.

Midnight Sam squirmed with pleasure: "The Professor, doc, was the best bloke this city has ever known. An institution he was, a bloody institution. Nobody came close. I feel privileged to have known him, privileged to have been his friend."

Doctor Jackson nodded and asked: "How about this Lady Jane? You mentioned a Lady Jane. Who was she?"

Midnight jerked his head from the pillow: "Who *is* she, you mean, doc, who *is* she … not who *was* she. Lady Jane is alive and well and …," he trailed, battling with himself, " … and I'm going to find her."

Midnight Sam slumped back exhausted and closed his eyes and Doctor Jackson got up from the bed, straightened his shoulders and studied his clip-board for the next patient. But the medic could not help smiling.

****

Three days later the ban on visitors was lifted. Midnight Sam was moved into a small side ward with seven other beds, five of them occupied, and a steady stream of vagrants began to shamble self-consciously down the antiseptic corridors in search of their mate.

"We thought dat you was a fuckin' gonner," said Mickey the Mouth, shaking his head and sitting down heavily on the side of the bed. A nurse, two beds away, looked up sharply and the Irishman whipped a hand to his mouth: "Sorry, nurse. Didn't mean to say dat, sorry my darling." The nurse shot Mickey a disapproving look and continued plumping the bedclothes. Mickey turned to Midnight: "How you doing Sammy? Dey say you had a heart attack, touch-and-fuckin' go, old Welshie told us. Tought you was a gonner, we did, tought you was a gonner. Getting our black ties out for d'funeral, we was."

Midnight smiled weakly: "You haven't got a black tie, Mickey. You've never had a black tie in your life. In fact, you haven't got a tie, not in any colour."

"Dat I fuckin' have," The Mouth lied belligerently, but too softly for the nurse to hear.

Midnight turned to Tattoo Terry: "What have you done to your mouth, Tatts?"

Tattoo Terry made a strange noise, somewhere between a grunt and a whistle.

"He hasn't been able to speak for two days," explained Mickey, stretching across Midnight to clap Tatts on the shoulder. Tatts, who was sitting on the other side of the bed, nodded and made as if to speak but shook his head, wincing at the pain.

"He went to see dat tattoist bloke on the canel boat – Bert whatever-his-fucking-name-is – and it cost him a pretty penny, I can tell you. And just look at the fuckin' state of him."

"Not another tattoo?" Midnight asked.

"Oh no, Sammy, dat would be too fuckin' simple. And where d'fuck would he put it? Oh no, dis time our Tatts here decided to branch out. He only went and had his fuckin' lips pierced. Jesus Christ! You should see the d'fucking' state of his mouth. Disgusting. I don't tink he'll ever be able to speak again, which …"

Tattoo Terry made a gargling sound and glared at the Irishman, but Mickey continued, unabashed: "… which, considering d'fact dat he's never said anything worth listening to in his entire life, perhaps wouldn't be a bad ting at all."

The conversation swung back and forth with Tatts, between much moaning and many sharp intakes of breath, managing to devour the bunch of grapes they had brought for Midnight. Finally, after an hour, a nurse marched up to the bed with a ferocious determination which had the patient's visitors on their feet before a word was spoken. With commendable casualness, Mickey produced a bottle of Lucozade from the muddle of his clothing and asked the nurse: "Will it be okay if I leave dis for d'patient? Help build up his strength and all dat." The nurse nodded impatiently and began to busy herself with another patient's bed chart. She hadn't noticed that the seal on the Lucozade bottle had been broken or that, despite the yellow cellophane clinging to the bottle, the contents were darker than they should have been.

Brian Davies was a man with a different mission: he remembered only too well visiting another of his 'residents' – The Professor – in the same hospital more than two years ago. The Prof had been badly beaten up and robbed and the day centre manager had taken it upon himself to create a safe and secure environment for the man when he came out of hospital. So Brian had converted the basement at the night shelter into a small but cosy one-bedroomed flat, which soon became known as The Prof's Parlour.

"Another week, they reckon, and you'll be coming home," Brian said, emphasising the word 'home.'

Midnight Sam, who was sitting upright with a copy of the Evening News open at the puzzle page (he'd already completed the newspaper's advanced Sudoko grid), repeated the word 'home' with a dismissive snort.

"Home," he shook his head, still staring down at the newspaper. "Where is … home?"

Brian Davies bristled: "Home, Midnight Samuel Midaka, at least until you are well, will be in The Prof's Parlour. No ifs, no buts, young man, it's The Prof's Parlour for you. No argument!"

Midnight Sam did not look up from the newspaper: "Okay, Welshie, just so long as I don't end up like The Prof."

"We all do, one day, Sam."

"But not yet, Welshie, not yet," Midnight Sam smiled directly into the older man's eyes.

"Okay," Brian Davies conceded, "okay then, not yet."

28

ASSISTANT Chief Constable Tim Butler scanned Detective Sergeant Chris Sellwood's personnel file, turned wearily around on his swivel chair and looked out across the glittering concrete jungle of Bradford by night.

The red, internal telephone on his desk buzzed softly and Butler reached for the handset, listened for a couple of seconds and then nodded: "Okay, send him in." He replaced the receiver, stood up and faced the window again, legs apart. A muffled double knock on the door and Chris Sellwood walked into the room.

"Take a seat, Sellwood," said the ACC, his back still to the room, hands resting on hips a shade over-theatrically. "Tough old city this," he mused, "tough and bloody ugly."

"It's not *all* ugly, sir," Sellwood replied. "Some of the villains we have to deal with … well yes, *they're* the tough and ugly ones."

"You mean the Gordon Blacklocks of the world," Butler said suavely, grateful for an opportunity to get straight to the point. He turned to face the detective. Sellwood raised his eyebrows and stared at his hands, which he noticed to his annoyance were clasped meekly on his lap. He unclasped them and rearranged himself in the chair. He met the ACC's steady gaze. Not waiting for the young detective to reply, Butler continued: "He's sticking to his guns, you know. Adamant that you assaulted him, that you hit him first. He's going to press charges. At least that's what his solicitor's saying. But he'll probably run out of steam – they normally do – when the trial date gets closer. He'll have other things on his mind then …," Butler paused, folded the fingers of both hands together and rested his chin on his thumbs. Sellwood said nothing.

"Listen Chris, you and I both know what an evil bastard Blacklock is – 22 previous convictions, 12 for crimes of violence and three of those for actual bodily harm – and we both know that he is going down for three to four, maybe more if old Plunkett is sitting. What is going to happen to Blacklock is not the issue." A pause, a rather sad pause. "The issue is you."

"You've read my report, sir. It's all in my report. I don't know what else I can add." A stubbornness, a finality in the tone. But Chris Sellwood knew the ACC was no fool. The man had bloodied himself in the East End of London. Butler was not one of the new breed of limp-wristed, university degree career coppers, brilliant at paperwork and jargon, who flooded the higher echelons of the Force. He was a real policeman, a hands-on bobby, the sort who could sort out a knife fight in a druggy, down town boozer on his own and not think to radio for back-up … as a matter of pride.

"You had a warrant to arrest Blacklock and your inspector had specifically ordered you to execute that warrant, with two other officers, the following day. But you disobeyed that order and went to arrest him, on your own, the night before. You knowingly disobeyed an order, detective sergeant, and that is a disciplinary matter."

Chris Sellwood bristled but said nothing.

"Look, Chris, I know all about your association with Blacklock's ex-partner – and I know there is nothing improper – but it all goes to suggest that you were in danger of putting your heart well and truly before your head."

Sellwood frowned: "He resisted arrest, sir, he pulled a knife on me."

Butler glowered at the junior officer above the prism of his hands: "No he did not, detective sergeant, no he bloody well did not. You lost your temper and you punched him in the face. He fell down the fire escape, fractured two ribs and sprained his ankle; he was also heavily concussed. And then you, young fellow, got hold of a kitchen knife, wiped it clean of your prints, covered it with Mister Blacklock's and left it on the floor beside him. That is what happened, or something pretty much like that, and you damn well know it."

Sellwood repeated stubbornly: "He resisted arrest, sir. He pulled a knife on me."

Butler shook his head despairingly.

"I've told you what happened, sir, and there's nothing more I can really say. If you want me to resign, then I will, of course. If that makes things easier …"

"No, I don't want you to resign. You're a bloody good copper, but I don't like being lied to."

Sellwood did not flinch. He was too far in to change tack now.

"I've told you the truth, sir. I can't tell you anything else."

The assistant chief constable leaned back in his chair and closed his eyes: "Okay, okay, but you know there will be an internal investigation after the trial and if the findings go a certain way, you may well find yourself looking for another job."

Sellwood nodded: "Is that all, sir?"

****

Amy Brown died on December 12th but her body was not discovered until six days later and only then because the landlord of the Rose and Crown reckoned she owed him £150. He put a shoulder to the door of the squalid room on the third floor of his pub and discovered the body. A syringe, half full of coagulated blood, lay besides the body which was naked apart from a black thong and a pair of fishnet hold-ups which hadn't held up too well. The young mother lay in a large pool of blood, dried and black, and a halo of vomit fanned out from her face, which wore a grotesquely angelic expression. The stench in the small, airless room was appalling.

Detectives prised the mobile phone from her right hand, stiff with rigor mortis. The battery had run out, but she had clearly been trying to contact somebody before she died. A post mortem examination revealed a potentially lethal dose of heroin, traces of cocaine and the fact that Amy Brown was two-and-a-half months pregnant. The official cause of death was a massive haemorrhage from the femoral artery, the site of her last injection. Why she chose such a location and at such a depth remained a mystery.

****

Lady Jane collected Emily from nursery at five o'clock in the afternoon. It was one of those stone-cold, grey winter days, too cold to rain, too cold to snow. And yet Emily was far from cold; she was warm, bright and bubbly, her face pink and glowing, her breath steaming and gay. Hanging on to Lady Jane's arm, she babbled excitedly on about the forthcoming school Nativity Play and, pausing for dramatic effect, she pulled Lady's hand to a halt, heaved her little shoulders with consummate pride and announced: "I'm going to be Mary, Aunty Jane, I'm going to be the Mother of Jesus."

Lady Jane forced a bright smile down at the four-year-old. She made all the right noises but Emily, of course, knew that something was wrong. They both lapsed into silence for the rest of the journey home. The wind howled a little, the cold stung their cheeks and their footsteps rang out on the hard pavement. But not another word was spoken until they got home.

"Why are you sad, Aunty Jane?" asked Emily, sitting on a kitchen chair and swinging her legs. Lady was preparing a cup of tea for herself and a glass of milk for Emily. She carried the two mugs over to the kitchen table, pulled up a stool opposite the child and sat down.

"I'm sad, my darling, because something very sad has happened," she began and Emily stopped swinging her legs. "Do you remember that video we watched a couple of weeks ago? The Lion King, I think it was called?" Emily nodded. "Well ...," Lady paused, pushed her stool back, extended both arms and continued, "… come and sit on Aunty Jane's knee." But Emily shook her head, mouth down-turned, and started to swing her legs again. "Do you remember what happened to Simba's daddy?" Lady Jane paused again, the hurt and compassion on her face palpable. "There was an accident and Simba's daddy died and went to heaven."

"It was not an accident, Aunty Jane. It was the other lion, the nasty one – Scarface Claw – he made Simba's daddy die. It was his fault."

"Yes you're right my darling, of course you are. But do you remember how Simba grew up to be a great lion, to be The Lion King, and how his father looked down on him from heaven. Do you remember how Simba lived happily ever after?"

Emily nodded slowly and waited.

"Something very sad has happened my darling."

"Has my mummy died?" Emily asked.

Lady leaned across the table: "Yes, my darling, mummy has gone to heaven."

There was a pause. Emily was deep in thought and her legs slowed.

"So, you're my mummy now," she said calmly, quite logically and, to Lady Jane's bewilderment, quite unemotionally. Lady was in turmoil. She had not anticipated such a reaction. She had rehearsed for everything else – the tears, the fears, the tantrums – but not for this.

"No my love, I'm not your mummy. I'm your Aunty Jane and I'll always be your Aunty Jane. And I'll always be here to look after you and to love you. But I am not your mummy."

That did it. Emily slid from her stool and stamped both feet on the floor, one after the other, raw anger in her face: "You *are* my mummy, you *are*, you *are*, you *are*." And then she ran, helter-skelter, out of the kitchen and into her bedroom, slamming the door behind her. Lady could hear the sobbing but she remained where she was. There was nothing more she could do, there was nothing more she could say. There was nothing more anybody else in the world could do or say.

29

GORDON Blacklock stood trial at Bradford Crown Court, charged with assault occasioning grievous bodily harm, resisting arrest and possessing an offensive weapon. The time-estimate for the proceedings was two weeks.

"This is not going to be easy Jane," Chris Sellwood told the key prosecution witness over a coffee in a little café just around the corner from the courthouse. "The defence are going to be hard on you. They will paint you as black as they can and they will drag up your past, I'm afraid. They will say you made the whole thing up to get back at the defendant. They will suggest that you are a lesbian and that you had a sexual relationship with Amy, who sadly is not here to refute that allegation. They will say that Emily broke her nose accidentally while you were attacking the defendant. They will probably make out that it was your fault. It isn't going to be easy, Jane."

Lady stirred her coffee and blinked: "I know it isn't going to be easy, Chris, but I'll be okay. I know the truth, I know what happened … and that is what I'll say." She reached across the table and patted the detective's hands. "More to the point … how about you? What are you going to say, my love?"

Chris shrugged and looked over Lady's shoulder at the wall: "*You* know what really happened. You're the only person apart from my wife who does. And I am going to lie, lie through my teeth, to make sure that bastard goes down and for a bloody long time."

"And then what, Chris?"

"And then I'm going to resign, quit this bloody lousy job, do something else with my life," he said, a bright but frightened smile on his face.

"I feel so guilty, Chris. This is my fault. If you'd never met me, then this would never have happened." Lady shook her head, close to tears.

Sellwood squeezed her hand: "Lady, you have got nothing to feel guilty about, nothing at all. There is so much more to this than Gordon bloody Blacklock. Maybe I should thank him. I don't want to be a copper for the rest of my working life. Not sure what else I want to do though, but I'm young enough to change direction. Just like you, Lady Jane, I've got a future and the future's bright …"

"The future's orange?" Lady grinned sadly.

****

Defence barrister Michael Hamilton QC rose with difficulty to cross-examine Lady Jane, a hard and whimsical smile on his face. He was a short, rotund, barrel of a man, in his late sixties with a blotchy red face (blotchier after lunch-time adjournments), thinning grey hair and hooded, bright blue, intelligent but feral eyes which betrayed no hint of emotion. His voice – deliberately and effectively deep and resonant – carried across the courtrooms of the country with effortless volume. Hamilton was every court reporter's dream. No mumbling, no hurried oratory, no inaudible submissions. With him it was loud and clear every time. He was a feared, loathed but admired character of the courts. Rude, arrogant, outrageous and comically irritable. He somehow managed to make "Yes, your honour," whenever he addressed the judge, sound like an insult.

Hamilton cross-examined Lady Jane at 2pm, after the lunch adjournment, not a good time for the witness as the barrister had, true to form, consumed a bottle of Moet champagne and a double portion of chips at a nearby restaurant. His face was very red.

"When did you first realise that your friend Amy Brown was a prostitute and a heroin addict?" Hamilton began with no polite preamble.

"I don't remember the exact date but I knew she was an addict as soon as I met her. As far as being a prostitute, I only found that out later." Jane paused and sighed: "Heroin addicts will do anything for their next fix … I should know, I used to be one." The admission took Hamilton by surprise: he was intending to bring that one up himself, at an opportune moment. He had already been out-manoeuvred. A small frown creased his forehead.

"Nevertheless you knew she sold herself for sex and she was injecting … despite the fact she had a daughter, a girl aged four."

"Yes, yes I did," Jane answered levelly.

"And you knew that your friend had lesbian tendencies."

"No, not really. I did know that she had reached a point in her life when she didn't really care what happened to her. To be honest, I don't think she did have lesbian tendencies and I think I would have picked up on that."

The judge intervened suavely: "Where are you going with this line of questioning, Mister Hamilton? I presume it is relevant to the case …?"

Hamilton loved that sort of question. It gave him an opportunity to put the judge in his or her place. It was, in legal circles, a well-known fact that the grouchy old barrister had always yearned to be a judge himself, but the ultimate accolade had ever eluded him.

Clutching the lapels of his voluminous robe and arching his back to his full height of five feet and six inches, Hamilton barked: "Your honour, I am simply seeking to establish that this witness had a close – I am not exactly sure *how* close – relationship with Amy Brown, the mother of the little girl who was allegedly assaulted by the defendant. And that she would do anything, and I mean anything, to protect that *relationship*." Hamilton pronounced the word in such a lascivious way that there could be no doubt as to its meaning. The barrister paused, cleared his throat, whispered to one of his legal team sitting behind him, turned back to face the witness box and asked: "Are you a lesbian, Miss Hicks?"

Lady Jane shook her head: "No, as a matter of fact I am not."

"It appears there was some argument between you and the defendant …"

"Gordon wanted me back, he didn't like my friendship with Amy and Emily … he is a very jealous man, your honour," Lady turned to face the judge, who gave the witness a small but reassuring smile.

"Never mind all that," Hamilton snorted. "Mister Blacklock wanted to distance you from such an unsavoury relationship and you flew at him in a rage, madam, a violent rage. Was *that* not the case?"

Lady Jane waited until she was sure the barrister had finished and then she replied, in a magnificent tone: "Firstly you tell me to 'never mind all that' as if Gordon Blacklock being a dangerous and violently jealous man is of no consequence …"

The judge cut in diplomatically: "Will the witness please restrict herself to answering counsel's questions … however unfair they might seem … and try to refrain from voicing opinions. Please continue, Mister Hamilton." But the jury had heard Lady's words too.

"Grateful, Your Honour," Hamilton puffed out his chest and continued: "Do you agree that you lost your temper with the defendant and that you attacked him?"

"He grabbed hold of me and told me I was going with him. Emily came running down the path and he called her a brat and said she should be put into care."

"That is not the way it was madam," boomed the barrister, "that is not what happened, is it, Miss Hicks?"

Lady Jane met Hamilton's withering and practised stare and then suddenly she realised, with a warm flood of memory, that she was only dealing with another bully: "I'm afraid it is, Mister Hamilton – that is your name, I take it? – I'm afraid that is exactly what happened." The judge suppressed a smile at the subtle reversal of roles.

"You rained blows on this defendant in a totally unprovoked attack, despite the fact that a vulnerable four-year-old child was in close proximity. And during your frenzied outburst the poor child found herself in the crossfire, so to speak. She sustained a broken nose. It was, was it not madam, an unfortunate accident, an accident brought on by your own violent behaviour?"

Lady Jane felt an icy chill of controlled anger deep in the pit of her stomach and she replied in a calm, precise manner which irritated Hamilton enormously but which arrowed straight to the hearts of the eight women and four men sitting opposite in the jury box.

"No Mister Hamilton, I'm afraid you are wrong. It was 'unfortunate,' to use your own words, but it was by no means an accident. True, Gordon and I did have a tussle …"

"That's all very well, madam, but the point is …," the barrister interrupted, wheezing with annoyance, but then found himself interrupted by the judge.

"Please permit the witness to answer your question, Mister Hamilton." Gentle, polite but omnipotent.

Lady Jane continued as if unaware of the interruption: "While we were struggling, Emily came between us and tried to pull Gordon away from me. Gordon deliberately struck her across the side of the head and she fell to the ground. That is what happened, Mister Hamilton."

"So you say, madam, so you say. But why on earth don't you just tell us what *really* happened? The jury are entitled to the truth. It was indeed an accident, but not at all the way you …"

The judge lost his patience: "Mister Hamilton, the witness has answered your question. It is time to move on. Do you have any further questions for this witness?"

Hamilton shuddered with suppressed rage but answered, with exaggerated politeness: "As Your Honour wishes … I do have a couple more questions." The barrister hesitated for dramatic effect and continued: "Do you know Detective Sergeant Christopher Sellwood?"

Lady: "Yes, I do."

"And would you call him a friend?"

Lady nodded, determined to tell the truth but suddenly fearful that Hamilton had an ulterior motive for this new line of questioning: "Yes, yes I would."

"A good friend?"

"Yes, a good friend."

"And you do know, of course, that Detective Sergeant Sellwood is the senior officer in this case, don't you?"

Lady raised her head and stared defiantly across at the barrister: "Yes, I do."

"No further questions, Your Honour," Michael Hamilton QC sat down heavily and raised his eyebrows to the jury.

****

"I swear by Almighty God, that the evidence I shall give, shall be the truth, the whole truth and nothing but the truth." Sellwood handed the bible back to the court usher and clasped his hands behind his back, facing the judge.

The detective gave his version of events on the night he arrested Blacklock, telling the truth but not the whole truth and definitely adding something but the truth. Almost an hour elapsed before the prosecuting barrister said: "No more questions detective sergeant, but would you remain there as I'm sure my learned friend will have some questions for you."

Hamilton cleared his throat, bounced to his feet with surprising agility and gripped both sides of the lectern with his pink and podgy hands.

"Why, detective sergeant, did you take it upon yourself to visit the defendant's home in the middle of the night to arrest him – *on your own?*" The barrister spoke the last three words slowly and accusingly, his head turned away from the witness, his cold and feral eyes staring at the jury.

"I have already explained that I made a mistake … I was worried that the suspect might have been warned off and I was eager to make the arrest. I felt at the time that I should strike while the iron was hot. With the benefit of hindsight, I should have waited until the morning."

"Nothing to do with 'striking while the iron was hot' was it detective sergeant. That is a load of rubbish, is it not, officer? It was because you were determined to teach the defendant a lesson for something the previous witness – your friend – had told you that he'd done. You didn't want your colleagues anywhere near, so you could take the law into your own hands." Sellwood remained impassive and said nothing. "Why did you punch the defendant in the face with such force that you broke one of your own fingers and my client's nose? Was it because you had been told he had broken the little girl's nose, so you decided to break his? Was that not the rationale behind your actions, Detective Sergeant Sellwood? An act of unprovoked violence, an act of revenge, as you saw it?"

"I struck the suspect because he was coming at me with a knife and there was no room to restrain him," the detective said flatly, not rising to the bait but aware that eight women and four men were watching him closely. "I was also afraid he might get away – he had been in hiding for a long time – and, of course, I deemed him to be a dangerous man … a dangerous man who was armed with a knife."

Hamilton pursed his lips and caressed one of his chins: "Armed with a knife, was he?" He stroked the corners of his mouth and repeated, with mock reflection: "Armed with a knife?" And then softer, a statement heavy with sarcasm: "Armed with a knife." A long pause, a restrained chuckle, a brilliantly executed disbelieving shake of the head and then, in a formal and respectful tone: "No more questions, Your Honour."

Chris Sellwood turned and stepped down from the witness stand, buttoned his jacket and caught Lady Jane's eye. She smiled almost maternally from the back row of the public gallery.

****

Solemn-faced with the importance of their roles, the jury members filed back into their seats. The court clerk rose and asked: "Would the foreman please stand?"

A tall man in a tweed jacket and rumpled shirt adjusted his spectacles and rose.

"Have you reached a verdict on which you are all agreed on any of the three counts? Please answer 'yes' or 'no.'"

"Yes."

"On count one (assault occasioning actual bodily harm) do you find the defendant guilty or not guilty?"

"Guilty."

Blacklock craned forwards, turned his head sharply and glowered at Lady Jane, who refused to meet his stare.

"On count two (resisting arrest) do you find the defendant guilty or not guilty?"

A pause and then: "Not guilty."

"On count three (possessing an offensive weapon with intent) do you find the defendant guilty or not guilty?"

"Not guilty."

"Is that the verdict of you all?"

"Yes."

"Thank you, please sit down."

The prosecuting barrister rose eloquently to his feet, braced himself on the lectern, studied the sheaf of papers in front of him and addressed the judge: "The defendant has, Your Honour, an extensive list of previous convictions, mostly for offences of violence. Common assault, assault occasioning actual bodily harm and one previous matter of assault occasioning grievous bodily harm. He has served two periods in custody. There are also a number of offences of dishonesty, threatening words and behaviour, drunk and disorderly and affray."

"Thank you," said the judge with a polite and curt nod, although he already knew of the defendant's lengthy antecedent history. And, anticipating Michael Hamilton's next question (the defence barrister had shot to his feet) the judge added: "I am not going to request a pre-sentence report from the probation service. I intend to proceed to sentence immediately." Hamilton jutted his jaw forwards but sat down without a word.

"Stand up, please, Mister Blacklock," the judge's voice was devoid of emotion. "You are a violent man and a bully. Yours is an unenviable history of violence, mainly against women. But on this occasion, you – a large and powerful man – turned your violence upon a four-year-old girl. You deliberately struck her in the face and you broke her nose. You could quite easily have killed her. You will go to prison for five years. You will serve half of that time. Take him down."

Flanked by two Reliance security guards, Gordon Blacklock was ushered towards the back door of the dock. But just before he disappeared, he stopped, strained against the guards and fixed Lady Jane with a cold and withering look.

"See you later Janey. Don't worry, I'll find you. Wherever you fuckin' are, Janey, I'll find you."

30

MAY that year was everything the month of May should be: mild of manners, bright and breezy, pale blue skies laced with cotton-wool clouds and new life springing from the April-irrigated earth, new life thrusting out from the trees and from the hedgerows. New life.

Midnight Sam, thinner and quieter now after a winter of forced hibernation and recuperation, sat alone on the park bench which overlooked The Tree in the park. Although it was a warm and kindly day he wore his navy blue donkey jacket, the two remaining buttons unfastened in deference to the sunshine. He offered his face to the sun and closed his eyes for a few seconds, shivering in the warmth.

For him it had been a long, long winter, mostly spent sitting quietly in The Professor's old armchair in The Parlour or shuffling hesitantly into the tiny kitchen to make himself a mug of coffee (against doctor's orders) or to pour himself a small glass of cider (again against doctor's orders) or to heat up the never-ending supply of homemade beef and vegetable stew (courtesy of The Mitre and most definitely *not* against doctor's orders).

Since Midnight's heart attack a change of lifestyle had been forced upon him. Strictly policed by Brian Davies and benignly policed by Bishop John, but not so strictly or benignly policed by Mickey the Mouth and Tattoo Terry. The day centre doctor called to see him each Wednesday, checked that he was taking his medication and gave him the once-over: blood pressure, temperature, stethoscope over the heart.

And slowly but surely, Midnight Sam made his recovery. The rest, medication, comfort and, last but by no means least, Mrs Bobby's wholesome stew, brought the street-drinker back from the brink. But what really saved Midnight from an early grave was his substantial reduction in alcohol consumption. The stark choice had been spelled out to him by the centre doctor, by Brian Davies and by Bishop John and this time he listened: continue drinking and die within a matter of months or stop drinking and live. Ever a creature of compromise, Midnight balanced the words of Brian Davies, Bishop John and his doctor against the interesting advice from Tatts and The Mouth. One two-litre bottle of medium strength cider every day, apart from Sundays, when he would abstain, save for half a bottle of red wine as a nightcap. And, to Midnight's credit, he moreorless stuck to this new regime. To non-drinkers this might be considered an excessive amount of alcohol, to regular drinkers it might be deemed average … but to street drinkers it was tantamount to turning teetotal!

Midnight leaned back on the park bench and listened to the birds; he frowned with pleasure when he heard the muffled call of an early cuckoo. He remembered the first time he met Lady Jane: she was sitting on the same bench, nervous and frightened and desperate for a drink. He had handed her his bottle and suffered the cold, black eyes of Gordon Blacklock. He recalled how Blacklock had pulled her away roughly and how she had half-turned to treat him to a small, sad smile of gratitude.

Midnight thought about Lady all the time now, suffering regular dark and despairing moments when he wondered whether or not she was still alive. But somehow he knew she was. He wondered what had happened to her, where she was, how she was, whether she was still with that violent man of hers. *Of hers?* The words stuck in his throat and filled him with sorrow and then disgust and finally with anger. He hated the thought of Lady Jane being with Blacklock.

Midnight opened his eyes with a start, sat upright and shook his head. He rummaged around in the back pocket of his jeans and pulled out a crumpled envelope. He extracted the letter – the first he had received from anybody for as long as he could remember – and unfolded the single sheet of writing paper.

'Dear Sam,

Derek and I heard about your illness. Brian Davies from the night shelter wrote to us and told us how poorly you have been. We do hope that you are on the road to recovery.

We often talk about you – all good, I assure you! – and about those two nights you spent with us last year. You gave us both such hope, Sam, and you cheered us up no end.

We still miss Jane desperately of course and we worry about her all the time.

Please take really good care of yourself – Derek and I are very fond of you, you know – and we are keeping our fingers crossed that you will find our daughter. For your sake as well as for ours.

God bless, Sam,

Martha Hicks.'

Midnight stared at the letter, folded the sheet of paper carefully, reverently and tucked it back into the envelope. He felt frightened and unworthy of such trust. He shuffled the envelope into the back pocket of his jeans and stared across at The Tree: the old oak wore the beginnings of its summer clothes.

Midnight heard the cuckoo again, closer and more distinct this time and a sweet breeze ruffled the leaves on The Tree. He looked up through the spreading branches into the powder blue sky and closed his eyes, allowing memories to crowd his mind: The Gambia, Paradise Island, Madiyanna Lodge, the old hammock he had once swung upon and dreamed upon when he was a boy. The breeze made him think he was cold and he pulled the lapels of his donkey jacket together. He recalled his meeting with Bishop John earlier that day.

"I can't help thinking, Your Holiness, that Lady Jane might not want to have anything to do with me. What if she doesn't remember who the bloody hell I am – begging your pardon, bishop? What do I do then?"

Midnight cautiously sipped the ecclesiastical Harveys Bristol Cream. He reasoned with himself: he had only consumed one of his statutory two litres of cider so far that day and therefore a schooner or two of the bishop's sherry would surely do no harm?

Bishop John fussed with his evil old briar, disappeared behind a cloud of yellow-grey smoke and leaned back in his armchair.

"Faint heart, Midnight, faint heart ..."

"But I so want to win this fair lady, Your Worship, I really do. I'm a little nervous ... that's all. To be frank, I'm shit scared ... begging your pardon."

Bishop John inspected his pipe, which had bolted like an ignited weed and died accordingly, and he rubbed his chin. Midnight noticed vaguely that the bishop had forgotten to shave that day.

"Let me tell you something, Midnight," the bishop began slowly and deliberately as if about to deliver one of his sermons. Midnight waited. "Do you remember your sponsored fancy dress walk for National Homeless Week *a couple of years back?"* Midnight nodded. *"I remember your costume. Who could forget it? An interesting blend of cultures. Sioux Indian and Zulu set off magnificently with a Winnie the Pooh scarf. Fascinating blend of cultures, fascinating ..."* Bishop John trailed with a smile of wistful nostalgia. *"Lady Jane was waiting with quite a reception party at the Great West Window of the Cathedral,"* the bishop continued. *"And the first person she congratulated was you. She walked straight passed the rest of us and gave you a hug and kissed you on the forehead. One of the reasons I remember it so well is that most of your warpaint ended up on her face. But another reason why that little episode stuck in my mind is the look she gave you, Midnight ..."*

"Look? What look? What do you mean, Your Highness?"

Bishop John picked up his pipe again, inspected the bowl, changed his mind and tossed it back at the ashtray. It missed and fell on to the floor, spilling charred tobacco on to the threadbare carpet. Midnight made to pick it up but the bishop stayed him with an outstretched hand.

"There was love in that look, Midnight Sam. Or, at the very least, deep affection."

"Or perhaps kindness, Bishop John," Midnight said. "It might have been just kindness ... Lady Jane was a very kind person."

"No, no, no," the bishop shook his head quite vehemently, reached for his schooner of sherry, drained half of it and put the glass back on the coffee table, precariously close to the edge.

The cathedral bell struck four and Midnight opened his eyes, mouthing the number of chimes to himself silently. He shook his head, forced himself back to the present and looked across to the park entrance, some hundred yards distant. Tattoo Terry and Mickey the Mouth were zig-zagging across the road which ran alongside the park and they were heading for the gates. Mickey looked none too steady on his feet but Tatts seemed reasonably okay, save the occasional lurch.

The Irishman stopped at the park gates, sagged sideways against one of the stone pillars, pulled a bottle of cider from a coat pocket, offered it to Tatts who declined and tilted it to his own lips with the infinite and studied concentration of the drunk. Tatts saw Midnight, raised an arm in greeting and struck out towards his friend. Mickey weaved his way resolutely behind Tatts towards The Tree.

"We've come to escort you to The Mitre," Tattoo Terry mimicked a courtly tone. "At least, I have," he added, looking over his shoulder at the Irishman, who was wearing an expression of dull but fierce intensity as he endeavoured unsuccessfully to walk in a straight line.

Midnight Sam grinned at the spectacle. He was glad to see them and relieved at a semblance of his old routine. It was a Thursday, his first Thursday 'out' since he had had his heart attack. And Thursday was benefits day.

Midnight stood up, allowed Tatts to link arms and they both shuffled across the park towards the road. It was not until they reached the gates that they realised they had left Mickey behind. The Irishman was slumped on the park bench, trying to coax Carolina Moon out of his mouth organ. He had forgotten about them, so Midnight and Tatts wisely chose to forget about him too.

"It's funny, you know …," mused Midnight.

"What's funny, Sammy?"

"Couple of years ago, I was doing exactly what we're doing now – linking arms with The Professor and helping him from the park to the pub. Déjà vu."

"What?"

"Nothing Tatts. It's just an expression. It means I've been here before."

Tattoo Terry frowned: "Of course you have – we all have – we meet up at The Tree a couple of times a week. I don't know what you're on about, Midnight."

"Never mind, Tatts."

****

Two months later Brian Davies knocked excitedly on the door of The Parlour. It was mid-afternoon, Midnight's nap time (sternly suggested by the centre manager himself), but the news was too important to wait. A sleepy Midnight Sam, dressed only in bright red boxer shorts, opened the door and peered out into the stairwell.

Brian Davies waved a letter and Midnight, after scratching the back of his head, took the sheet of paper and began to read with an ever-deepening frown of concentration.

"Who is Detective Sergeant Chris Sellwood?" he asked finally. "How does he know about Lady Jane?" Midnight did not look up from the letter which he held tightly in both hands, frightened that it would blow away.

"You're not the only person who has been looking for Lady Jane, you know. Quite a few people have been … on the case … I think the expression is. Including that young detective who arrested The Professor, the one who came to the funeral. He's always felt bad about what happened, although it was hardly his fault. There was nothing else he could have done at the time.

"Well, when you told me about the birthday card Lady sent her parents from Bradford I went to see him. He used the police computer system which links up with every force in the country and, after feeding in Gordon Blacklock's name, he eventually tracked down Lady Jane. Bingo!"

Midnight Sam was in shock but he managed, in a faltering tone: "So why doesn't he just tell me where she is? Why does he want to see me first?"

"Detective Sergeant Sellwood is clearly a close friend of Lady Jane and it appears that he's been, well, sort-of protecting her. He wants to make sure … well, she's been through a lot and … he's probably worried that …" Brian Davies floundered, but Midnight came to the rescue.

"He wants to make sure that I'm not just another Gordon Blacklock," he said and the centre manager nodded with relief.

"Something like that, Midnight," he said.

Midnight Sam handed the letter back to Brian Davies, rubbed his face with both hands and closed his eyes.

"I'm scared, Welshie," he whispered.

"But you'll go … won't you?"

"Yes, I'll go."

31

JANE HICKS knelt in front of Emily, adjusted the little girl's crisp, new school uniform and whispered in her ear: "I love you." Emily threw her arms briefly around the neck of her adoptive mother, before she scampered, bright-eyed and excited, through the gates of Salcombe Primary School into the bustling playground … and into her future.

With bitter-sweet emotions, Jane stood by the school gates and watched Emily disappear into a group of children. Ironically, the little girl flourished since the death of her mother and had become almost an extrovert. Jane marvelled at the transformation and harboured a secret, warm glow of pride. But she was ever-watchful of her charge. There were moments, moments of wistful detachment.

A teacher emerged from the schoolhouse, clapped her hands briskly and blew a whistle. Jane turned and slipped away, the last grown-up to leave.

Not for the first time that summer, Jane felt that she surely must be dreaming: so much had happened since Gordon Blacklock had been sent to prison, so much of her life had changed, changed beyond her wildest expectations. She could hardly believe the past four months, the enormous transition – her summer of transformation, her summer of content.

"I've got a good friend in Salcombe, Jane, bloke called Pete," Chris Sellwood told her two days after the trial. "He owns half a dozen houseboats which he rents out in the summer. His daughter used to help him but she got herself married and moved to Plymouth. He's in a bit of a pickle. I've spoken to him and he is very keen ..."

"You mean a job?" Jane asked incredulously. "Is this friend of yours offering me a job? But he doesn't know me, he doesn't know anything about me."

"I've told him about you. And it's not charity, Jane. He is really desperate for someone to look after his houseboats during the season. Cleaning, getting rid of the rubbish, changing the bedding and the towels, replacing the Calor Gas cannisters, topping up the water tanks ... that sort of thing. Nothing very glamorous, I'm afraid."

"But why me?"

The detective took a long time to answer: "Because I recommended you and because I know you would be brilliant at it ... and because you're a good swimmer should you fall in (a gruff chuckle to mask his embarrassment) ... and because ... well, just because ... "

"Because what, Chris?" Jane asked mischievously, resting her hand on his arm.

"Just because, Lady Jane," Chris Sellwood said with finality.

Jane walked down the steep hill into Salcombe town, lost in thought. It was a beautiful late September morning. A cloudless sky, the winding tidal estuary a picture postcard blue and a dozen seagulls wheeling between the sun and the sea, exposing their soft and snowy-white bellies but with eyes as black and as hard as coal. And cries as hopeless as hell.

"But where would I live? And more importantly, what about Emily?"

"You'd live on one of the houseboats – there's one Pete never lets out – and Emily would live with you."

"Is there a primary school in Salcombe, Chris? This is not just about me you know, in fact it's not really about me at all. It's about Emily. I have a responsibility for Emily now."

The detective nodded: "I know and of course there's a school there. I asked Pete. One of my first questions, in fact. And I beg to differ that this is not about you. Naturally it's about Emily. But make no mistake, this is very much about you too."

Jane frowned, but she was beginning to feel the first stirrings of excitement: "You say that this Pete wants help during the season. So what would happen in the winter? What would I do then?"

The detective raised a finger: "Pete runs a marine store which is open all year round. Salcombe's not just a holiday resort – it's a working seaside town with a modest fishing and boat-building industry. He'd like you to work in the shop off-season …that's if you wanted to."

Jane continued down the steps to Whitestrands Quay, a sudden sea breeze ruffling her hair. She boat-hopped until she reached her small motor launch which she reversed expertly out into the harbour. She steered across the mouth of Batson Creek, around Snapes Point and into Kingsbridge estuary.

Jane and Emily's home for the past three months – a lovably ugly, blue-and-white houseboat called Quiet Waters – was moored in the middle of a stretch of water known as The Bag. The vessel rose high and rather ridiculous at her permanent anchorage amidst an array of sleeker craft.

Quiet Waters was Pete Johnson's White Elephant – an unlettable houseboat. The paintwork was atrocious, chunks of surface rust flaked away at a touch and the plumbing made an irritating and untraceable din, for some perverse reason especially late at night. The ageing tub listed to starboard and creaked with the swell of the tide. A faint but unmistakeable smell – the dank and damp odour of decay – hung in the air. Nevertheless Jane loved the disintegrating hulk and turned it into a warm and friendly and surprisingly comfortable home for the two of them.

A covered 'patio' foredeck, large enough to accommodate a small, white, plastic table and four chairs, led through ill-fitting, sliding glass doors, to the living room, furnished modestly with a sofa, an armchair, a round pine dining table, four dining chairs, a glass-fronted display cabinet and a cupboard, upon which sat a portable television set and a CD player. Jane had brightened up the room with framed photographs of Emily and Amy, a couple of sheepskin rugs, a framed painting of Padstow harbour (which Chris Sellwood had given her as a Christmas present) and several vases of fresh flowers, mostly lilies. A narrow corridor led to a small galley kitchen, adequately equipped with cooker, fridge, sink unit, work surfaces, wall and floor cupboards. Off the corridor to the right was a tiny bathroom with a hip bath, toilet and washbasin; and to the left were two cabins – one with a cramped double bed and the other with bunk beds. Emily slept, depending on her mood, on the top or the bottom berth. Jane had transformed Emily's miniscule cabin into a kiddies' wonderland: tinkling mobiles, brightly-painted walls and ceiling, cuddly toys everywhere, a shocking pink, shag-pile rug on the uneven floor and Winnie the Pooh curtains covering the single port-hole.

Quiet Waters measured 33 feet in length and 12 feet across the beam. The flat roof had been canvas-screened to form a crude sundeck with access via a fixed, iron ladder from the tiny aft-deck. Besides the designer yachts and cruisers, the houseboat was kept permanent company by bad-tempered, inquisitive swans and shoals of large, lazy fish constantly on the lookout for tit-bits.

Steep fields, dotted with cows and sheep, sloped down to the water's edge and, apart from the lapping and gurgling of the sea and the clinking of rigging against the masts of a myriad boats, there was hardly ever a sound. And at night, with the modest illuminations of Salcombe town barely visible, the sky became a soul-tingling miracle of stars. Black, infinite and comforting in its enormity.

Emily's nightmares were becoming less frequent. Once or twice a week now as opposed to once or twice every night. But they were still distressing, for both the little girl and for Jane, who would pluck Emily, glistening with sweat and shivering with fear, from her soaking bunk bed, hold the child close to her chest and take her out on to the foredeck, beneath the glittering blanket of stars. She would cuddle Emily close in her arms, pick damp locks of hair from her forehead and whisper into the little girl's ear: "It will be all right my darling, it will be all right." Over and over and over again. Eventually the blank but unseeing eyes would register reality and the nightmare would slither back to the dark place from whence it had emerged.

"What do you dream about, my darling – I mean, when you have those horrid nightmares?" Jane asked once, when they were having breakfast.

"That man, Aunty Jane, that man who hurt me. He's going to hurt me again and he's going to hurt *you*. I try to run away but I can't move my legs and then he comes after me and I don't know where you are, Aunty Jane, I don't know where you are …," the words tumbled out and Emily's chest began to heave as she relived the recurring nightmare.

Jane closed her eyes briefly with guilt at having aroused the nocturnal terrors.

"I don't like men, Aunty Jane ... they're not nice ... they make me frightened."

"But you like Uncle Chris, my darling," said Jane soothingly, stroking Emily's knee. "There are nice men as well as nasty men. There are kind and good men.

"But Uncle Chris has *got* a mummy," said Emily with the simplistic wisdom of a child and Jane nodded in agreement.

"But I do know another nice man, a kind and good man – and he doesn't have a mummy," said Jane, surprised at herself. "He was a friend of mine once, a very good friend. You would like him. He makes people laugh."

"Would he make me laugh? Would he be silly and do funny things?"

Jane nodded: "Oh yes my darling, he would be silly and he would do funny things ... and he would love you *so* very much." She turned away.

"Why are you crying, Aunty Jane?"

Jane composed herself, blinked her eyes and smiled that rare and radiant smile of hers, a smile which The Professor had once said "could light up the world."

"Let me tell you about Midnight Sam ..." she began.

****

In the first week of October, Samuel Midaka caught a train to Totnes, the Virgin Inter-City from Glasgow to Penzance. Brian Davies had given him £100 spending money for the trip and Tattoo Terry and

Mickey the Mouth had contributed a bottle of red wine for their friend and a bottle of white wine for Lady Jane.

Sam peered out of the window. What was he going to say to her? What was he going to do? But, more to the point, what was she going to say to him, what was she going to do? Would she laugh at him, would she be kind but tell him that he was being ridiculous, that there was no point, that he might as well turn around and head straight back to the wasteground? His heart skipped a beat at the thought of 'going back.' He realised, with a degree of astonishment, that he did not want to go back, not now, not ever. Not back to the wasteground.

Okay, he had been a no-hoper, he had been cheerfully drinking himself to death, he had been well on the way to becoming just another statistic. He had been Midnight Sam – lovable, scatty, booze-befuddled Midnight Sam. But, for Chrissake, he was a young man (mathematically at least) and there was life ahead of him. Surely … ?

****

Samuel Midaka sat on the low wall above Whitestrands Quay, overlooking the harbour. It was a grey but gentle afternoon and Salcombe had been given back to the locals. The sounds and the smells were different now and the town was quieter, more the way an ordinary little town should be. The narrow streets echoed again and the tiny town car park was almost empty again. Seagulls seemed bolder and people kinder.

Cats crossed the road slowly, bolder and unseen dogs barked conversations at one another, across the rooftops.

Samuel noticed none of this; his main concern was the quickening beat of his damaged heart. He inspected the wristwatch Brian Davies had given him and noticed that his hands were shaking.

Emily skipped within a couple of feet of him, an important satchel slung across her shoulders, as she made her way down to the pontoon quay below.

Jane Hicks was a dozen paces behind, a carrier bag of shopping in each hand. She was too intent on watching Emily, who had a habit of leaping fearlessly from boat to boat, to notice him and she walked passed without a sideways glance.

"Lady?" he called in a small voice.

Jane froze and placed both bags of shopping carefully on to the ground. She heaved her shoulders, raised her head to the heavens, eyes closed, and only then did she turn around to face the man she loved.

"Midnight," she whispered and took a step towards him, but hesitated.

Samuel Midaka stood up and spread his arms in a helpless gesture.

Jane suddenly frowned, put her hands on her hips and said, a touch frostily: "What the hell took you so long?"

END